THE
GLASS
HOUSE

First published 2022 by
FREMANTLE PRESS

Fremantle Press Inc. trading as Fremantle Press
PO Box 158, North Fremantle, Western Australia, 6159
fremantlepress.com.au

Cover image by Erin Cadigan / Arcangel, arcangel.com
Cover design by Nada Backovic, nadabackovic.com
Printed and bound by IPG

 A catalogue record for this
book is available from the
NATIONAL
LIBRARY National Library of Australia
OF AUSTRALIA

ISBN 9781760991791 (paperback)
ISBN 9781760991807 (ebook)

Fremantle Press is supported by the State Government through the
Department of Local Government, Sport and Cultural Industries.

Fremantle Press respectfully acknowledges the Whadjuk people of the
Noongar nation as the Traditional Owners and Custodians of the land
where we work in Walyalup.

THE GLASS HOUSE

BROOKE DUNNELL

 FREMANTLE PRESS

Brooke Dunnell is a writer, mentor and workshop facilitator. Her short fiction has been widely published, including in the mini-collection *Female(s and) Dogs*, which was a finalist for the 2020 Carmel Bird Digital Literary Award and shortlisted for the 2021 Woollahra Digital Literary Award. The unpublished manuscript for *The Glass House* was the winner of the 2021 Fogarty Literary Award. Brooke has a PhD in Creative Writing from the University of Western Australia and lives in Boorloo (Perth) with her husband and two dogs.

For my parents

– ONE –

Rowan had wanted the two of them to tell Evie together. If only one parent was there, he argued, she might get the wrong impression. Both of them being present would demonstrate a united front: we will be separate but also connected. Together, although apart.

Julia thought that was dramatic. 'It's only for a few weeks.' She was clicking around the internet for her ticket, unable to decide whether it was worth the extra cost to catch a flight leaving at midday rather than the crack of dawn. 'If you make it into a big deal, she'll get suspicious it's something more.'

'If I'm there, I can calm her fear.'

'If you're there, you'll *create* her fear.'

They gazed at one another, a détente. Rowan cleared his throat. 'It isn't something more, is it?'

Julia sighed and selected the early flight. 'No,' she told the laptop. 'I don't think so.'

'And you'll tell Evie that?'

'I don't lie,' she reminded her husband.

Which was not strictly an answer to his question, but at least it was honest.

Evie was Rowan's daughter, Julia's stepdaughter, but to the extent she could know what it was like to have a child of her own, it felt like the girl was hers. They'd met when Julia was twenty-five and Evie three; she felt they'd grown up together. If only one thing would bring Julia back from her trip, it was the greatest teenager in the world.

On the afternoon Julia chose to tell her, the two of them walked to the Botanic Gardens for an iced chocolate by the lake. Evie wore her school blazer and hat and Julia's heart clenched to see the happy girl sucking on her spoon, brackets of dark sauce collecting in the corners of her mouth. Their drinks were almost finished by the time she brought herself to say, 'So there's something we have to chat about, okay?'

Evie's cheeks flushed. She removed the spoon and lay it on the table. 'Oh, God.'

'What?' The girl's anxiety transferred instantly. Julia's heart pounded. 'What is it?'

'You're asking me?' Evie objected. 'You're the one dropping the bomb. *We have to talk.* That's how you cardiac arrest a person.'

'I didn't mean to frighten you,' Julia said. On the lake, one duck chased another, climbing on its back and pushing it below the surface. The aggression was unsettling. 'It's not as serious as that, I promise.'

Evie removed her hat and shook it. The hair below was

perfect even after being squashed under straw all afternoon, the skin of her forehead creamy and clear. Weren't fourteen-year-olds supposed to be pink and yellow with pimples, hunched in permanent angst? Evie replaced the hat. 'Well, what is it?'

'I have to go to Perth for a little while.'

'Oh.' Evie's shoulders relaxed. 'Is it Grandpa Don?'

Julia nodded. Her father was a ninety-two-year-old widower whose children now lived in the Eastern States, a four- or five-hour flight if something were to go wrong. Don remained in the family home, a late seventies build full of hazards: a step-down lounge and a step-up dining room, cabinets and coffee tables with thin glass panels, tiles with the unforgiving texture of cliff rocks. Since his wife's death, Don had accepted minor assistance in the form of grocery delivery and a cleaning service, but it was getting beyond him now. Julia and her brother had agreed.

'Is he sick?' Evie asked.

'Just old. He can't take care of himself anymore.'

Evie nodded, but she didn't know. Her mother Samara's parents had died when she was young, and Rowan's were in their mid-sixties, in robust good health, living their sea change down on Phillip Island. Julia's blood pressure and resting heart rate would be more worrisome than her mother-in-law's.

'How long will you be gone?' Evie asked.

'I don't know yet. A couple of weeks. Not too long.'

'Will you bring Grandpa Don back to stay here?'

Julia was startled. 'Why would I do that?'

'Because he doesn't have anyone.'

Julia looked back at the lake. Though there were dozens of ducks, all more or less identical, she felt she recognised the vicious one gliding around the water, its bill proudly erect. The victim duck was nowhere to be seen.

'He wouldn't want to move here,' she told her stepdaughter. 'He's very set in his ways.'

Nodding sombrely, Evie used the metal straw to vacuum up the rest of her drink. Julia's own flat white was going cold, so she finished the last two-thirds of it in a few quick swallows, displaying yet again that she was not a true Melburnian.

The temperature had dropped while they were in the park, and they bent forward into the chill breeze for their walk back, the light disappearing around them. Evie reached for her hand as they crossed the road and Julia's chest warmed. But Don needed her more than her stepdaughter did. Evie was young, but she could protect herself and had a father and mother, both ready to defend her to the death. All Don had was Julia and Paul, and Paul couldn't get much time off work.

They weaved south-east towards the flat on Fawkner Street, Evie still happy to hold hands even though she was a teenager and they were safe on the footpath. They swung arms, quiet in the darkening afternoon, and Julia told herself it would all be okay. She'd go and sort her father out, and then she'd come back and things would return to normal.

But Evie was sharp, alert to the subtlest of changes. 'And you and Dad are okay?' she asked as Julia tapped her fob to the panel by the gate. Rowan's bike was chained to the nearby rack; he'd be upstairs, watching out the window as they came up the street.

Julia pushed open the door, their conversation paused by the buzzer. 'Hey,' she said when it went quiet again, catching her stepdaughter's arm before she could go ahead to the stairwell. 'You don't have to worry about that.'

Evie nodded, her cheeks pink, breath warm and chocolatey. Julia folded her into a hug and the girl accepted readily, their bodies swishing back and forth like a windscreen wiper. When they touched, it was sweet but there always had to be movement, slightly exaggerated, in the way of little kids: swinging hands, rocking hugs. Evie could be still and unselfconscious only with her mother.

Julia released her stepdaughter and watched her leap up the stairs three at a time, light and bounding until she rounded the corner and disappeared.

Though Julia never felt completely at ease around Evie's mother, their relationship was a good one: civil, verging on friendly. They had little in common, but there were always the topics of Rowan and Evie to fall back on: his minor flaws, her major accomplishments. Samara was also happy to talk about herself, and Julia to listen. Like the older sister she'd never had, Samara was the one in charge: of Evie, of Rowan, still, and certainly of Julia. The idea of not having Samara in her life felt reckless to Julia, like leaving one job without another lined up. She would need Samara to write her a good reference.

The two women waited in the living room while Rowan helped Evie pack for the week at her mother's. Samara sat in the very centre of the sofa as if draped in massive skirts that required accommodation, her chin lifted slightly to show off the slim line of her throat. Julia placed a glass of water on the coffee table and took a chair opposite, feeling plain in her T-shirt and leggings. 'They won't be long, I'm sure.'

Samara sipped her water, then sat back. 'So. Back to Perth for a while.'

Julia nodded, unsurprised that she already knew. Samara, of course, knew everything.

'How long has it been?'

She counted back to the end of 2017. 'A year — no, almost a year and a half.' The realisation was guilt-inducing. 'Too long.'

'Don't beat yourself up,' Samara instructed. 'You're not your father's keeper.'

Julia felt some reprieve. 'Still. He's old. Someone needs to look after him.'

Samara nodded, unconvinced. She rearranged the lavallière at her throat so that the tails settled in a more flattering way over her breasts. 'And some space to yourself might be good,' she commented, not meeting Julia's eye.

Julia was flustered. How much had Rowan told her? It was one of the small battles of their marriage, to get him to keep things private from his ex-wife. The door they kept open for Evie's sake was too slowly shut for Julia's comfort. Ro found the habit impossible to break; he and Samara had grown up together, they were friends before they were lovers, and because of their daughter they were bonded forever. It was Samara's impeccable discretion that prevented Julia from being continually embarrassed.

'This place is so small,' Samara groaned when Julia didn't reply. 'Is Ro ever going to move out?'

Grateful for the neat sidestep, Julia smiled weakly. 'Maybe in a box.'

'I hope it feels cavernous for him without you around,' Samara said. 'Then he'll realise what he's missing.'

Her tone was distant, the verbal equivalent of shuffling papers at a desk, but with Samara it was the words that mattered, not the delivery. Julia was touched.

Evie appeared in the doorway with thumbs hooked into the straps of her backpack, Rowan behind her. 'Hi, Mum.'

Samara stood and opened her arms. They hugged side-on, cheekbones touching. Evie had so many of her mother's features: the heart-shaped face and thick eyelashes, the elegant ears, fingers, ankles. Now when she stood up straight, she was an inch taller than Samara and only two inches shorter than Rowan, slender and long-limbed like both of them, with the shine of health in her hair and nails. When her stepdaughter was little, Julia had longed for some stranger to remark on how alike they looked, wanting not only the compliment but to observe Evie's reaction. Probably she would have laughed, though not meanly. No one would actually mistake the two of them for blood relatives.

Mother and daughter stood with their arms wrapped around each other's waists. 'How do you feel about Julia's news?' Samara asked.

Evie shrugged. 'I mean, it's got to be done.'

'But you're allowed to have feelings.'

Samara was a mediator in divorce settlements for the

painfully wealthy. She wore five-hundred-dollar dresses and encouraged former spouses to let it out with love. 'Only respect can live in this room,' she lectured, according to Evie. Sometimes crisis meetings were called during school holidays and the teenager had to sit in her mother's office, listening through the door. 'Respect and radical honesty. Let's break this thing clean.' By the end of the process, some of the couples wanted to get back together, which meant another fat fee for Samara when things went down the toilet again.

'I have feelings,' Evie countered. 'They're just not the most important thing right now.'

The three adults stared at one another, unsure how they'd created such a perfect, empathetic being.

Julia was careful never to initiate physical contact with her stepdaughter in front of Samara, so she was grateful when Evie stopped to hug her as they left. She tucked her head to fit under Evie's chin and held her tightly. 'I'll see you before I go, okay? This isn't goodbye.'

'I know,' Evie said, releasing her with a soft smile. 'You worry too much, Jules.'

Watching Samara and Evie descend the stairs, Julia had the urge to call her stepdaughter back, to beg her to come on the trip to Perth. She imagined the cheer and efficiency with which Evie would greet the task. *Come on, Grandpa Don,* she'd say, brushing the old man's shoulder with a benevolent hand. *It's got to be done.* Even he couldn't argue with that.

The hours after Evie went to Samara's stretched through the flat. It was the only time the space ever felt too big. Julia slipped out to the balcony, but the night had fallen silent. Evie's departure left a vacuum so big the whole suburb suffered.

She turned and looked back at Rowan in the kitchenette, cobbling together a stir-fry for two. His shoulders drooped and his hair was flattened, as if a great weight was sucking him down. As he straightened from his search through the vegetable drawer, their eyes met. There was an empty second in which his expression didn't change, like his glance had fallen on a stranger, before his lips pulled into a pained smile. He pointed down at the chopping board and mouthed, *Food?*

Julia sighed very softly, so it was almost indistinguishable from an exhalation, then nodded. The sliding door squealed on its runner as she went back inside the flat.

For the last few weeks, they'd been sleeping separately when they were alone. There was an inflatable mattress that Rowan would set up on Evie's bedroom floor the night she went to her mother's, folding it back into the hall cupboard at the end of the week. When Evie was with them Rowan acted like nothing had changed, slipping his arms around Julia in their bed like he always did. The routine had been established wordlessly and now Julia felt like the time for talking about it had passed. In a few days she'd be gone, and he wouldn't have to leave their bed to get space for himself.

Rowan carried the mattress to Evie's room and Julia followed, watching as he unrolled it and plugged the cord into the wall. The fan was loud. The thing lurched from side to side as it filled with air, the top layer lifting and dimpling to resemble a real bed. Rowan excused himself, stepping past her to get the spare sheets and doona, switching off the power with practised efficiency. In a few minutes the bed was made. He sat on the end and began removing his shoes.

'Ro,' she said from the doorway.

'Hmmm?'

When she began speaking, she'd meant to ask why he wanted to sleep in here, separate from her, but what came out of her mouth was, 'I don't think we should talk while I'm away.'

He looked up with alarm. She was relieved she could still evoke that reaction. 'What? Why?'

'So we have a chance to think.'

'Think about what?'

Julia stared. As if he didn't know.

'I don't think *less* communication is a solution.' His voice was unsteady as he shoved at the heel of his sneaker.

'It's not meant to be a solution.'

'What is it, then?' He kicked the shoe off and it hit the wall, though not hard. 'A punishment?'

'A bit of insight, maybe.' She took a breath. 'Into what it might be like to be apart.'

'We *will* be apart.'

'You know what I mean.' She scrubbed at her forehead with the heel of her hand. 'Apart for good.'

Barefoot, Rowan rose and stepped towards her. She gazed up at him. He was a handsome man. He was her husband. She gripped the doorframe.

'I don't want to be apart from you,' he said. 'Not even for a few weeks.'

When she first suggested going back to Perth to help

Don, Rowan had accepted it without argument, though also without enthusiasm. Julia had tried to see the situation as a blessing in disguise, a chance to pull some things together, and she'd assumed he was thinking the same. That was part of her problem: believing she knew what was going on in her husband's mind. Believing that because she felt something, he did too.

'I'm not saying it'll be forever,' she told him. 'I think it will help. Because if we see how it sucks to be apart —'

'I know it's going to suck,' he argued, reaching for the hip that wasn't pressed into the wall and pulling it towards him. 'You don't need to give me the silent treatment to make that clear.'

'It's not the silent treatment.'

'It seems juvenile. *I'm not talking to you!*' His eyes widened as his pitch rose. It was the voice he used to impersonate the nastier girls at Evie's school. *'You can't be my friend anymore!'*

Julia had a flash of memory, disappearing just as she recognised it, like a thought that leads into a dream. She shook her head. 'It's not that.'

He was standing right up against her now, hand moving to the small of her back to pull her towards him. She breathed in: cotton, fading aftershave, light sweat. He was lean and athletic, a head taller than her, stubble darkening his chin in the late hour. 'I hate all of this,' he murmured. 'It's fucked.'

She put her forehead against his chest, not sure whether to slide her hand below the waistband of his shorts, or just sit on the carpet and cry.

– TWO –

The domestic airport had been a destination back when Julia was a child. If a family friend or relative was flying into Perth the whole family drove out, paying through the nose for parking so they could wait in the terminal for the plane. Julia had liked climbing the stairs to the gates alongside the passengers. She wanted people to think she was going somewhere.

The departure lounge had been fishbowl-shaped back then, with a handful of gates and an overpriced coffee shop. Julia liked to find her own little dead area, a sliver of space behind a bollard or next to a drink machine and away from service counters and seats. She set herself up with her knees on the dusty carpet and elbows on the windowsill, staring down to the tarmac below. The best was when she spotted a plane as a dot in the distance and watched it all the way through to the rumbling rush of the landing, and then its nose followed the line to the gate where her family was waiting. It felt like being chosen.

The airport had grown over the years she'd been away. Every time she returned to see her father, there were new shops, different walkways, changed entrances. Now, instead of departing from the centre of the building, passengers had to go around the back, as if they were sneaking out.

Exiting the aerobridge, it seemed like several planes had landed at once. Someone wheeled a cabin bag over Julia's foot. When she was finally able to funnel her way onto the escalators, she held the handrail and leaned back. She'd heard a story once of someone tripping right at the top of a staircase, hands tucked too deep in their pockets to break the fall. Now whenever she went down a set of steps, Julia had to blink away the image of a skull cracked like an egg on the floor.

An ad over the baggage claim read *Welcome to Perth!*, the colours leached with age. So she was in the right place. An old sign used to adorn the highway leaving the airport: *Welcome to Perth, A City for People*. She and Paul used to joke about what else a city could be for. Sheep? Ghosts?

That same highway was a lane wider now, Julia noticed from the taxi. There were new buildings on either side, office space and retail, half with leasing details posted in the windows. All of this couldn't have appeared since her last visit; it must have been under construction for years without her paying attention. She hadn't travelled to Perth by herself since she married Rowan.

Chatting into his headset the whole time, the driver took a route Julia could decipher, but only just, like someone speaking in the simple French you studied in primary school. They headed west along the newly widened highway, then south on a dual carriageway, and then right onto another resurfaced arterial, the old traffic-lit intersections replaced by flyovers. She kept thinking she was in the north-eastern suburbs of Melbourne and having to correct herself. It had the same vague familiarity to it.

A shuttered corner store, its advertising for the local newspaper faded from the sun. A brightly coloured childcare centre built on what had always been a vacant block. The trees that used to line the footpath outside the dentist's office, now all cut to stumps. Someone had painted blotchy white teeth on the bark.

The sign for their street appeared. Still chatting, the driver turned. Julia had been back ten or twelve times in the past decade, but she couldn't remember feeling like this before. As if every little change had happened at once.

The driver stopped and pulled the handbrake. Julia fumbled in her wallet, imagining her father watching through a crack in the curtains. 'Thank you,' she said, reaching between the seats to swipe her card at the machine. The driver nodded at her in the rear-view mirror, his conversation uninterrupted, and drove off as soon as the boot was closed.

The wheels of Julia's suitcase rumbled like distant thunder over the uneven driveway as she walked up to the house. She tried to view the building dispassionately, like a real estate agent: two-car garage on the right, front lounge with bay window on the left. Between them was the low overhang of the front entryway, the heavy wooden door framed by twin panels of rosin-yellow decorative glass. To the unaware, the house would appear empty; the mission-brown roller doors of the garage pulled down, the light from the front room blocked by heavy drapes. The main windowpane had a coffee-coloured tint in which Julia could see her reflection, as if she were inside already, gazing out.

Unlike the roads and shops, the house hadn't changed at all. It was the same one her father had built when her mother accepted his proposal; the one they moved into two days after their wedding, the walls and windows uncovered. Under the low roof outside the door, it even smelled the same: of overcooked pasta and towels half-damp in the dryer.

She had a spare key in her bag but knocked instead, sure that Don was home. As she waited, she looked up into the eaves and saw the corners grey with spiderwebs, thin water stains along the outside edge.

The door opened and there was her father, stooped almost to her height. Melancholy filled her. He'd always insisted on good posture.

'Oh,' he said, seeming mildly surprised, though she'd rung from the cab rank to say she'd arrived. He leaned into his walking stick, the handle tucked against his hip at a forty-five-degree angle, rubber stopper on the other end barely catching the ground. 'Already, is it?'

She kissed his cheek, scratchy with stubble. He wore a shirt of thick navy canvas buttoned to the neck, which seemed clean but had a faint musty whiff. His white hair was too long around his ears and had yellowed a little. Sebum shone on his scalp. 'How are you, Dad?'

'Ninety-two,' he said, either mishearing her or trying to be droll. Shuffling aside so she could enter, he hunched into the alcove created by his bedroom doorframe, his back against the closed door. 'That cabbie,' he went on as Julia pulled her suitcase inside, 'a woman, was it?'

'A man.'

He snuffled. 'Bit of help with your luggage too much to ask?'

'It's fine, Dad.'

'I hope you didn't give him a tip.'

The wheels clacked as Julia moved along the hallway to the wing of smaller bedrooms: Paul's, hers, and a spare. Don's slippers scuffed behind her. 'Not that one,' he yelped as she stopped outside her childhood room. 'There's been a reconfiguration.' He nodded to the last door. 'I thought you'd be more comfortable.'

So, one space in the house *had* changed in the past forty years, Julia noted as she stepped inside. The room had always been a dumping ground for things that didn't fit elsewhere: the family PC and printer, Paul's fitness equipment, their mother's sewing machine. Now all the junk was gone, replaced with a neat double bed and a dressing table, like a proper guest bedroom. The quilt was still crosshatched from being folded up in its packaging. 'Dad! When did you do this?'

'Do you like it?'

'It's very nice.' She touched the metal bedframe, which squeaked. Later she'd have to find the allen key to tighten it up. 'Well done.'

'Thought you'd like somewhere comfortable to stay.'

When she and Rowan had come in the past, they slept in Paul's old bunk beds, squeezing their luggage around the oversized furniture. The couple of times Evie had joined them she was next door, in Julia's room. She wished her father had done this years ago, so the new furniture could get some use. He wouldn't be able to take it with him.

'You've put a lot of effort in,' she said cautiously.

Don lifted his chin so she could see the ropes of his throat, bristled with white. 'The furniture people put it together for an extra fee.'

'That's great.'

Relaxing a little, Don brushed the end of the bed with his spare hand, the other braced against his stick. 'I thought, something fresh and new.'

'Lovely.'

'I liked the yellow. Cheery.'

Julia nodded. Flooded with sudden tiredness, she sat on the bed and yawned. 'Goodness,' she said.

'Would you like a little nap?'

'I don't know.' She picked up the pillows and smelled them: brand new. On the plane she'd had a middle seat and had to stay rigid, elbows bent into her waist to avoid disrupting the passengers on either side. 'I shouldn't. I need to adjust to the time difference.'

Don pushed his hand through the air in a dismissive gesture. 'You torture yourself.'

'No,' Julia argued, but the idea of trying to stay awake did seem overwhelming. She'd woken up at the equivalent of two a.m. in Perth for the early flight, and there were still hours to go until sunset. Hours in which she'd have to be in this house; hours without contacting Rowan beyond the brief message she sent when the plane touched down. She lifted her legs from the floor and stretched along the mattress, which was firm but not unpleasantly so. It rustled underneath her. 'Just a power nap,' she said. 'Get me up in an hour, okay, Dad?'

Nodding, Don reversed towards the door. 'Pull that curtain,' he said, and Julia half-rose from the bed to see that the flimsy net curtains that used to adorn this room had been replaced by heavy block-outs. When she drew them closed everything darkened sweetly, like the day had been cancelled. He added unnecessarily, 'They're new, too.'

The afternoon passed in long, scattered dreams like clouds, and when Julia woke it was dark. There was no lamp in the guestroom, so she had to find the light switch, blinking against the brightness.

Her stomach felt gnarled. She had no idea of the time, but she'd last eaten a dry croissant on the aeroplane very early in the morning. Opening the bedroom door, the light spilled out into the hallway, showing the treacherous route to the back part of the house: a chunky telephone table piled with old *Yellow Pages*, crushed sneakers lined up along the skirting board, a mat with lumps of air caught underneath at the entrance to the kitchen. How did her father navigate this obstacle course every single day?

Guessing that she'd wake hungry, Don had left a cling-wrapped plate of cheese and crackers on the bench. Julia ate it all, tapping the last knob of cheese along the porcelain to catch any crumbs. When she was finished, she took the plate to the sink, found a plastic cup and filled it with tap water, draining it in a few deep swallows.

The back third of her childhood home had full-length windows that looked out onto the backyard. The night was a deep grey, but Julia could make out the terracotta-bricked patio and lawn beyond, both dry and bare. Right near the back fence was the old Hills hoist, drooping to the right from when Paul used it to play Superman. Squinting, Julia saw a couple of items pegged out there, spinning slowly in the dark.

Footsteps tapped their way down from the front bedroom: Her father had always slept lightly. Julia shook her head. The dull *teck* sound of the stick was missing, meaning Don had risked a trip through the house with nothing to break his fall. Worse, he seemed to be moving much faster than he should, like he'd forgotten she was there and was racing to confront a burglar. Turning to face him, she put her hands on her hips and opened her mouth.

A dog stood there, peeking its snout into the kitchen. It was mid-sized, with a deep-brown coat. Seeing her, its tail waved. It walked over to the breakfast bar and sat down, panting gently.

Dad doesn't have a dog, Julia thought, then reconsidered. *No one told me Dad got a dog.* Somehow, in the weeks before she came to help him leave, her father had found a housemate.

'Hey, mate,' she murmured, offering the animal the back of

her wrist to sniff. It licked her arm gently and she took a hold of its collar, bright yellow with a paw-shaped tag. 'Biscuit,' she read. Thrumming its tail in recognition, the dog reached up with its front paws and revealed himself to be a boy. 'Well, there you go.' Scratching his jaw, she wondered where Biscuit had been when she got here, then remembered her father standing in the entryway with his bedroom door shut tight.

Straightening, she checked the clock and groaned. It was half-past ten and she was wide awake. If she'd felt intimidated by the endlessness of time earlier in the day, then it was much worse now, with the light gone, the silence, the appearance of a random dog. Despair sucked at her like the undertow of a wave. This was all too much, too much.

No, too big. The house was too big: that was the beginning and the end of the problem. It was a typical home for the outer suburbs, four bedrooms and two bathrooms on a seven-hundred-square-metre block, with plenty of entertaining space inside and out. Even Samara's smart California bungalow didn't boast those dimensions. But instead of a middle-aged go-getter and an active teenager, this place housed only a reclusive ninety-two-year-old – and a dog, apparently. How many rooms could Don actually need? Julia ticked them off: his bedroom and toilet, the front room where he watched telly, the kitchen, the laundry. More than half the house was barely used.

But it did have a use, her father would argue; it held his stuff. The detritus of forty years of marriage, parenthood, widowerhood. Don wasn't a hoarder, but he was not organised, not tidy. Take this back area, for a start. One end of the breakfast table was piled with appliances, and the junk from the guestroom had been left on various chairs. To counteract the eternal cold of the slate floor, mats of various shapes and sizes had been scattered all over, ground down and dirty, their edges curling up like dead leaves. The long curtains meant to cover the back windows had hooks missing in a few places, so they didn't sit flat against the rod, but gaped and bagged instead.

The house was great for children, at least those born in the eighties. Skidding Hot Wheels over the rocky landscape of the floor and jumping from chairs with arms extended to swat the slats holding up the raked ceiling. A deep bath where you could get your whole head below the surface, then crack your eyes open to find sunken toys. Slipping into the walk-in pantry or laundry cupboard for hide-and-seek, crouching low so the seeker didn't see your shadow through the louvred doors. The big backyard, the narrow gap behind the shed, the shed itself with her father's woodworking tools, had been a whole universe for her and Paul to enjoy. Now the idea of her ageing father alone in the same one filled Julia with fear.

But he hadn't been alone, she tried to remind herself, still holding the edge of the bench. There were things in place to help him continue to be independent. His groceries were delivered, as were his medications and library books, and someone came twice a week to clean. A white button hung from a cord around his neck, ready to be squeezed in case of emergency. Julia wasn't sure what happened when it was deployed, if an agency would try to call Don first or just send someone right away, but she knew what the subscription cost per month and had an app on her phone that connected to the device's battery, so she was alerted if the power was running low.

All of it had taken years to set up, the result of many battles with Don to get him to see sense. The wins had been exhausting and only mildly satisfying. Julia and Paul knew how their father flouted the arrangements: he cancelled the cleaner if he didn't want to see anyone, he 'forgot' to loop the emergency button around his neck. Even if he'd bow down and do what they wanted, the arrangements were no longer fit for purpose. Julia was here to finalise them all, leaving her father unaided in his echoing cavern of memories. Don might consider that a victory, but even he must have known it was pyrrhic. They had to cancel the helpers because his needs were too great. It was time for him to move to a smaller place, somewhere with permanent, onsite care.

Knowing for weeks that she needed to go, Julia had put it off, booking her flight and telling Evie at the last possible moment. She didn't expect the process to be easy, but there was one advantage: he'd actually agreed to leave. Paul couldn't give up the time to help, so it had been his task to talk their father into it. Somehow, seven years after losing his wife and at least a year since he could be said to be able to look after himself, Don had been convinced. Julia didn't know how her brother had managed it.

'Come on,' she whispered to the dog, leading him to the back door and sliding it open. Biscuit went outside, pissed obediently and came back in again, following her up the hallway. Her father's bedroom door was cracked open, his deep, regular snores seeping out, and the dog slid through the gap.

Don Lambett letting a dog in his room. Julia couldn't believe it.

She returned to the guestroom and got back under the sheets. Staring up at the ceiling – beige with age and patterned with tea-coloured stains, watermarks in the corners from cracked tiles or who knew the fuck what – she imagined everything else that piled and suffocated and jammed this house: the possessions, the dog, her father, the past.

– THREE –

Julia dozed for a few hours, getting up and returning to the kitchen when she heard her father moving around. The space was both too vast and too crowded for him to negotiate. He sat down at the breakfast table as soon as she told him to, face drooping with relief, one arm fussing around the base of his chair in a way he thought was subtle.

'I know you have a dog there,' she said, switching on the kettle.

Don seemed surprised. Had he expected to be able to hide the animal from her? For how long?

'Biscuit,' he said.

At first Julia thought he was putting in his order, then remembered the name on the dog's tag. 'When were you going to mention it?'

'Him,' Don corrected sulkily.

'Mention *him*.'

Instead of answering, he shifted his hand, so the dog

had to come out from under the table. Both of them looked recalcitrant.

Julia had to search for the instant coffee, finding the jar on a high shelf beside the rangehood. Grease coated the glass. 'Is this your coffee, Dad?'

Don nodded.

'Is it the only jar?'

His shoulders rolled with discomfort. 'I don't know. Use it if it's in date.'

She unscrewed it. The contents smelled as she expected, caffeine and dirt. She'd never been able to talk her father into more gourmet coffee experiences; he thought it was all fancy-pantsy nonsense. Taking out a teaspoon, she covered the bottom of two mugs with the freeze-dried crystals as the kettle rumbled.

Julia took note as she assembled their breakfast. Don's fridge door was full of old sauce bottles and dressings, but the shelves were mostly bare. The contents of the vegetable drawer were disintegrating, the liquids pooling yellowish in the bottom. The pantry was similar, stocked well with spices and staples but low on the items she actually imagined her father eating: tinned spaghetti, pineapple chunks, instant soup. When the toast popped, she spread butter to the corners of each slice, then carried the plates and mugs to the breakfast table. Nodding his thanks, Don lifted his coffee with both hands and hunched over it slightly, as if needing the warmth.

'How long have you had Biscuit?' she asked, clicking for the dog. He slunk over and accepted a scratch under the chin.

'A while,' Don muttered.

'He's an adult dog.'

Don bit into his toast and chewed noisily, jaw pulsing like a piston.

'You didn't get yourself a puppy, is what I'm saying.'

'You've missed your calling as a detective.'

Julia persisted. 'Where did he come from?'

'He needed a new owner.'

'Someone gave him up?'

Don tore the toasted bread away from its crust, which he offered to Biscuit.

'I don't want to offend you, Dad,' she began. Her father stiffened, his gaze sliding past her and fixing on the hallway beyond, as if waiting for someone else to show up and tell her off for him. 'But are you able to give him all the care he needs?'

'It's not dangerous,' he told the room, 'to feed a dog bread.'

'I don't mean right now. I mean the vet and stuff.'

'He hasn't needed the vet. He's a healthy dog.'

'But he might, one day.' No response. 'Does he get walks? Because you can't —'

'He goes out in the backyard. He has a whale of a time back there.'

Julia sighed.

The dog watched fretfully from his position next to Don's chair, as if he feared getting turfed out again. Surely Biscuit had been a resident long enough to know Don was top dog in this house. Julia peeled her own stiff crust from her toast and held it out to Biscuit, who took it gently and lay down on the floor.

'I have kibble for him,' Don said. 'Dog biscuits.'

'Okay.'

'He has his own bed. A dish of water in the laundry.'

'I believe you, Dad.'

He settled slightly, lifting his second piece of toast with a twitching hand. As he ate, Julia observed him discreetly, the way she had the pantry, trying to assess the lay of the land. He wasn't dressed, though she couldn't expect him to be at six in the morning. As with the shirt he'd worn the day before, his old tartan dressing-gown seemed mostly clean, though there was a dark spot on one lapel, maybe old. His sandpapery stubble was even. His teeth were in.

'You're staring,' he commented.

'It's good to see you, you know.'

He chewed non-committedly.

'Are you pleased to have me home?'

'Of course.'

'I'm not cramping your style?' Tears jumped into her eyes for a second, but she blinked them away.

His eyes drifted over to her, neither warm nor cool. Their whites looked faintly yolky, the same way his hair did. 'This is your house too,' he said. 'You're always welcome.'

The desire to speak to Rowan throbbed like a toothache. Instead, Julia rang Paul. He answered quickly.

'Jules. I thought you'd ring yesterday. I was worried.'

'Sorry,' she said. 'I was asleep.'

'All day?'

'Pretty much.'

'How's Dad?'

'Well, he's fine.'

Paul latched onto the insincerity. 'What's wrong?'

'Did you know he got a dog?'

There were voices in the background. 'Hang on,' Paul instructed. After some scraping sounds, like furniture moving, the line quietened. 'A dog?'

Julia described Biscuit coming down to the kitchen in the night, how attached the two of them seemed. 'Dad's very defensive about it,' she said.

'What a surprise.'

'I don't know if he was trying to hide Biscuit from me when I got here, but —'

'Of course he was.'

The siblings went silent for a while. Julia imagined she could hear the gentle wash of waves. Paul lived two streets back from Bronte Beach, in a flat about the same size as Rowan and Julia's, though it only had to fit one person.

'I don't know,' Julia said at last.

'Look, ignore the dog,' Paul decided. 'Just keep going with the plan. He hasn't changed his mind, has he?'

'He didn't say anything about that.'

'Good. He's not safe there.'

'I know,' Julia said. She wanted to describe the packed hallway and impractical pantry, but Paul had been here more recently than she had. He was the one who'd made the decision that enough was enough.

As she ended the call, Julia felt a rush of resentment. Immediately, she tried to chase it away. It was logic that had led them to this arrangement, where Julia moved in to sort out their father while Paul continued with his regular life. He managed a trendy bar in Darlinghurst and could only get back to Perth for snippets of time, sometimes just a night, never more than a week. Julia and Rowan had their own business, so she was more flexible, able to go where she was most needed. It was just how things had turned out. It was not a commentary on Paul being a man or Julia being a woman, or on Julia being old and dull while her brother's life was fast-paced and glamorous. It certainly wasn't, she reminded herself, because Paul was single and successful while Julia was just a part-time stepmother without small children of her own. Even if it felt that way.

Her father and Biscuit were in the front room, the dog lying on the carpet by Don's favourite recliner. She was pleased to see her father had washed and dressed, albeit in the same heavy shirt from the day before. His hair was stuck down to his head like papier-mâché and his forehead glistened.

When they were little, Julia and Paul couldn't come into this room unless they were invited. They had the TV room just off the kitchen; this was the adult space. Their mother would sit on the carpet, legs bent to the side like a mermaid, and do jigsaw puzzles while Don stretched out to read. The pinewood hutch, a wedding gift, took up most of one wall, a small flat-screened television perched on its lowest shelf. In its glass cabinets were the good china and the good wine, all untouched and dusty.

Julia put her hands on her hips. 'Can we have a quick chat?'

'Now?' Don asked.

'I just need to work out a couple of things.'

Sighing, he muted his morning news program and wriggled higher against the backrest. 'Chat away, then.'

'The cleaners, do they still come on Mondays?'

Don blinked. Snuffling softly, Biscuit rolled onto his back.

Julia raised her voice, though she knew her father's hearing had nothing to do with it. 'The people who clean the house,' she said. 'Is that still on a Monday?'

'No.'

'No? What day is it?'

'None of them.'

Julia's hands slid from her hips and gripped the hem of her shirt. 'What?'

'I called to cancel,' Don said. 'Free them up to help somebody else.'

'You were entitled to that assistance.'

'It's not a matter of entitled.' He looked at the remote control. 'People don't always get what they deserve.'

Julia shook her head. If the cleaners had gone, it was a bit early, but the service would have been wrapped up soon anyway. 'What about groceries?'

'What about them?'

'When are they delivered?'

The dog whined and arched his back, and Julia bent forward to rub the base of his ribs. A leg kicked in ecstasy.

'There was one last week,' Don said, but before she could ask the exact day, he went on, 'but that's all finished now.'

She stopped scratching the dog's stomach. 'Why?'

Don looked at her pointedly.

'Dad.' She breathed in through her nose, out through her mouth. 'I could have used the help.'

'It can go towards someone who needs it.'

'The shopping isn't subsidised like the cleaners. You pay for the delivery.'

'Well.' Don shrugged shortly, his shoulders heaping up to his ears and tumbling away. 'Save money, then.'

'We have a lot of work to do,' she said, trying to sound patient. Giving up hope of her return, Biscuit rolled back over and lay his snout on his paws. 'It would have been helpful to get some stuff taken care of.'

Don picked up the remote and aimed it at her. 'I'm missing this,' he said.

She looked back at the television screen. A man in a grey suit was mopping a small square of floor, eyes shining with delight. Two women in shift dresses stood alongside him, hands held to their chests as if viewing a miracle.

The walls were pressing in; she couldn't breathe. Julia hurried through the house, dragged the patio door open and burst outside. In daylight the true neglect of the backyard was revealed: the overgrown grass burned to straw by the summer sun, the only living things tall, thorny weeds topped with yellow flowers. The outdoor furniture was coated in grime. All around, looking like neat brown stones, were fossilised discs of dogshit, so old and untouched they could have been carbon-dated to reveal the exact moment Biscuit had first arrived. It would be a more direct way of learning the truth than asking her father.

This had been his pride and joy, once. Every weekend Don

would strip to a Bonds singlet and stubbies and mow this lawn to a fine emerald carpet, sweep the patio bricks and wipe down the chairs. In the evenings he put on barbeques, lamb chops and fat sausages, chunks of margarine-daubed corn wrapped in foil. The outdoor table sat ten, and they often invited family friends and their kids, passing mayo-thick salads and crusty bread rolls up and down. Afterwards their mother would call Julia and Paul to help her with the dishes, Goldie's face dewy from light wine and conversation. Even before she died, whenever Julia tried to picture their mother, this was the image she summoned: Goldie Lambett, younger than Julia is now, drying her hands on a tea towel and laughing, accompanied by cicada music and the smell of mozzie coils.

Julia knew she must be simplifying, but in her mind, Goldie was always happy. By name, by nature, Julia supposed. Her mother's only ever job had been in the home and, as far as her children knew, she'd relished it, singing to herself as she cooked, stopping to hug them if they appeared while she was cleaning. 'Neat and sweet,' Don had called her. He'd taken joy from his wife, and why not? She was almost thirty years younger than her husband, who'd been a white-collar bachelor until he met his colleague's daughter. He should have been alone his whole life, maybe. Not as punishment, just by temperament. What had attracted that bright happy woman to the stern, immovable older man?

Julia had never been afraid of her father: he wasn't mean or violent, just grumpy. She was wary of him instead, knowing how he could suck the fun from a thing with his negativity. It was almost like he did it on purpose, and Goldie seemed to find this charming. It was no use complaining to her when Don hurt your feelings: even as she soothed you, Goldie would be genuinely perplexed. 'Your father doesn't mean it,' she said. As if it was all part of some elaborate joke, Julia thought, that no one got but her mother.

Despite their mutual besottedness, Julia's parents didn't have an egalitarian relationship. Don was so much older that he'd retired when Paul entered primary school, and Goldie, in her mid-thirties, had simply added him to her list of people to care for. As a teenager, Julia had watched her mother bring trays of tea and biscuits up to Don in the front room, and it made her swear against marrying someone like him. 'Let him get it himself,' she told her mother once, stopping her in the hallway. 'He's not decrepit.'

Goldie shook Julia off. 'One day you'll be in love,' she said lightly, 'and you'll do things like this too.'

In love, Julia had thought with horror. How was it possible?

Now she guessed that most children must be like she was, baulking at the idea of their parents having a relationship that excluded them. The four Lambetts were together so often, and yet her mother's prime concern was always her husband. Julia was jealous. She wanted Goldie to herself.

Because Don was so much older, there had always been the notion – subconscious, stuffed all the way down, a blink of light in a coal chute – that he'd die first, and earlier, leaving the children alone with Goldie. It wasn't that Julia wanted it; it was the natural order of things. Don had had a long, good life. But that was not the way it had gone.

Standing in the backyard, frustration collected and

throbbed in Julia's limbs. Another selfish, unfair thought, though she had to acknowledge it to give the pain somewhere to go: this should have been her mother's job.

- FOUR -

In the afternoon, overwhelmed by the scale of the project ahead of her, Julia returned to the kitchen. Her father claimed food had been delivered in the past week, but she couldn't find evidence of this. Many of the cans and jars that lined the pantry were stuck to the shelves with rust or old leaks; they could have been bought a decade ago, back when Goldie was alive. Levering up tins of baked beans, Julia looked for their used-by dates, but they were blurred by dust and time.

Still, they wouldn't starve, even if the prehistoric stuff turned out to be inedible: there was white bread, plain crackers, cheese, butter. Frozen meals were stacked in the freezer, replicas of the food Goldie used to cook. On the countertop was a bowl of apples, her father's favourite fruit.

Julia shut the fridge. She'd had toast and butter for breakfast, a cheese sandwich for lunch. If she was going to clear out this house, she'd need more fuel than dairy and bread.

'Dad.' She leaned into the lounge, where he was onto his

seventh hour of television. 'I'm going to the shops.'

Her father struggled up from where he'd slid along the recliner's slippery vinyl. 'What for?'

'Food. Coffee.' *Everything*, she thought.

'Oh, well. Take the Commodore.'

'Does it run?' Her father hadn't driven regularly for years.

'One way to find out. Hey,' he called as she reached for the door handle, 'we need teabags, all right? And how about a cake.' She looked around to find him smiling, his eyelids softly collapsed. 'Might as well celebrate, eh?'

She'd learned to drive in her father's old Holden, broad as a bus, with a manual transmission and hand-wound windows. It was parked on the front lawn, the grass beneath its tyres sandy and dying. She had to turn the key twice, but it burst to life all right, as if it just needed a wake-up call to get moving. The fuel gauge was full and an air freshener hung from the rear-view mirror. Don had prepared it for her, maybe on the same day he'd bought the new furniture for the guestroom.

The route to the closest supermarket was scored into her brain, but Julia had to go slowly, recalling how to use the gearstick and the heavy clunking clutch. In the shopping centre car park, she took a bay on the periphery and peered at the white structure with its flat, blue roof, the signage in neon eighties script. The whole complex had been shut from Saturday lunchtime through to Monday morning when she was little, but now it was three o'clock on a Sunday and everything was open.

There used to be a fabric store here that sold their school uniform; Julia and Paul had tried on items behind a wispy white curtain with Goldie positioned to hide their embarrassed silhouettes. According to the directory by the automatic doors, that shop had been replaced by a health food store. Julia wondered how much of a market there was for that stuff around here. Her dad certainly wouldn't be interested.

She got a trolley from the corral and entered the independent grocery store. In Melbourne, she and Rowan did their shopping at Prahran Market, wandering from vendor to vendor: meat from the butcher, fish from the fishmonger, fruit from open crates. Here the selection was more limited, but it was all the same basic stuff. She shopped like a hungry person without a list, because that's what she was. Mangoes and apricots went into the cart, good brie and prosciutto, hummus, Greek yoghurt, chicken breasts, fresh pasta. Aisle after aisle, she pulled down items with the urgency of bringing in washing ahead of a storm. Breadcrumbs. Rock salt. Soy sauce. Pralines. She sensed the black clouds assembling in the distance.

Another trolley turned into her aisle, and Julia tried to shrink out of the way. The shop was a rabbit warren, the narrow aisles blocked by oversized endcaps and ageing shoppers letting their trolleys roll off as they chose between brands of oats.

As she passed, the customer grabbed the side of Julia's trolley. 'Julia, oh my God, is that you?'

She looked up and recognition pinged through her, only to be replaced by the swift plummeting sensation of dread. 'Hi.'

Davina Weir – if Weir was still her last name – had been in Julia's year at primary school. They were close back then, their mothers very good friends, and the Weir family were regulars at backyard summer barbeques. Julia and Paul had even stayed with their family for a week once, when Goldie had been in hospital and Don was still at work.

The adult Davina was as tall as Rowan, with soft, pale skin. Her hair was shoulder-length, the ends dyed bright purple, and her mulberry nail polish was chipped at the edges. The makeup and hair dye layered over twenty-five years should have made Davina feel foreign to Julia, but she didn't. The Davina she'd once known floated very close to the surface.

Lunging for a hug, Davina whacked a hip against the corner of her trolley. 'Ow, shit!' she shouted, grinning and rubbing the spot with one hand as she leaned over again, more carefully this time. Julia sucked in her stomach so their abdomens didn't touch, though there was quick, squeamish contact between her throat and Davina's pillowy breasts. 'Julia, what the fuck, what are you doing here?'

'Shopping,' she said. The single loud *HA!* of Davina's laughter was jarring and familiar at the same time. 'I'm staying with Dad for a bit.'

'You live in Melbourne, right?' The hug ended. Davina put both hands on the end of Julia's trolley again, holding it in place.

'That's right.'

There was a pause in which Julia could have explained, but she didn't. 'Is this still your local, then?' she asked, smiling to show Davina she wasn't judging her. She remembered Davina always being very conscious of judgement.

'Talk about turning into your parents,' Davina said, although they hadn't been. 'I even live on Stewart Ave.'

'Near the Wessels' house?' Julia asked. Kimmie Wessels

had been another girl at school. The three of them used to walk together every day, trailed by Paul, and Davina's little sister. Kimmie, who was an only child, would get annoyed and say they were going to be late, but Davina never hurried once.

'Number twenty-two.'

That meant nothing to Julia, who didn't remember the Wessels' house number, just their street. 'Are Kimmie's parents still there?'

'They all went back to Cape Town a zillion years ago.' Davina rolled her eyes, always wide and expressive. Beneath them was old liner, slightly smudged, a little sexy for a Sunday afternoon. 'You're staying with Don? How is he?'

'Old,' Julia said. 'You know how it goes.'

'But he's well?'

'As good as you can expect.' Julia wondered if Davina knew her mother had died. She must, because Goldie and Pam Weir had been friends even after the two girls fell out of touch. It felt awkward to bring it up, though, so she said, 'He's slowing down. He got a dog.'

'You guys are spending some time together, then?'

Not wanting to mention the need to find a low-care facility and pack the house, she only nodded.

Davina's eyes went to Julia's ring finger. When she raised them again, they were tinged pink with emotion. 'Oh my God, it's so good to see you, really.'

'Yeah.' Julia shifted her weight. 'It's been a really long time.'

Davina reached into her pocket and pulled out a large,

older-model phone, the screen tarnished and cracked in a corner. 'Give us your number, we'll catch up properly,' she ordered. 'You're here for a little while?'

Julia rose onto her toes to see how she was being classified in Davina's phonebook. *Julia L.* 'I don't know how long yet.'

'More than a week? I'm kind of busy for the next few days, but after that.' Davina tapped her nail against the plastic.

'More than a week.'

'Great.' Davina's thumb hovered. 'Hit me.'

As she recited her phone number, Julia briefly considered switching the final two digits, but she wouldn't put it past Davina to descend on Don's house, either pissed off or oblivious, if she couldn't get in touch. Or she'd be the kind to check the number as soon as she got it. She imagined Davina hitting 'call' from a metre away and Julia's phone staying silent.

'Done!' Davina crowed, putting the device away. She gazed at Julia. 'What do you know! Julia Lambett herself.'

She smiled weakly. 'In the flesh.'

Davina gave another single punching hoot of mirth. 'I'll be in touch,' she said. 'We'll go out.' Fluttering her fingers in farewell, she pushed her trolley past Julia's and sashayed down the aisle.

Julia had planned to go to a bakery for the cake her father wanted, but she felt the energy zapped out of her, disappearing into the colourful ends of Davina's hair and fingers. Slumped over the trolley, she went to the supermarket's bakehouse and found a jam sponge, then dragged her feet to the checkouts. Davina wasn't there.

Putting her items on the belt, Julia realised she'd never considered the possibility of running into old ghosts. Really, it was inevitable. This was where she'd spent the first twenty years of her life, and though she'd moved farther and farther away over the years – to a flat near the train line, then a share house on the coast, and then to the Eastern States – there were plenty who hadn't. When Goldie was still alive, there were always stories of who she'd seen at the shop or the park, what the gossip was at the community hall and the library and the playing fields. It was like an invisible fence penned in most of the kids Julia and Paul had grown up with, restricting them to the immediate area or a few suburbs away, at most. Even if they had managed to escape, their parents were still in the family home, just like Don, acting surprised when their adult kids had to move back in because they couldn't afford real estate.

On her trips to Perth with Rowan and Evie, she'd never bumped into people she knew, but then they'd only really used Don's house as a base. As soon as they woke in the mornings, they were in the Commodore, driving to the city or to the beach, wandering around Fremantle or Subiaco or Hillarys, day trips to the hills or the Swan Valley. Acting like tourists, and tourists never knew anyone.

Driving home, Julia sat erect, hands at ten and two like a police car was breathing down her neck. Her eyes roamed the footpaths for other blasts from the past. In the taxi from the airport, she'd been preoccupied by all the things that seemed to have changed; what she should have been aware of was everything that hadn't.

'I ran into Davina Weir today.'

It was the brief lull between dinner and dessert. Julia had served grilled salmon with a quinoa salad, and though her father questioned if the dots among the grain were maggots ('The dots *are* the grains, Dad'), he finished enough to satisfy her. She picked up the sponge cake from the kitchen bench and its plastic packaging crackled.

'Who?'

'Davina Weir.' Julia put the cake on the table and went back for a knife and plates. 'You remember, her mother was friends with Mum.'

'Pamela Weir.'

'That's right.'

Don lifted his nose and sniffed. Noticing, Biscuit got up and did the same, hoping to smell something he liked. 'Silly woman.'

'Mrs Weir? Why?'

He waited until she was sitting down to answer. 'When your mother died,' he began, reaching to massage the dog's ear, 'she sent an absolutely enormous bunch of flowers. I don't know what she could have spent on them. Looked like the tail of a peacock. They could barely get it through the door.'

Julia unpackaged the cake and the dog sat up higher, looking at it longingly. At least someone was interested: it was dry, the cream yellow in the light. She wished she'd had the energy to go to the bakery after all. 'That sounds nice of her,' she said distractedly, picking up the knife.

'She never went to the funeral.'

Slicing into the stiff sponge, Julia had no idea if her father was right. She'd only ever been able to summon Goldie's funeral in small flashes, like lightning in a blackout. She knew Don and Paul had been there, and Rowan, never letting go of her hand, but beyond that you could say anything about the day, and she'd have to take your word for it. Five hundred mourners? A percussion flash mob? Sure, maybe, if you say so. 'Some people don't do well at funerals. They'd been such good friends—'

'They hadn't spoken for a while,' Don interrupted, accepting his plate. 'That woman never had any sense.'

Julia hadn't known that. She wasn't surprised Goldie never said anything; though she liked to gossip, it was all lighthearted. When things were serious her mother could be discreet to the point of pain. 'Well, maybe she felt embarrassed to go.' Julia took a small slice for herself. 'Unwelcome,' she said pointedly.

'Too right,' Don said. 'She wasn't welcome.'

She exhaled so hard some of the icing sugar drifted from the cake onto the tablecloth. 'So she sent flowers instead.' Julia didn't know why she was trying to stand up for Pamela Weir. 'Anyway, I was just saying. Davina was at the shop.'

Don nodded and swallowed, his Adam's apple moving jerkily. 'She was there.'

'Who?'

'That Davina. She came to the funeral.'

Julia lowered her fork. 'She did?'

'Stood at the back.' He shrugged and cut a wedge of sponge with the side of his fork, unfussed by its tastelessness and texture. 'Didn't go to the wake, though. Or not that I saw.'

'Really,' Julia muttered, wondering.

When they'd finished their dessert, the two sat gazing at their plates for a moment, lost in thought. 'Well,' her father said after a while, jolting her to attention, 'that was welcome-back cake, so.' He coughed. 'Welcome back.'

- ☾ -

Evie Cheng crouches low to the floor, the slim aisle marked black with sparkling little points like the night sky. A dropped bottle rolls back and forth with the motion of the bus. Trying to help, she chases it to the front and stops at the yellow line, which must not be crossed under any circumstances. Death will result, or so the rumour goes.

The bottle clatters down the steps and hits the brush at the base of the door. The driver looks in the rear-view mirror. Back to your seat, please.

Evie drags her feet along the starry floor. Swinging out to the right as the bus goes left, she knocks a hip into the hard silver of a seat edge. Stumbling, she reaches for the pole that runs between the seat back and the ceiling.

The man sitting there turns. Hello. *A smile of recognition.* Hey, we know each other.

– FIVE –

The routine of work had set hard in Julia's bones. At four o'clock the next morning, Monday, she was awake, keeping herself in bed while everything in her pushed to get out, get dressed, get going.

She'd run Rowan's physiotherapy practice for the last ten years, helping to build it from a one-man operation to a niche but well-regarded clinic on the corner of Canterbury and Toorak roads. She was in the office six days a week, often from open until close, but dropping by even when she had time off to make sure things were ticking over. The only time she'd had more than a day or two away, she was holidaying with Rowan. Even then – touring Japan for their honeymoon, visiting the Gold Coast with Evie, days in Perth to see Don or staying in Sydney with Paul – they packed the itinerary. Rowan had an aversion to being idle and this had infected Julia as well, though she could resist the urge to be productive if what she was doing was valuable in some other way. Like her afternoon at the Botanic Gardens with Evie: if Rowan had been there, he would've ordered them all to power walk around the lake as soon as their drinks were finished.

Now she was on indefinite leave. Their longest-serving and most reliable receptionist, Sruthi, was taking on the tasks of office manager. Julia didn't have to worry about what was being done in her absence, at least not on the work front.

Still, she felt agitated. In the early years the business had low points; debts were high, patient loads low. She and Rowan hunched over the figures, wondering if they should give up the lease when it ran out. Toorak was a tough market; the residents all had their personal trainers and orthopaedists, and the rent pinched. Julia didn't tell Rowan, but she felt some relief at the idea of taking down the sign, locking the doors and walking away. After weeks of fifty or sixty hours at the desk, willing the phone to ring, wiping down surfaces until they threatened to lift away with the paper towels, the idea of waking to nothing on a Monday morning was sweet.

Later, when they got into a groove and Rowan was able to hire staff, the question became whether Julia might quit entirely, or at least go part-time. They could afford it, and less stress would surely be good for her. Rowan had pinched his thumb and forefinger around her wrist.

'You're wasting away,' he said, which had nothing to do with anything.

Again, the idea had fluttered around her head, beautiful and untouchable as a butterfly: days with no responsibilities;

becoming a lady who lunches. Even Samara had to work, although, like Rowan, she would have died without it. But in the end, Julia decided not to drop too many hours.

'When we have a baby,' she promised, 'then you can replace me.'

They'd shaken hands on it. The memory makes her skin prickle.

But thank God she hadn't taken the opportunity to step back, if this was what unemployment was like: no concrete need to get out of bed, none of the safety of knowing your tasks and how to achieve them, no gentle satisfaction at getting things done. Julia didn't always feel completely comfortable amongst their staff, especially recently, but she liked the office itself. She knew the coffee machine and photocopier settings back to front, the guy to call if one of the Pilates reformers started making a grinding sound, how to display the foam rollers in an aesthetically pleasing pyramid. On top of all that, being at work meant looking forward to going home. Now the pantry was fully stocked, Julia had nowhere to go.

The day sagged and spread. Julia was too awake to doze off and too drowsy for what she was there to do. She dragged herself to the kitchen to make meals for her father, returning to the guestroom in between to crawl onto the unmade bed and scroll through her phone. The inertia weighed down, heavier and heavier, so that she couldn't get up and be useful if she tried.

She pictured Rowan standing at the end of the bed, hands on his hips. Even when he tried to stand still, there were little pulses of energy in his thighs as the muscles prepared for action.

'What are we doing?' he'd say. 'What's all this?'

Julia wanted to answer his question, but they'd made that decision. And besides, she had no defence. Shaking his head in gentle dismay, he vanished to somewhere he could get things done.

Her father didn't ask her what she was doing. Between meals he returned to the front room, the dog padding after him. A couple of times during the afternoon the two of them passed the guestroom on their way through the house, the four footfalls of Biscuit and three from her father, and she wondered what they were up to. What they'd do if she didn't come out to make them more food. There were still those frozen dinners; probably Don would go through those, meal by meal, then wait, then starve.

If she'd behaved like this as a teenager her father would've been on her case, demanding she leave her bedroom door open and calling her out to the car to go on errands. He'd give her chores and watch while she completed them. In the evenings, if she tried to slip off to her room, he'd order her into the lounge and sit her on the couch while he and Goldie watched *Four Corners* or *The Bill*. He wouldn't allow her to be alone.

On Monday night she had the same dream that had woken her up at four a.m.: Evie on a bus, a strange man trying to speak to her. Julia tried so hard to see his face that her eyes opened into the darkness of the guestroom. Someone was breathing beside her. Biscuit sat on the floor, his chin resting on the mattress.

'Hey,' she whispered, once she had her bearings. She disentangled her hand from the sheets to stroke his snout. 'Hey mate, you okay?'

The end of the dog's tongue slid out for a moment, pink and broad as a slice of ham, delivering a gentle kiss to Julia's palm. She sat up, touched, but Biscuit turned and went back to the hallway, his toenails clicking as he moved off the carpet. It wasn't until Julia had rearranged her pillows and turned on her side, trying to fall back asleep, that she realised her father must have opened her door so the dog could go in.

It was just a matter of starting, Julia decided the next day. The journey of a thousand miles began with a single step, the eating of an elephant with a single bite, and all that. The house would not get sorted and packed by lying around looking through her phone.

And this was work, too. Even if it wasn't a job she ever would have chosen.

She decided on the kitchen, the space she'd inspected the most thoroughly. She had old boxes from the garage, the dirt and dead cockroaches tipped out, and a roll of large bin bags ready to go. The pantry doors whined open, the ancient contents cowering in the dusty yellow light.

She went shelf by shelf, telling herself not to marvel at the age of the items she brought down: rice with a nine-year-old best-before date; cans of soft drink with limited-edition designs for the Beijing Olympics. A line of decorative tins labelled *Flour*, *Sugar*, *Tea* were removed without looking under their lids. Nothing good could result. She tied the bag closed and pulled another off the roll.

Her father stayed at the other end of the house. She'd made him a thermos of tea to get him through till lunchtime, not wanting him to appear behind her and have his skull caved in by a falling bottle of soda water carbonated in the previous century.

She was methodical, patient. She wanted to blast loud music to clear her mind, but she needed to be alert to her father's call, so she settled on a single earphone and her jumbled thoughts. The challenge was not to think of Rowan. If she came close, she gave herself a little shake, like hitting a nerve in a game of Operation, and directed her mind elsewhere.

After Samara got the bungalow's kitchen renovated, she'd had a dinner party to show off the marvel of two ovens, six burners, integrated everything, and Julia and Rowan were invited. (This brief acknowledgement of Rowan didn't count, Julia decided, because she was really thinking about Samara.) Receiving the guided tour, Julia had made comparisons not with the pokey kitchen in their South Yarra flat but this one, her mother's, which was big and open and had been state-of-the-art when Don bought it for her. Goldie had selected from a catalogue the wall tiles with their raised vegetable motif, the carrots and onions and broccoli handpainted in Europe, or so they were told. Those veggies caught every splash and smear in their crevices, but Goldie wiped them down with love every night, making sure they shone under the trendy new downlights. Since she'd arrived, Julia had been trying to do the same, scrub off old marks and bits of grit from the last few Goldie-less years, but they didn't look like they used to.

BROOKE DUNNELL

To her surprise, the pantry was soon finished. Two shelves held the items Julia bought on her shopping trip, along with what could be salvaged from her father's ruins. Her elation peaked, then ran dry. Really, the problem had just been shifted to the bags and boxes scattered on the floor. The real order would come when things started leaving the house.

Midafternoon, her father and Biscuit came in. The dog stayed close to Don's side, as alert as Julia to the possibility of dirty crockery smashing on the hard floor and cutting his feet through his slippers. Julia snatched the plate from Don's hands. 'Dad! I would've come and got that.'

'I'm not a complete invalid,' he commented, untroubled. Leaning on his cane, he gazed into an open cupboard. 'Well.'

'I only just started on that one,' she said. 'Look at this!' She led him to the pantry. 'How long since you've seen it like that?'

Don was silent for a moment, gazing at the bare shelves. Biscuit went past him to sniff the recesses where food had been, turning back with a confused expression at finding only sticky surfaces and not the source of all those smells.

'What did you do with it all?' Don asked.

She pointed to the bags and boxes lined up in the adjoining TV room. 'Most of that needs a trip to the tip, but there's some that can be donated.'

'If it's edible, we'll eat it.'

She shook her head. 'Not food, Dad. Old utensils and things.'

His face knotted. 'Show me.'

Julia went and picked up a box she'd filled with mismatched drinkware. Other cupboards were still overflowing with them,

58

more than the two of them would need even if she didn't wash up for a week.

Don sat at the table and she put the box in front of him. With a shaking hand, he picked through the contents. 'We had to get these when you could hold your own drink,' he said, tapping a nail against a plastic cup that once looked like it was made of glass. Now it was cloudy, scratched around the rim. He put it aside and rested his fingertips on a mug with a faded print of a chairlift. 'We got that when we went to Thredbo.'

'Who went to Thredbo?'

'All of us.'

Julia vaguely remembered a driving holiday through country New South Wales. 'Do you want to keep it?' she asked.

He ignored her. 'That's from an old camping set,' he said, lifting a neon cup for a moment before putting it back. 'That one – I think your mother took it from a buffet. She liked the shape.'

Julia was stunned. 'Mum stole it?'

'It's hardly stealing. One glass? I suppose.' Dropping it the last couple of centimetres into the box, Don sat back and tapped his stick against the floor. Biscuit got up from where he'd been sleeping, his face wary. 'Anyway, that's fine. Send it to the Good Samaritans.'

'Dad.' She sat down beside him and tried to decipher his expression. 'Are you sure?'

'This is what you're here for, isn't it? The big clean-out.'

'I'm not getting rid of everything. There's stuff you can still keep.'

Don pushed his stick between two tiles and worked

himself up to a standing position. The effort was a lot for him. Closing his eyes, he put his free hand against the table to catch his breath. The other twisted tight around the stick's handle.

After a second, he opened his eyes. They were dry, even bright. He fixed them on Julia. 'What are you making for tea?'

'Oh.' Surprised, she had to think. 'Pasta. Is that okay?'

'That'd be lovely,' he said. 'If you didn't throw it all out.'

His eyelid trembled as he winked; he was trying.

Exhausted after her efforts in the kitchen, Julia was falling asleep when her phone lit up with an incoming text. Julia reached for it, hoping it would be Rowan. They hadn't said anything about sending one another messages, but she'd allow the technicality if he gave in first.

Her device didn't recognise the sender's number. *So when are we hanging out?*

Julia's brain was foggy and slow with the approach of sleep. As if realising not enough information had been given, the sender followed up quickly: *I can't believe we bumped into each other at IGA! So random.*

It was Davina. In the two days since their encounter, Julia had hoped she'd have second thoughts or just forget about it, like a normal person. They hadn't seen one another since they were kids. If there'd been reason to stay in touch, they would have.

A third message beeped: *It's Davina, obvs.*

The contraction was irritating. Julia shut down her screen and returned the phone to its charger, then rolled towards the wall. Didn't Davina know what it looked like, sending three unanswered texts in a row?

Now she couldn't sleep. She tried to will herself into the weariness of her body, the feeling of cool sheets after a refreshing shower. Though she'd worked all day, there was still so much of the kitchen left to do. Not to mention everything else.

She turned onto her other side. She was here for a reason, anyway, not to waste her time catching up with people. The quicker she sorted everything out, the quicker she'd be back in Melbourne with her husband. Sorting all of *that* out.

Her phone gave a final, dull-sounded ping. It was Davina again, with a single entreaty: *Jules?*

She couldn't bear it. The woman had come to her mother's funeral, hung around behind the pews. Snuck out without giving her condolences. Julia typed a swift, businesslike response, suggesting coffee later in the week, something that could be cut short if necessary. By then she'd definitely need a break, a reason to get out of the house.

As the text hurtled out into space, Julia felt something that was not quite déjà vu – it couldn't be, she'd never texted Davina before – but had that similar, tilting quality. That sense that what is happening is not quite real, but predetermined; you couldn't get out of it, even if you tried.

– SIX –

Davina Weir was Julia's first friend. The Lambetts and Weirs met at story time at the local library when the girls were five. Julia had been going all year, but Davina showed up to the last session before the Easter break wearing a white cardboard crown, long paper ears drooping down her back from the weight of glue and cotton wool. Julia gaped at her dress, Dorothy-of-Kansas blue-and-white gingham with a thick ruffle underneath, and Davina marched across the room and asked to be partners for the egg hunt.

It turned out there wasn't an egg hunt; Davina's mother made it up to get her to go. Furious, Davina dragged Julia to the food table and showed her how to plunge a clawed hand into the bowl of Cheezels so one hooked around each fingertip. 'Then do this,' Davina ordered, sucking the orange rings one at a time like lollipops. When the Cheezels were reduced to tight mushy wads, Davina tipped her head back and lifted her hand, letting the neon lumps slough off into her mouth.

Davina was back the following week. Her outfit was more normal but no less fascinating: knee-length denim shorts with flowers embroidered on the pockets, a sleeveless shirt that tied at the belly button and pale blue plastic shoes. Davina had older sisters, Julia learned, which was how she knew to dress like this. All Julia had was Goldie and Kmart.

The mothers saw their daughters together and stood near one another to watch. They were a full-sized version of the new friends: Davina and Pamela tall, and Goldie and Julia short; the Weirs with thick dark hair and the Lambetts wispy blonde. Pamela Weir was loud the way Davina was loud, her laugh echoing around the library. Once Julia turned around at the noise and saw her mother's little wrist caught in Pamela's hand the same way Davina held hers. Goldie looked back at her and smiled, her cheeks pink with energy.

Davina crouched over a box of books, her pale limbs stained grey at the elbows and knees. She followed Julia's line of sight. 'Is that your mum?'

'Yeah.' Feeling a rush of love for her mother, Julia waved.

Davina frowned and for a moment Julia was afraid she'd reject Goldie, say something awful about her rumpled jacket or thick ankles, but it was her own mother Davina was appraising. 'Mine's having a baby,' she said, disgusted, and Julia saw the wide curve of Pam's belly pushing against her blouse.

'Oh,' Julia said. In her household babies were a precious gift, but Davina was clearly unimpressed.

'She's old.' Davina flipped through the book in front of her so quickly the pages slapped together. 'It's probably a boy. My dad wants a boy.'

'How old is she?'

Davina rolled her eyes. 'Thirty-eight.'

Julia checked her own unpregnant mother. Pamela had released Goldie, but the two women stayed close together, the lump of baby almost touching Goldie's soft stomach. 'My mum's thirty-two next birthday,' she reported. 'Dad's taking her out for dinner.'

'If the baby's a girl, it'll be so funny,' Davina said, tossing the book back in the box. 'Dad thought I was going to be a boy, too. They were going to call me David and had to change it. I hate it. I'm going to change it when I'm sixteen.'

Julia was overwhelmed. Until this moment she hadn't been aware that you could hate your own name or get a new one or have a mother that was too old or prefer a particular type of baby. A couple of times Goldie had thought she might be having a baby, and she told Julia that if it ended up being true, all she wanted was for it to be healthy.

Davina described her two older sisters, Christie who was in year three and Tahlia in year two, then frowned in suspicion. 'Do you go to school?'

Julia shook her head. 'Not till next year.'

'Me too. We better be in the same class.'

Julia felt a thrilling shiver of fear.

The Weirs had come to story time for the next few weeks. At the beginning of June, the Lambetts were almost late because of a midday storm. Julia rushed into the library as soon as the station wagon stopped, slowing to a chicken-legged gait at the entrance so she didn't get told off for running. Everyone else was waiting in the children's section, but Davina wasn't there yet, so Julia went and sat on a plastic chair in the foyer. Goldie came in a couple of minutes later, shaking out her umbrella and putting it in the stand. 'Are they here?'

'Not yet.'

Goldie stood by Julia and faced the doors. Outside, the rain poured like buckets had been tipped out in the sky, the bitumen dark and swirling towards the drains.

When the triangle rang out for the start of story time Julia peeled herself off the chair and took her mother's hand. They stood on the far side of the circle, Goldie holding Julia's shoulders in front of her, squeezing them every so often. Julia's mother seemed shrunken and pale without the height and breadth of Pamela Weir to pull her up.

At the end of the story Julia and Goldie clapped faintly, then left the library without talking to anyone. The rain had eased to a miserable drizzle.

'No books this week?' Don asked when he got home from work. He yanked his tie free from his neck like it'd been choking him. The end of the kitchen table usually held the pile of borrowed books, but that night there was nothing on it.

'My friend wasn't there,' Julia said, and burst into tears.

Don held her on his lap, patting her warm, heaving back and letting her wipe her nose on his shirt. 'Who's this friend?' he asked Goldie, who was at the stove, listlessly stirring a stew. 'Is it a real person, or what?'

'Davina,' Goldie sighed. 'And her mother, Pam. We've enjoyed talking to them the past few weeks, but they weren't there today.'

Don adjusted Julia so her sharp knees didn't dig into his abdomen. 'Just today?'

'We thought we'd see them.'

'Well, that's nothing to worry about.' Don bounced his thigh. 'You'll just have to go back next week and see.'

The thought of the future heartened Julia. Running straight through the doors of the library into Davina's waiting arms, the two of them sealing themselves together with the force of their friendship. 'Right,' she said, looking at her mother. Goldie was gazing out the window, her face slowly smoothing out. Her eye caught Julia's and she smiled.

Encouraged by her father's lack of opposition, Julia continued sorting. Over the next couple of days she made it through all the shelves and drawers in the kitchen, into the deep laundry cupboards and out of the bathroom vanity. These areas felt somehow safer than trying to venture into any of the bedrooms, even though her findings were sometimes gross, as wet rooms tend to be. Once spaces were cleared, she returned with cleaning products to scrape up years of dirt and hair and crud. Sometimes, as in an archaeological dig, there were unexpected finds, like a rusted hairclip that had been Julia's favourite accessory in preschool, caught under a loose tile near the toilet. She tried not to think of what it meant for her to be the first person to find the clip in thirty years.

She still had the urge to talk to Rowan, but it had dulled. What was becoming almost unbearable was her desire to see Evie. Thursday night was when Evie switched between the two houses, and in a matter of hours she'd be re-entering the flat, schoolbag hanging from one shoulder and a smile on her face.

Picking Evie up from Samara's was usually Julia's task, and she took it seriously. No matter the condition of her office she'd be packed up by half-past five, a neat to-do list left for the following day. To avoid getting sweaty, she took the tram back to South Yarra instead of walking, heading straight for the car without entering the building. By the time she was on the way to Malvern it would well and truly be peak hour, the traffic snarled and agitated, but Julia would find herself tapping the wheel and humming, anticipation simmering in her belly.

Rowan would be late to get Evie; she knew that with certainty. It was why the job had fallen to her for the past few years. Rowan's appointments ran behind, or he'd get caught talking. It would annoy Samara, no doubt, but Julia felt worse for Evie, having to wait for her father and then sit next to him in the malodorous car. When they got to the flat, Rowan wouldn't have thought of dinner, but he didn't like to order anything either, so he'd make Evie come along to the supermarket when all she wanted to do was unpack and relax. He might even ask her to cook. *I've just got a couple of things to finish up,* he'd say, pulling out the laptop. *I'll be right with you.*

Julia scrubbed at the laundry trough, shaking her head. When she picked Evie up, she was always on time, and she let her stepdaughter pick the radio station on the drive back. Up at the flat, dinner would be one of Evie's favourites, all the ingredients ready to go.

She was happy to do it; her stepdaughter was always

gracious. And besides, as the only child of divorced parents, Evie had to uproot herself every week and resettle in a new environment. Julia just wanted to make things easier. In another world, one that ran on logic if not logistics, it would be Rowan and Samara who had to swap houses, with the week's custodial parent joining Evie in the big bungalow while the other retreated to the bachelor pad. Why was it the one who was least at fault who suffered the greatest consequences?

Arms aching, Julia stood back and surveyed her work. It was difficult to see improvements to such intentionally distressed surfaces, but at least she could smell lemons when she took a deep breath. She'd liberated seven mostly empty bottles of fabric softener and four old cans of spot remover from the cupboard above the dryer, and found a single child's sock, frog-green with black at the toes and heel. It all went straight in the bin.

Her phone beeped in her pocket. *So this happened*, the message said. A picture followed: Evie and Rowan sitting on a tram with their heads tilted together, a wry smile on the teenager's face. Julia's snorting gasp of laughter was more from consolation than humour, but she was warmed by the sight of Evie with her straw boater held at her chest, eyes mid-roll. Rowan's arm was around her, his grin genuine. He'd thought they were taking a happy selfie, not a sarcastic one.

He said driving wastes petrol, Evie continued. *We are having 'quality time'.* The phrase was punctuated by a little yellow emoji rolling its eyes even more elaborately than Evie was in the picture.

Julia's thumbs flew over her screen. *I'm cleaning Grandpa Don's bathroom by hand. How does a tram ride with your dad compare?*

We're gonna have cauliflower crust pizza, was Evie's response. *But I'll pray for you.*

Julia went back to the picture and zoomed in. Rowan's hair was dark with sweat, the collar of his polo shirt folded the wrong way against his neck. She looked for signs he wasn't coping without her, but maybe there weren't enough pixels for that.

She was about to close her app when a final note came through: *Dad and I love you Jules xxx*

Julia stared until her eyes stung with tears. *I dreamt about you,* she wanted to say. *I miss you both so much.* But that was too much to put on a child, even one as mature as Evie. Instead, she sent a row of kisses and switched her phone's screen off.

She'd often wondered if things would be different if Evie had siblings. She seemed to enjoy being an only child, knowing how to hold her own in a crowd of adults. Still, surely Evie would be just like Julia, who was almost six when she was presented with Paul and instantly understood the squashed little bug to be her responsibility. Evie would have been excellent in the role. *Would be,* Julia reminded herself. Would be.

She didn't know whether Rowan and Samara had intended to have more children than just Evie; it wasn't something Rowan ever talked to her about, and Samara certainly wouldn't. Either way, Evie's difficult birth had put a stop to it. Rowan told Julia about it quite early on, the two of them holding hands in the flat's dark bedroom. She was sleeping over; they didn't live together yet. According to Rowan, baby Evie had been bigger than expected and the labour had gone badly, so that once the delivery was complete, she and the mother had to be taken to different parts of the hospital for further care. Rowan didn't remember if he'd been instructed or had made the choice, but he'd followed Evie's nurses instead of those accompanying Samara, and that, he felt, had been the beginning of the end.

'I ended up being gone for a while. And she could have died,' Rowan had said. 'They both could have, or that was what I thought. But Samara went through it alone.'

'You went with your child,' Julia reassured him. 'A tiny defenceless baby.'

'Samara was defenceless, too.'

All Rowan described was blood soaking a big wet flower into the sheets below Samara's pelvis, and the urgent voices of the medical staff as they unhooked things and prepared for transport. 'It would have been so confusing,' Julia said. Rowan pinched his fingers tighter around hers. 'You acted on instinct.'

It wasn't that Samara resented him. Afterwards, she said he'd made the right decision. What had happened – and the two of them agreed on this – was that, in the moment when Samara went down one hallway and Rowan and the baby down the other, they'd realised that Evie was now the most important thing, and that the two of them could be separated in the need to protect her. Or at least that was how Julia understood it.

'And other stuff, too, you know,' Rowan continued. 'It just wasn't the same. We only talked about Evie. We didn't really know each other anymore. We didn't feel romantic.' He sounded regretful. 'We let the passion go.'

Julia guessed that it was hard to be intimate with someone when all you could see was blood and viscera pooling underneath them. When you'd watched them turn and walk in the other direction as your life ebbed away. By the time Evie turned one, her parents were separated.

The first time Rowan's ex-wife rose from a chair and extended an elegant hand in greeting, Julia had thought of that story: grey-faced and bleeding Samara on a bed, being wheeled away from her husband and baby so both their lives could be saved. As it turned out, by creating Evie and freeing Rowan, Samara had changed Julia's life too.

– SEVEN –

The café Davina had chosen was by the river, close to where they'd grown up. It was a long building with a pointed white roof and a wide wooden deck that faced the water. From the edge of the deck, the slope down the bank was fairly steep and sandy, dotted with rocks. A paved path wove down to the walking trail that followed the river.

Davina was already there when Julia arrived. She'd chosen a table out on the deck and sat with her back to the entrance, dark hair rippling in the wind. Julia considered turning and going home, maybe changing her phone number, smuggling her father onto a plane and taking him with her back to Melbourne.

Davina's head lifted, like she sensed something on the breeze. Looking around, she half-rose from her chair. 'Hey. Hello.'

They embraced and Julia saw foundation settling into the lines on Davina's forehead and specks of mascara dusting her cheekbones. She wondered what her own face betrayed. They were grown women now, there was no getting away from it, but the flash of light in Davina's eyes was the same as when they were five years old, and Julia wondered why she'd felt so reluctant to see her. Probably it was just being out of practice. During her time in Melbourne, she'd caught up with a few people from Perth, classmates from uni or colleagues from old workplaces, and though she'd been nervous beforehand, things always ended up fine.

It had taken her a long time – most of her adulthood, really – to understand that grown-up friendships could be conducted with much lower stakes than childhood ones, especially if you had a partner as a buffer. On non-Evie weekends, she and Rowan sometimes had brunch or coffee with another couple, and it could just be a distraction, an activity you might try out to pass the time. Like going rock-climbing or to an indoor trampoline park. You didn't have to pledge your whole life to it.

A regular at the café, Davina sat back in her chair and flicked through the menu, commenting on what was good, what time of day they stopped selling certain items. She kept flicking her wrist to check her watch, which hung loose and heavy like a bangle. It was like she couldn't keep the time in her mind.

A university-aged server came over with an iPad and Davina flirted mildly with him. She wouldn't get an espresso because it would keep her up all night; she wanted cheesecake, but she needed to keep an eye on her figure. At this comment the three of them paused for the server to appraise her. The sensation made Julia's stomach fill with an uneasy heat, though he'd barely looked her way.

'You can get the cheesecake,' he told Davina, winking.

When it was her turn, Julia ordered tea and a scone, fine with being thought of as a boring old granny. With one last glance at Davina, he took their menus and swaggered back into the building.

'He's my favourite,' Davina sighed happily. 'He's so much fun.'

'This place seems nice,' Julia said. 'How long's it been here?'

The corner of Davina's lip curled in amusement. 'Ages and ages.'

'Oh.'

'It was here when we were kids. They remodelled it.'

Julia's memory of the spot was of nothing but sand and thin grass, a relative barrenness above the lusher, tree-lined banks. She wondered if Davina was pulling her leg. 'We didn't really go to cafés much, I guess.'

'We came here together all the time.'

Her chest flushed with uncertainty and she turned in her chair to take in the vista. The outlook from the edge of the deck down to the river felt familiar, but that was all. The café itself could have been photoshopped into the scene.

'Maybe not with your parents, but Mum took us a lot. There was an adventure playground over there.' Davina pointed to a nearby sandpit, which also seemed too new.

'I guess my memory is bad.'

'That sucks. I feel like I remember everything.' Davina's eyes fixed on Julia's. 'We had an awesome childhood.'

Unsure how else to react, Julia nodded.

'It's why I wanted to live here. It's criminally overlooked, if you ask me.' She gestured towards the water. 'The river. The walking trails. It's really family friendly.'

'I was thinking that,' Julia said. 'About Dad's house.' The server came with a jug of water and two glasses, and Davina filled them both and passed one across the table. 'It's a waste to have one old man living in such a big space. It'd be better filled with people who can really enjoy it.' Lifting the glass, she wondered if it was fair to say her father didn't enjoy his house anymore. Enjoyment was too mild a concept. The house was not just the place Don preferred to be, it was his hard outer shell.

'Have you got a family?' Davina asked.

Stunned at the directness of the question, Julia took a moment to answer.

'You're wearing a ring,' Davina continued. 'Sorry. I peeked.'

'It's not peeking. It's jewellery.' The fingers on her right hand swivelled her engagement band around, as if to hide the small diamond from view. 'I'm married.'

'Oh my God,' Davina said, leaning deeply forward, 'tell me all about him. I'm tragically single,' she explained, waggling her own bare fingers. 'I need to live vicariously through you.'

Taking a deep breath, Julia proceeded slowly, allowing Davina a trickle of information rather than breaking down the whole dam. She described Rowan, their business, when they'd married. She talked about Evie at length but Samara only in passing, and she didn't say anything about not having contacted her husband for days.

As Julia spoke, the server returned with their order, but Davina didn't look at him once. She bent close to the table, chin propped on her curled hand and eyes boring into Julia's, as if she was sharing an encounter with celebrities or lions, or celebrities wielding lions, rather than the basic facts of her life.

'And that's pretty much it,' Julia finished, reaching for the small dish of cream.

Nodding, Davina sat back. The action reminded Julia, bizarrely, of someone slumping with exhaustion after an orgasm. 'So, no kids of your own?'

Julia kept her eyes down. 'Just Evie.'

'Was that …'

She tensed, waiting for Davina to complete her sentence, but she didn't. When Julia lifted the scone to her mouth Davina was staring at the river, her food untouched. Julia tried to follow her gaze, but there was nothing to see.

'How about you?' Julia asked. 'What's going on in your life?'

Davina gave her a big smile. She started with her sisters, their jobs and children and marriages and problems, seeming not to hold anything back: Tahlia's husband cheats, Christie cheats on her husband, a nephew is on drugs, a niece has trouble with the police. Julia's eyes goggled; she had to lower her scone. Unbothered, Davina moved on to people she assumed Julia remembered from school, though the names were only fleetingly familiar. Brendan Shelton broke his leg in a motorcycle accident and had to have the limb amputated below the knee. His wife Sadie Davies, three years behind them in school, had almost left him but got pregnant with twin boys instead. Colin Berman had gone to South America for some skateboarding thing and disappeared, probably on purpose, and his sister Liza was in jail for Centrelink fraud.

Julia was relieved when Davina excused herself to go to the toilet. Listening to her was exhausting. The need to sit still while paying close attention reminded Julia of long drives at twilight, having to be vigilant for a creature that might suddenly leap out in front of the car.

She wondered how Davina knew so much about all these people; if it was from social media, or what. Julia wasn't on Facebook herself, and Davina's reportage was a good reminder as to why.

The server came for their plates. Davina's food and drink had barely been touched, but before Julia could stop him, he'd cleared everything away. 'Would you ladies like anything else?' he asked, hand on their table number as if expecting a no.

Looking at her watch, Julia was surprised to see more than an hour had passed. 'Um,' she said, looking for Davina, but she didn't appear. 'Just water, I guess.'

When Davina returned, she didn't comment on the disappearance of her food. 'So,' she said, leaning forward again, the intense look returning to her face. 'What's going on with your dad?'

'What do you mean?'

'You want him out of his house?'

Julia shifted uncomfortably. 'I wouldn't put it like that.'

Davina waited.

'He's ninety-two. The house is huge. He needs somewhere more manageable.' Her neck prickled. Why was she justifying herself to someone she hadn't seen for decades?

Davina sat back. 'It must be painful to see him decline.'

Her sympathy surprised Julia. 'It is.'

Paul had visited Don in February. His bar was slammed from the middle of November through to the end of January, but after that he was able to fly to Perth. There he'd discovered that, unlike people who work in hospitality, the home-help service they'd hired had put in minimal effort over the break.

'The crumbs on the floor are an inch high,' Paul had shouted down the phone to Julia, who tried out the measurement with her forefinger and thumb. The air conditioner was leaking, he continued, and it was at least thirty degrees in the house. The fruit bowl and fridge were full of mush.

'Dad hasn't been eating properly,' Paul said. 'He's not in good condition.' Worse, her brother told her, Don hadn't had a single visitor since Christmas Eve. He'd been completely alone.

Julia had been horrified. It was her and Rowan's year to have Evie over the festive season, and they'd decided to stay in Melbourne and celebrate as a family. During that time she'd rung her father every couple of days and twice on Christmas, once with Rowan and Evie on speakerphone, and later just the two of them. Each time she'd pictured the usual Don on the other end, not a starving, dirty prisoner sweating into his unwashed sheets. Of course, Don hadn't once mentioned being all by himself.

When he couldn't get the right people on the phone Paul had driven straight to the home-help company's head office, demanding answers. Their father's liaison officer was startled and defensive, as Julia supposed you would be if a man banged on the front counter and accused you of neglect. The explanation Paul was given – in a partitioned office away from the customer floor, a security guard standing nearby in case he lost his shit again – was that Don had paused his twice-weekly service, telling the woman currently in the position to spend some time with her kids. 'He said his son was coming from Sydney,' the officer announced, keeping her face carefully blank. There was a note to prove it, photocopied and tucked into Don's file. 'He gave his cleaner a tip as well,' she continued. 'She bought chocolates for the office. It was lovely.'

'More bullshit from Dad,' Paul reported to Julia later. She'd never heard him sound so embarrassed, so furious. 'He doesn't think he did anything wrong.' Don's argument had apparently been that the hard-working helpers deserved a holiday like anyone else, that he was capable of looking after himself for a bit. Paul had almost exploded, telling him it was clear he couldn't. 'It's beyond a joke, Jules,' he said. 'It's got to be the end of the road. We can't let this happen again. It's *neglect*. Even if it is self-inflicted.'

Julia felt dizzy at the prospect. 'What are we supposed to do? Have him declared insane? He won't go anywhere.'

Paul said he'd talk to their father and get back to her. Like that would do any good, Julia had thought: when it came to a rock and a hard place, Don Lambett was the rock. But then Paul had called a final time, just before he left Perth. Their father would move out of the house, but Julia needed to facilitate it. She'd been so stunned, she'd agreed.

Julia didn't tell Davina any of this.

'What does Rowan think about you being here?' Davina asked.

'He understands.'

'Still.' Davina paused meaningfully. 'It can't be easy.'

Julia's eyes burned. A single tear leaked out and she wiped it away. 'It isn't.'

Davina stood up and walked around the table, kneeling beside Julia to embrace her. The pressure was so comforting that if she hadn't been sitting down Julia would've collapsed against the other woman, using her long, soft body for support. It was the first real hug she'd had since she got to Perth. When they pulled apart, she blamed the emotions it stirred up for her quick agreement to having dinner at Davina's the following week.

That night Julia made chicken salad. Don ate slowly, spearing several of the same item onto his fork for each bite: a mouthful of snow peas, then a mouthful of asparagus, then a mouthful of chicken. He would eat her food, but he did it his way.

Julia filled Biscuit's bowl with kibble. 'I might start walking him,' she suggested. 'Get us both out of the house.'

'Please yourself,' Don murmured, chasing lettuce around his plate.

'How old do you think he is?'

'Eight and a half.'

Julia was surprised at her father's certainty. 'How do you know that?'

Don scowled and kept eating.

'What breed is he then?' she challenged.

'A bitsa.' When Julia didn't seem to understand, Don grunted. 'Bits-a-this, bits-a-that. He's a mutt.'

'A mix.'

Don rolled his eyes.

'Well, whatever. He still needs exercise.'

'He has a backyard,' he said tersely, stabbing through a cherry tomato so that it exploded. 'But you can walk him.'

After a while, Don seemed to realise how aggressive he'd been. 'So.' He swallowed. 'Did you have a pleasant afternoon?'

'I did.'

'What did you do?'

Julia had decided not to tell him about seeing Davina. 'I had coffee at that café by the river.' She peered at him. 'It's been done up, but we used to go there as kids.'

Her father shrugged.

'Do you remember? It had the adventure playground, I think.'

'That was really more your mother's business,' Don said. 'I just brought home the bacon.' He cleared his throat. 'But it's good you took a break today. You've been working very hard.'

'It's fine,' Julia said. 'It's what I'm here for.'

'Well, you want to pace yourself. There's plenty of time.'

The idea of slowing down made Julia feel strangled. She wanted this over as soon as possible; she wanted to return to her family. She wanted the comfort of knowing her father was somewhere safe. 'I'm going to start calling places next week,' she said. 'See what might be available for you to look at.'

Jabbing his fork into chunks of cucumber, her father did not reply.

- ☾ -

Hello. Hey, we know each other.

Nodding quickly, Evie slithers back to the second-last row, palm pressed against her throbbing hip. Risks a peek back down the aisle to where the man is sitting, but he isn't turning to look. Sees his short brown hair, shining in the sunlight. The curve of one ear and his thick denim jacket.

There's ten minutes until the bus reaches the shopping centre. Is the man who knows her, who she knows, going there too? Her heart hot and sick in her chest. She imagines him getting off at the same stop and waiting to talk to her again. Would this be good or bad?

A few blocks before her stop, his arm goes up and presses the button. A soft ding and the light above the driver illuminates: bus stopping. *The man stands as the vehicle slows and sidesteps to the nearby exit without looking back. With the snap of the opening doors he is gone, heeled boots ringing down the corrugated metal steps.*

– EIGHT –

It was meant to be an Evie weekend.

Evie weekends were always packed. On the Saturday, the two of them had a girls' breakfast on Chapel Street while Rowan worked, followed by family runs around the Tan, festivals or markets, movies, theatre, dinner in the city. Sundays were for day trips: St Kilda on the tram or a drive to the Dandenongs or Mornington, then outdoor yoga as the sun set, homemade pizzas, Chinese tea. Julia got down on the living-room carpet and painted Evie's toenails while they watched reality TV, careful with the brush so the colour didn't smudge. Side by side on the lounge, they tipped their heads to balance sheet masks and cucumber slices, reducing their chat to murmurs so nothing slipped off.

Julia was still dreaming in anxious flashes about Evie on a bus, an ominous shape claiming to know her. Waking, she reminded herself that her stepdaughter took trams and trains, not buses. And anyway, Evie's instinct for self-protection was more refined than anyone's.

The first time Julia looked after Evie by herself she'd taken the four-year-old to a playground and sat with other parents while the little girl barrelled into the crowd. Evie wore an orange beanie, which was how Julia kept an eye on her among the swarms of children, but then she had a sneezing fit from the tree sap and opened her eyes to find the beanie gone. Panicking, Julia ran into the playground, thinking of crime shows and Madeleine McCann. Rowan would never forgive her; Julia would never forgive herself.

As soon as she passed the climbing frame, there was Evie, facing off with a boy her size who was grabbing for the beanie. Julia opened her mouth, but little Evie had it under control, drawing herself to full height and shouting in the boy's face: 'No! Leave me alone! You don't have permission!'

Seeing Julia, the boy had turned to her beseechingly, his hand on the pompom. 'I just want to *look.*'

'No!' Evie yelled again, yanking backwards and away from his grabbing paws. 'No! I don't have to let you! It's *mine!*'

The boy's mother had come and crouched down in front of him. Julia followed Evie to a corner of the sandpit. 'It's not your fault if that boy's mad at you,' she told her. 'You did the right thing.'

Evie lifted her chin with pride. 'I don't care.' She patted the beanie. 'It's my hat.'

Ten years later, she was just as forthright, just as determined, just as assertive at ordering people out of her personal space. If there was a malevolent force around, on a bus or otherwise, Evie would fight back. 'You know what you do,' she once told Julia, 'if you're in a crowd and some loser tries to rub his junk on you?'

'Move away?' Julia guessed. Seeing her stepdaughter's dubious look, she tried again. 'Call for help?'

'You have to make a *scene*,' Evie said. 'Draw attention. Humiliate him like he deserves.' She raised her voice to demonstrate. 'Like, *Excuse me, what the fuck are you doing, are you sexually harassing me?* And you know what you say if someone flashes you?' she continued breathlessly. 'You go, *Take your tiny dick somewhere else, fuckface!*'

Julia had laughed. 'Is all the swearing necessary?'

'It attracts attention.' Pulling Julia to her feet, Evie got her to practise the way she said the schoolgirls did on the junior oval, digging their heels into imaginary testicles and shouting into the wind. Screaming *Get the fuck away from me or I'll call the police* at the blank, stupid face of the wall, Julia had felt exhilarated. She never would have been brave enough at Evie's age.

Browns. Browns and oranges and mustard yellows. The inside of her father's house was like being trapped in an old beer bottle.

Julia scrubbed the shower. The wall tiles were porridge-coloured, a row at eye level accented with flowers in brown and orange. The floor tiles were orange. The taps were plastic and beige.

She knelt in the bath, which had discoloured around the drain. There were pictures somewhere of her in here holding her baby brother, suds up to their waists. When the film was developed Goldie saw that Paul had been weeing at the time, the arc of urine cutting through the bubbles like a burst of chardonnay. Thirty years later the house's windowpanes had discoloured to the same shade.

Julia sprayed glass cleaner onto the mirror. The light fixture sputtered a little overhead, releasing a faint, endless buzz. She'd cleaned this bathroom just the day before, and the day before that. Now she was procrastinating. There was still most of the house to sort through, not to mention all the other arrangements that had to be made: care-home inspections, real estate agents, movers. When she tried to keep it all in her mind at once it made her panic and want to clean, so here she was.

She swiped at her reflection. Her skin was pale, darkening to mauve under her eyes. At first, she was startled at the greyness of her hair under the harsh lighting, then realised she could shake the discolouration loose into the sink. Dust and slivers of fibreglass from the deteriorating mirror. There was no such thing as truly clean, especially since this room would continue to be used as long as she was here, dust and hair and skin cells floating off her or getting sucked in from the hallway. Even if it was the final time, a last scrubbing before departure, she'd still be excreting microscopic parts of herself onto the just-cleaned surfaces. They could demolish the house, and she and her parents and brother would be smashed up in the rubble. They were in all the systems: the brickwork, the water, the soil. They'd lived there for too long.

Julia threw the plastic bottle into the bin. She was well and truly losing it now. If only she could talk to Rowan or Evie.

She was meant to be using the time to decide what she wanted, what their future would be, but it had been a little over a week and she'd got nowhere. At least in Melbourne she'd had some idea that not speaking to Rowan would help. Now their future beyond Julia's time in Perth was just a big empty circle in the centre of her mind, like the sun. It was impossible to look at it directly.

The light in the house darkened from the straw yellow of animal fat to a darker, flaxy plasma. Julia stepped into her sneakers and went to put the lead on Biscuit, who licked at her face with delight.

'Be safe,' Don mumbled, eyes on his favourite gameshow.

'Will you have a look at some stuff while we're gone?' As she moved through the house cleaning and sorting, Julia had set aside any items she thought her father might find important. A pile sat in the recliner that had been Goldie's.

'I'll get to it,' he grumbled. 'Keep your hat on.'

It was early autumn, warm days and cooler evenings. Julia walked quickly, the dog keeping pace. Usually, she relished the late afternoon breeze on her skin, tacky with sweat and dirt, but the westerly hadn't come in today and the air sat heavy and still.

They took a winding path towards the river, houses and street names sparking faint memories: she'd been to a birthday party at that house, there used to be a phone box at that corner there. Children played in yards while their parents washed cars on lawns or roamed the verge with watering cans. It was a family friendly place, like Davina had said. It was nice. Still, Julia wore sunglasses and kept her chin tucked. She wasn't interested in running into anyone else she knew.

As they got close to the river, there was a metallic smell. Kids liked to nick trolleys from the shops and push them down the slope into the water. Old ones lay on their side, stuck in the muck, half-sunken cages. For a while, Julia remembered, there were several submerged in a row. The more daring kids used it to cross to the other bank without having to walk around to the footbridge.

There was so much she remembered, it was unsettling that she still couldn't recall an old café or an adventure playground.

The river path had been resurfaced and widened, two lanes painted in white to instil order. This was a popular exercise spot, it seemed, despite the clouds of mosquitoes and sharp, briny odour. Joggers and cyclists fought for space, weaving their way past Julia and Biscuit with short pants of frustration. Julia wrapped the lead around her knuckles so that the dog was pulled close, out of people's way.

They reached a white tree with a trunk that grew semi-horizontally and used it as a point to turn back. Coming towards them was an older woman, her T-shirt faded orange, lumbering along on the wrong side of the path. Julia tried to shift out of her way, then realised she was heading for them on purpose. The woman caught her eye and called, 'Hello!'

Julia squinted, not recognising her. 'Hi.'

When she reached them, the woman squatted, groaning slightly, and reached for Biscuit. 'Beautiful doggy!' He put his snout in the air and closed his eyes, accepting the adoration. 'I've been watching that lovely long tail bob from side to side. Isn't she gorgeous?'

'Thank you,' Julia said, wondering why, if the woman had been staring up Biscuit's arse for so long, she hadn't figured out he was male.

Both knees on the path, the woman leaned forward and cupped the dog's jowls. 'Is she friendly?' the woman asked.

A bit late for that, Julia thought. 'Very friendly. Biscuit, sit.'

The dog's rump attached itself to the ground as if magnetised.

'Oh, wonderful. What else does she do?' Before Julia could respond, the woman offered her hand. 'Shake, doggy!'

Biscuit lifted a front paw and touched it to the woman's palm.

'Marvellous!' she enthused. 'Lie down! Now, roll over! Play dead!' The dog did all three, ending up sprawled, spread-eagled, on the grass. 'My,' the woman said, 'you've taught her well!'

Julia, who hadn't taught the dog a thing, could only shrug.

The performance over, Biscuit sat up. The woman stroked his jaw, seeming unbothered by the threads of slaver hanging from it. It took Julia a moment to realise she was humming something under her breath, a song, or maybe a spell. Biscuit's eyes rolled towards the heavens.

The woman paused in her palpations. 'Do you have children?'

'A stepdaughter,' Julia said.

'Children of your own?'

Julia pulled her lips back in a false smile. 'No.'

The woman began the process of getting up, arranging her palms and feet in various combinations against the earth like she was playing a game of Twister. Instead of offering to help, Julia busied herself with stroking the knobby tip of Biscuit's skull and rubbing spit back into his fur. Once standing, the woman let out a heavy sigh and reached for the dog again. 'People these days treat their animals like children. But they are not children.'

Julia nodded.

'Dogs are dogs. Children are children.'

'I know,' Julia said. 'I have a stepdaughter.'

The woman looked mournful. 'You said so, yes.' Finally, she pulled her hands back from Biscuit. 'Thank you for letting me meet her. She's a beautiful doggy.'

'He,' Julia said. The woman's brow scrunched. 'He's a boy.'

'Yes,' she said, as if this were obvious. 'Goodbye.'

The woman swept past them, T-shirt fabric squeaking under her pumping arms.

After a few moments, Julia was roused by the soft pull of the dog against the lead. The light feeling in her limbs from the earlier part of the walk was gone; now Julia felt as stiff and creaky as if she were made of tin. She plodded after Biscuit back up the slope and all the way to the house.

When they got in, Don was in his chair with the footrest stowed, hands squeezing the armrests like he was about to get up. The television was off. Stopping in front of him, Julia saw the deep grimace on his face. 'Dad?' she asked, bending to his eye-level. 'You okay?'

'Fine,' he grunted. Biscuit put his front paws on Don's bony knees and was rewarded with a scratch behind the ear.

'You looked …' Julia began, but her father's expression had cleared, his grip relaxed. Biscuit dropped down to the carpet and closed his eyes. 'It doesn't matter.'

Don picked up the remote control and the TV came to life. Julia stepped out of his way. 'Did you know the dog can do tricks?' she asked.

He flicked back and forth through the channels so that images flashed on the screen at a dizzying rate. 'Like what?'

'Sit, lay down, that stuff.' Hearing the words, the dog's ear twitched.

'I told you he was well behaved.'

The room smelled faintly sour, and Julia itched to pull the curtain back, open a window. 'His last owner must've been really good,' she said. 'I don't understand why they gave him up.'

'One has nothing to do with the other.'

'But to just abandon him …' Julia trailed off, throat tight. Biscuit was asleep, one paw quivering like he was dreaming of a good dig.

'They left him in good hands.'

Great hands, Julia thought. Hands that could feed and pat the dog, but little else.

About to leave the room, Julia noticed a crocheted rug draped over the small pile on the chair beside Don's. 'What's this?' she asked. 'Out of sight, out of mind, is that it?'

Her father's jaw stiffened. 'You could say so.'

'You were happy to go through the mugs and things the other day.'

He snorted, as if the differences were obvious.

'I'm not asking you to do much,' she said. 'I can decide on most of it. This is the tip of the iceberg.'

Don found a news program and cranked up the volume. 'I'll get to it.'

Julia looked over her shoulder. On the screen a queue of grey sheep moved up a ramp into a truck. Saliva leaked beneath her tongue, tasting like the river. 'Dad.'

'I said I'll get to it.'

'It's not that.' She didn't know what it was. Sweat poured from under her arms and along her hairline. Her inhalations dragged against rocks of emotion in her throat.

Her father muted the television. 'Sit down. You've gone pale as anything.'

She curled up on the squat, shiny sofa wedged perpendicular to the hutch. It was the kids' sofa, the only piece of furniture in this room she and Paul had been allowed to use. When their parents had guests, this was where they sat to show off their good behaviour. 'I'm fine,' she told Don.

He raised a white eyebrow. 'How long since you spoke to Rowan?'

'A few days.' It was just rounding down.

Don glanced at the TV. Now the sheep were on a large ship, the ocean around it wide and green. He switched it off. 'Your mother and I, when we were married, not once did we have more than two days apart.'

Julia believed this. There'd been the odd night Don was away, doing something for work or fishing with her uncle, but it was never for long. Goldie was always at home, that old tea towel clumped in her hands.

'We talked, your mother and I. We talked about everything.'

More likely Don had talked, and Goldie listened. Julia could see how her mother's gentle smile and hums of encouragement would lead a person to believe they were having a conversation.

'Well, it can't be helped,' she said, trying to keep her tone steady. 'I need to be here at the moment.'

On her way out of the room she wondered if her father understood the irony of instructing her to stay close to her husband, when he was the reason that they were apart. Not that she blamed him for their problems. Really, the need to come to Perth had been flukishly convenient, given what had happened between her and Rowan. But Don didn't need to know any of that.

– NINE –

On Wednesday, Julia walked to Davina's as the sun went down, the sky rippling with jacaranda purple and blood orange. The evening felt soft and empty. Glancing into windows as she passed, Julia was presented with fragments of twilight life in the suburb where she'd grown up. The figures in the homes all glowed from individual light sources: televisions, laptops, tablets, stovetops and, in one case, a man with his polo collar loosened, leaning to light a candle on a dining room sideboard. It made her feel melancholy, the way everyone seemed so separated, but she knew she was just romanticising the past. As kids, she and Paul had a TV room separate from their parents', and they would have thought nothing of bringing a Game Boy to the dinner table if only Don would let them.

The route was the same one she used to take to primary school. After two blocks she passed the Weirs' old house, which unlike most of the others was dark, its windows covered. It was half the size of the Lambetts', despite having contained twice as many children. When they met at story time, Davina had shared a bedroom with her second-eldest sister; later she was put in the smallest room with Lou. She'd hated that, being exiled with a dumb baby while Christie and Tahlia were together. She swore she could hear them plotting against her through the wall.

Some work had been done to the place, Julia noticed. Actual bitumen had been laid over the dead grass where the Weir family van had always been parked, and the old pool fence at the side had been replaced by frameless glass. The letterbox was different – a pelican with a huge tin beak to hold the mail. She wondered who lived there now, whether it looked any different inside.

When she got to Stewart Avenue, Julia hesitated outside number twenty-two, looking at the other homes on the street. It was disorienting that she couldn't remember which had been the Wessels', even though she and Kimmie Wessels had been friends for years.

As she was trying to recover her memories, the door opened and a young woman emerged. 'Can I help you?'

That was the problem, Julia realised with relief; she had the wrong house. Maybe even the wrong street. 'Sorry, I'm just—'

'Are you Davina's friend?'

Surprised, she said, 'That's right. Julia.'

The younger woman nodded, the massive bun on top of her head bobbing precariously. 'She thought you might be wandering around.' She spun elegantly on the ball of her foot. 'Come in.'

So, Davina had a housemate, despite being in her mid-thirties. Julia tried not to judge; you could never know a person's situation, and Davina hadn't said anything about what she did for work. Or maybe this woman was Davina's partner, though she seemed quite a bit younger. And anyway, Julia remembered, Davina had said she was single.

Inside, the layout of the house was similar to the Lambetts', its long central corridor lined with closed doors. From behind one leaked the bubbling dings of a video game. There was a cheery yellow rectangle of light where the hallway ended at the kitchen. Davina was at the stove, her back to them, so the younger woman tapped her shoulder. 'Your mate's here,' she shouted over the exhaust fan.

Davina turned and grinned, and a small jet of warmth filled Julia's stomach. 'Jules!' she cried. 'You're right on time. I'm almost done.'

Julia surveyed the stovetop. Each burner hosted a pot or pan, its contents bubbling away. The kitchen island was lined with plates and bowls and the oven glowed as it cooked yet more food. 'Can I help with anything? This looks amazing.'

'No, no, you're the guest!' Davina turned to her housemate, who slouched in the doorway, thumbing her mobile. 'Bill, can you keep Jules company for a few minutes? Grab a bottle of wine.'

Sliding the phone into her pocket, the younger woman went to the shelf above the fridge, gathered the stems of three wineglasses in the crooks of her fingers and nodded at an adjoining archway. 'Through here.'

The dining room furniture was up-to-the-second trendy, the seats made of clear plastic to make the space look bigger.

Their shape reminded Julia of school chairs. Davina's housemate poured the wine, filling two glasses and wetting the bottom of the third. She set the full ones down and took the other. 'I'm Billie,' she said, reaching across the table.

'Julia Lambett.' Billie's hand was warm. When they let go, she ran a palm over her head, to check the height and buoyancy of her bun. Satisfied, she sipped her splash of wine.

Julia tried not to stare, but she was fascinated by the younger woman's makeup. The top half of her face was elaborately done, her eyelids shimmering in multicoloured shades with thick black wings drawn at the corners. From her nose down, the skin was untouched, her lips pale and chin raw with spots, like she'd been interrupted in the middle of putting it on.

'So, you knew Davina when she was a kid.'

Julia nodded. 'We went to school together. Our mothers were good friends.'

Billie leaned forward. 'What's the goss?'

'Pardon?' Why did Julia feel like an old maid in front of this woman? She tried to relax.

'What was she like back then?'

Julia imagined Davina as a little girl, crashing around the library like the pinball in a machine. The day Mrs Weir brought the new baby to story time, Davina had caught up with Julia on her way out of the building and wrenched her back. 'Don't you think it's so funny,' she breathed in her ear, 'that they had a girl when they really wanted a boy?'

'I guess,' Julia had said. Goldie was striding ahead, into the car park.

'My dad cried when Lou was born,' Davina said. Grinning like a lizard, she let go of Julia. 'See you next week.'

'Cheeky,' Julia said now, in response to Billie's question. The younger woman's smile at this word mirrored Davina's, and Julia wanted to cry out, *Like that! It was just like that!* Instead she swallowed wine and looked around the room. 'This is nice.'

'She just redid it.'

'Right.' Julia nodded. 'So do you rent, or ...?'

Footsteps grew in the kitchen and Julia turned, expecting to see Davina. Instead, a boy of ten or eleven stood in the doorway, dressed in a long soccer jersey and giant sneakers. He stared blankly at them. 'Hi.'

He must have been the source of the video game noises, though Julia was confused as to how he fit in. Maybe a nephew? 'I'm Julia.'

Raising one machete-shaped eyebrow, Billie sipped her wine.

'This is Jax.' Davina appeared, holding a dish, and placed her free hand on the boy's shoulder. 'Have a seat, sweetie,' she told him, putting the plate in the centre of the table. It was piled with mini quiches, supermarket-bought and heated in the oven. 'Here's the first course.' Davina's skin was flushed with excitement. '*Bon appétit,* hey?'

'Can I have a Coke?' Jax was staring at the wineglasses.

Davina ran the back of her hand across her forehead. 'Sure, sweetie. Just let me—'

'Billie's having wine,' he interrupted.

'Only a little,' Billie objected, shaking her glass to show how low the volume was. 'It's a special occasion.'

'Don't stress,' Davina said airily, returning to the kitchen. 'Everyone gets what they want.'

Jax's eyes fell on Julia. He seemed determined, but not troublesome; a kid who tattled just to make things fair. Paul had been the same. 'You're sitting in my chair,' he announced.

Billie rolled her eyes.

'I like to sit there,' Jax continued. He reached for a quiche.

'Do you want me to move?' Julia asked.

He chewed for a moment before shaking his head. 'It doesn't matter.' A chunk of pastry ejected from his mouth and slid down his chin.

'Then why'd you say it?' Billie upended her wineglass to catch the last drops, then splashed in more from the bottle.

'You're having more wine,' Jax said tonelessly.

She sneered at him. 'So what?'

They were siblings, Julia realised. She was glad to have figured it out. 'I have a little brother too,' she told Billie, then realised how paralysingly boring this was.

'Yeah. Paul.' Seeing Julia's surprise, Billie shrugged. 'Davina told us.'

'*Davina*,' Jax echoed. He pushed another quiche into his mouth.

Davina started bringing through the main course, dish after dish of meats, salads, breads, until the table was crowded. She laughed as she passed around clean plates. 'I guess I got carried away!'

Jax immediately began serving himself, but Billie loosened her grip so that the empty plate listed. 'How much did this cost?'

'That's not for you to worry about.'

'How much did it cost, Mum?'

Mum? Julia sucked a few droplets of wine into her windpipe and began to cough. 'All right?' Davina asked her.

'Fine,' Julia croaked. She drank water until the itch in her throat was soothed. 'Went down the wrong way.'

Balancing the base of her own plate on her fingertips, Davina placed a spoonful from each dish around the edge, like the marks on a clock face. Billie was still waiting for a response, and at last Davina gave it. 'We're celebrating,' she told her daughter, offering a pair of tongs.

Billie sighed, the exhalation rushing sharply through her teeth, but she straightened her plate and began serving herself.

Now that she knew, Julia couldn't believe she hadn't seen the resemblance between the two women earlier. Maybe the eye makeup had thrown her off. 'So, Billie,' she asked, 'what do you do with yourself?' Trying to work out how old she was. At a guess, Julia would've said twenty-three, but that would mean Davina gave birth at thirteen. Though Billie could be a stepdaughter, or a foster child.

'I'm at TAFE,' Billie said. 'Cosmetology.'

'Makeup, not spaceships,' Jax explained.

'How long's the course?'

'I'm almost finished.' Billie rubbed her nose with her sleeve and reached for her wineglass.

'And you want to be a makeup artist?'

She shrugged. 'I guess.'

Davina rolled her eyes good-naturedly. She'd barely eaten. In fact, none of the women had; it was only Jax who was making progress, pushing forkfuls into his mouth at a regular clip.

'My stepdaughter doesn't really use makeup yet,' Julia told the table, aware again that this was not an interesting thing to say. 'She's fourteen.'

'Billie started wearing lipstick in primary school,' Davina said. 'She always carried a tube in her backpack.'

'I had to,' Billie said. 'Otherwise Jax would eat it.'

Julia waited for a clue as to whether this was a joke or not, but none came. 'It looks like you know what you're doing with that cat's-eye, anyway. I always end up blinking.'

'Goldie never wore makeup,' Davina commented. 'It would have been hard for you to learn.'

'It might look good on you.' Billie reached for the wine bottle again. 'Give you some colour. You look kind of young.'

Davina laughed her bullet-like *HA!* 'Older women want to look younger, though. You'll know when you're our age.'

Julia took the opportunity to jump in. 'How old are you, Billie? Out of interest.'

Billie sipped her wine before answering. 'Seventeen.'

'I'm eleven,' Jax announced as he went back for seconds.

'The same age gap as you and Paul,' Davina said.

'Yes.'

'A girl and then a boy, too. Isn't that crazy?'

'It is a coincidence,' Julia said faintly, trying to do the maths in her mind. Davina Weir had a child at nineteen. How come that gossip had never reached Julia?

Davina carried the barely touched food back to the kitchen, reappearing with a towering pavlova and carton of Ben and Jerry's. Scowling, Billie grabbed the ice-cream from her. 'This is twelve dollars a tub.'

Her mother ignored her. 'I'll just get the bowls. Sit, sit!' she called to Julia, who hadn't even tried to stand. 'You're our guest!'

'It's twelve dollars,' Billie repeated as Davina left the room. 'Naomi buys it sometimes. But *she* has the money.'

Unsure who Naomi was, Julia said, 'It's very decadent.'

'My darling daughter.' Davina carried a stack of bowls and spoons in one hand and a can of instant whipped cream in the other. Billie's young forehead wrinkled in outrage. 'You're not an accountant. You don't have to worry. Just enjoy it.'

A bowl of dessert was placed in front of Billie, but she made no move to lift her spoon. The four of them watched as the cone of cream Davina had sprayed on top drooped further and further to one side, finally sliding into a puddle beside the meringue. Jax finished his own bowl and then, without asking, reached for his sister's.

When the table had been cleared, the children went to their rooms and Davina led Julia out the back, where they sat on either end of a wooden swing bench. Davina had brought more wine, and she refilled Julia's glass.

'Just us adults now,' she said with a sigh.

'I didn't know you had kids.'

Davina shrugged. 'It's not my entire life.'

'You must've had Billie young.'

'I was having fun.' She winked. 'It was a bit like, *whoops!*'

Julia's chest burned and she swallowed wine to cool it. Davina poured more. 'Who would've known sex ed classes would turn out to be true?' she continued. 'It only takes one time.'

'I was always scared of that,' Julia murmured. With her boyfriends before Rowan she'd been paranoid, doubling up with the pill and condoms, imagining the looks on Goldie and Don's faces if she came home pregnant. She wondered how the Weirs had reacted to Davina's news.

'You're smarter than me. I always thought, *It won't happen, I'm special.*'

Julia's thoughts about having a baby had been the inverse: *It'll happen eventually. I'm no different from anyone else.* She'd been wrong, too.

'Turns out I'm quite fertile,' Davina was saying. 'I get it from Pamela, I guess. My sisters are the same.'

The burning sensation returned. Julia tried to focus on the backyard, which was narrower than she'd expected, the grass long and weedy like at Don's, but without the landmines of old dog poo. There was a pond in one corner, the plastic netting around it sagging towards the water.

'Goldie had some problems,' Davina continued. 'I guess that might also run in the family.'

It took Julia a moment to catch on. 'My mum?'

'She had some miscarriages. Pamela told me.' Davina's hand wrapping around her forearm was a shock. 'It's not Goldie's fault. No one talked about it back then.'

Julia shook her off and downed her wine again. 'I know it wouldn't have been her fault,' she said, her voice husky.

Davina emptied the bottle into Julia's glass. 'You looked kind of funny the other day when we were talking about it.' She sipped from her own, mostly full, glass. 'Tell me if I'm way off, though. I'm not trying to be rude.'

She always said that when she was being her rudest, Julia remembered. 'Way off about what?' She stared at the crappy fencing around the pond. If Davina's children were younger, it could've been fatal.

'If you want a baby and can't have one.'

Julia had never heard it stated so nakedly before. Instead of just heat behind her sternum, there was now actual pain; a clenching and twisting like Davina had shirtfronted her, got right in her face. 'That's kind of private.'

'Okay. I understand.'

'I mean, I don't ...' Julia shook her head.

'It's fine if you don't want to talk about it.'

'There isn't anything to say,' Julia lied.

Davina raised her hand in submission. 'Okay. Okay.'

Finishing her wine, Julia stood up. The grass in the yard bent to one side in a sudden wind and her leg muscles trembled. 'I'd better go. I don't like to leave Don for too long.'

'Hey.' Davina's expression was soft. 'I didn't mean to upset you.'

'I think I've had too much wine.' The lawn hadn't moved; it was Julia who'd been hit by an invisible force. She leaned against a post. 'I'm not a big drinker.'

Davina looked concerned. 'Are you going to be sick?'

'I just need to go home.'

'You want a lift?'

Shaking her head, Julia stumbled to the back door. 'The fresh air will be good. Don't worry.'

She called out weak goodbyes to the kids as she went down the hallway, unsurprised when neither came out to farewell her. The front door had a complicated set of locks and she had to wait, agitated, for Davina to catch up and open it for her.

'Are you sure you're all right?' Davina asked, putting a hand to Julia's shoulder. 'You can stay the night if you need to.'

'I've got to get back. Thanks for dinner.'

Julia hurried along the driveway, gulping air. Slowly the bobbing earth smoothed out. She had her bearings now, at least a bit. Walking down the middle of the silent street, she felt relief when she could turn the corner and leave Davina and her fuckery behind.

– TEN –

Julia and Goldie kept going to story time after the Weirs disappeared. Each week Goldie would park the car and look in the rear-view mirror at Julia, still buckled into the backseat. 'Maybe today,' she said, raising her eyebrows. 'What do you reckon?'

'Maybe,' Julia echoed. As they approached the library hand-in-hand, Julia found her anticipation harder and harder to suppress. The squat oyster-coloured building seemed to shimmer with promise. Davina and Pamela hadn't said they were going anywhere, and the Lambetts weren't used to people who didn't say goodbye.

As the weeks passed, Julia had found it easier to manage her cycling disappointment. Her father stopped noticing their mooning faces and asking if the little friends had shown up this time. (It showed how much he knew: Pamela and Davina weren't little *at all*.) Julia was back to laughing at the stories and borrowing books. But pulling up to the library still gave her that Cinderella-at-the-ball feeling, waiting for the prince to stop talking to the other ladies and lock his eyes on her.

The day the Weirs came back they slid into story time late, stopping just inside the door. Davina's hair had been cut in a thick wedge below her ears and she wore a see-through plastic raincoat, though the sky that day was clear. Pamela Weir looked taller than ever.

The session broke up and Davina ambled over to Julia, her raincoat crackling. Julia's heart pounded. The prince, the prince was approaching!

'I lost a library book,' Davina commented when they were finally face-to-face. Her hair stuck out at the sides.

Julia felt breathless. 'Is that why you've been away?'

Davina squinted with confusion, then took Julia's hand. Her palm was hot and moist. 'Come on,' Davina said, but instead of the children's section she pulled her over to Pamela. Julia looked around for her own mother, but Goldie had been waylaid by someone far less interesting than the Weirs.

'Julia,' Pamela said. Julia was amazed she remembered. 'How are you?'

'Fine,' Julia squeaked, but Davina cut in.

'She wants to meet the baby,' she said, reaching for the bulge at Pamela's waist.

Horrified, Julia expected Davina to pull up her mother's shirt and expose her bare tummy, or worse. 'No,' she said. 'I mean—'

It turned out to be worse. Expressionless, Pamela Weir slid her hands under the collar of her black top. Grimacing, she gripped something, then drew it out of her midsection.

Julia swallowed a shriek. She didn't know much about having babies, but she was pretty sure women had to go to hospital to get them out, not just reach down into their bellies whenever someone told them to.

'Lou,' Davina announced as her mother revealed a baby in a lime-green onesie, a matching scrunchy band sliding off the hairless, egg-shaped head. Davina smiled gleefully. 'Another girl!'

'Yes, yes,' Pamela said tiredly. As she bent down to show off the baby, some of the fabric around her tummy sagged down. Lou had been taken not from the inside of Pamela's body, Julia realised, but out of a cotton carrier the same colour as her shirt. She felt cool with relief.

The baby had eyes like Davina's.

'Hi,' Julia said, holding out a finger like she'd seen on TV. Instead of wrapping her tiny hand around it, Lou squawked in dismay.

'She's hungry,' Pamela Weir said, shifting her to the crook of one arm and reaching her other hand towards her collar bone.

Just when Julia thought she was safe from seeing the hidden parts of her friend's mother, suddenly Mrs Weir's bare breast was there, round and white under the library lights. She slid Lou over to the big pink dummy in the centre and the little face clamped right on it.

Looking around, Julia couldn't see either Davina or Goldie. Her palms sweated as she watched the baby suckle with its fierce red lips, the rich colours blending with the mother's body in a mass of raw wetness, like the inside of something private. Mrs Weir stared into space, humming faintly.

There was a baby in her own mother's belly now; Don and Goldie had told her about it a few days earlier. It would be a Christmas present, Goldie said, taking Julia's hand and pressing it to her tummy, which was hard and seemed to return the pressure. They were quite sure that this baby would actually be born, but just in case, they'd asked Julia to keep the secret a little bit longer. Watching Mrs Weir feed Lou, she bit down on her lip so as not to tell.

The temperature had dropped since she'd left Don's house, and Julia stuffed her hands in her armpits to gather warmth. Once she was no longer on Stewart Avenue, she kept to people's verges instead of walking on the road, conscious that she was wearing dark colours on a moonless night. The houses that had been so brightly lit earlier in the evening were now dark and shut.

This was why she didn't seek out people from her past, why she didn't succumb to nostalgia and other assorted crap. Two times she'd lifted her face and looked people in the eye since she got back, and what had it earned her? A stickybeak down at the river telling her life wouldn't be the same without a child, and now Davina. Davina with her endless revelations: she had two kids of her own. Goldie had problems conceiving. She'd looked into Julia's soul and seen that a similar thing was happening to her; worse, she'd asked about it. Julia hated that urge some people had, when they realised someone was uncomfortable, to keep digging at it, trying to uncover the seed. Like there wasn't a reason it was buried in the first place.

It was pretty rich coming from Davina, who hadn't even mentioned her own children until she'd shoved them in Julia's face. In fact, she was yet to share anything truly personal, beyond a bit of gossip about her sisters. She'd said nothing about the father of her kids, her job, not even her parents.

Julia was on a roll now, silently choreographing her argument as she power walked towards her father's. Speaking of Pamela Weir, what was this shit about the two women falling out so badly she'd skipped Goldie's funeral? It can't have been her mother's doing, Julia thought, panting a little with exertion. She'd been a saint.

Pamela, on the other hand. Goldie had been thrilled by her friend's brashness, but as Julia grew closer to the Weirs, she'd found it disorienting. She wasn't used to a mother who snapped at her children, who was sarcastic, who said things about her husband when he wasn't there and when he was, her mouth pressed into a thin line, the lips worn away from chain-smoking. Once, playing with Davina, Julia had come across Pamela Weir lying facedown on the carpet, arms spread out like she was skydiving.

'I'm wondering how I got here,' was her answer when Julia asked if she was okay. 'I'm wondering what's the point.'

Mr Weir had appeared behind them just when Julia was beginning to panic. 'You leave this to me,' he said, smiling broadly. At least he knew how to act around children.

That was the week she and Paul stayed with the Weirs so Don could be with Goldie in hospital. Before they went, Julia had been excited about the holiday at her friend's house, but she'd never been so happy to come back home.

No doubt it was Pamela who'd done something to turn Goldie away. It must've been bad, too, because Goldie could forgive a lot. And this was a woman Goldie had confided in about her problems having another baby.

Allegedly, Julia reminded herself. According to Davina, if she could be believed.

Don's house came into view. Filtered through the amber glass in the windows, the lamps in the front room gave off an eggy light. When Julia let herself in, her father was fully reclined, one hand hanging down to touch the dog's head. A late-night show was muted on the TV.

She hesitated. If Don was asleep, she should rouse him, get him into bed. A ninety-two-year-old couldn't spend the whole night in a chair, especially if he'd already been there all day. But she feared the indignity of waking him, seeing him in that vulnerable state. In a week and a half, she hadn't yet entered her father's bedroom.

There was also the chance of stumbling on something that couldn't be undone. As long as all she could see was the top of his head and one slack arm, Julia was safe; the worst could be put off.

The dog snorted suddenly and got up, causing Don to lift his hand. Julia exhaled. He was awake.

'That you?' he asked. Mucus tumbled in his throat.

'You're still up.'

Don reached for the button and the chair slowly moved upright. 'I was dozing,' he said. 'Didn't want to go to bed till you were home.'

Like when she was a teenager, Julia thought, sitting on the sofa. When he'd realised Goldie wouldn't sleep without both her children safe in their beds, Don took over the watch, reading by lamplight until he heard a key in the lock. 'That's sweet.'

'That's parenthood.'

Biscuit crossed the room and touched his chin to Julia's knee. She cupped both ears and rubbed behind them. 'You guys have a fun night?'

'Riveting,' her father said, watching the dog. 'Softball interviews with politicians, a bloody awful musical performance. There was a quiz afterwards and none of the contestants knew a thing. How was yours?'

'All right.' She stopped scratching Biscuit and he wandered back over to Don. 'I had dinner at Davina Weir's.'

She hadn't told her father what she was doing before she left, just said she'd be out and reheated a frozen meal for him. His plate was on the television tray, scraped clean. She wondered if he'd got up at all while she was gone.

Don's eyebrows rose with recognition. 'The one from the supermarket.'

'That's her.'

He made a noise deep in his chest. 'What does she have to say for herself?'

'Not much.' Julia stared at her laced fingers. 'She's got two kids.'

'Oh, right.'

'Did you know?'

'It sounds familiar.'

'The oldest was seventeen. Davina must've had her as a teenager.'

Julia looked up when her father didn't respond, but he was staring into space. Biscuit had lowered himself over the old man's slippered feet and gone back to sleep. 'She had a boy as well,' she added. 'Younger.'

Don nodded.

They sat quietly, listening to the dog's soft snores. Julia considered asking her father about Goldie, whether she'd had miscarriages like Davina claimed. She'd thought about it on the walk home. The age gap between Julia and Paul was wider than most, but her parents were careful and her father was older, and together that could slow things down. She knew her mother had wanted a second child, telling Julia that babies were precious and wonderful. Julia had imagined a feather floating down from the sky, a matter of magic and fate and luck if it landed on your shoulder. And it did; they'd had Paul.

She decided to play it halfway. 'Davina didn't mention her mother. She didn't say anything about Pamela and Mum fighting.'

'Why would she? It was ages ago.'

Julia was confused. When her father mentioned it the other day, she'd got the impression the women fell out just before Goldie died. 'How long?'

'I don't know. How old are you?' Don screwed up his face in irritation. 'Twenty years? More?'

'Really?'

He waved a hand. 'Donkey's years. Forever.'

Julia couldn't believe it. She was certain she'd asked her mother about Pamela Weir much more recently than that, as an adult. But if Don was right, they hadn't been friends since Julia and Davina were teenagers. 'So, why'd she send a big bouquet to the funeral?'

'Exactly!' Don punched his thigh in triumph. 'I told you, the woman needs her head read.'

Julia waited as her father made his way to his feet, then shuffled to the step and heaved himself up. Biscuit followed, ready to break his fall. 'Goodnight,' Don called over his shoulder.

'Night, Dad,' she said. He and the dog went into his room, leaving the door cracked open a little behind them. She waited until his light went off, glad for another day without seeing her father naked or hurt or frightened, without having to spoonfeed him or push a bundle of paper towels down the dirty crack of his bum. Not having to face him at his weakest, because that would mean facing herself and what she wasn't prepared to do.

The shock when Goldie died had been massive, seismic. Not only before Don, but far before her time; barely fifty-six, her lungs thrashed by influenza that turned into pneumonia and drowned her overnight. Don also had the flu and moved into Paul's old room because his cough was worse than hers and she needed rest. When he checked in the morning, she was dead.

Don still slept in their bed. He'd only let Julia throw away the sheets.

Julia was living in Melbourne, Paul in Sydney. He'd caught

a flight to Tullamarine so they could go on to Perth together, hands clutched so tight she caught another passenger looking at them fondly. It had been a few months since Julia last saw her mother; not nearly long enough for Goldie to go from the neat, smiling person she'd always been, to dead. Goldie's hair was barely grey.

By the time of the funeral Don had recovered from the flu, the way people were meant to. He was in his mid-eighties and he'd got through with Panadol and throat lozenges.

Their father had always been old; he was the same age when Julia was born as Goldie had been when she died. On top of that, his personality felt old, forged by war and the Depression. When his wife died, Don's ageing had accelerated rapidly. His children were shocked it had anywhere left to go. The flesh disappeared from his chest and shoulders, his neck skin draped like a curtain. Brushing a hand across his back as they walked into the funeral service, Julia had felt the ribs and thin connecting tissue of a cooked chicken with all the meat picked off.

Lying in the guest bed after seeing Davina, Julia tried to remember things Goldie had said: about Pamela Weir, about trouble having children. About anything. Her mother just stood there, mute, hands clasped at her stomach – the damn tea towel had been set down, at least – a gentle smile on her face. *I'm worried about your father,* was all she'd say. *He's got a bad cough.*

That was invented: Julia hadn't spoken to her parents when they were sick. She guessed they hadn't wanted to worry her. It meant she hadn't seen Goldie even a little bit diminished, moving through the house in a nightdress, face pale and hair ragged.

Paul hadn't suffered Julia's denial. He was younger, more used to things being unpredictable. He thought she was as rigid as their father. 'People die,' he said. In the front pew of the chapel, he kept his arm around Julia as she cried. The photograph they'd chosen to display was the one that most closely resembled the Goldie that Julia held in her heart. During their meeting with the celebrant, Paul picked up the frame. 'She looks like the Mona Lisa.'

'No, she doesn't,' Julia snapped. 'She looks beautiful.'

'The Mona Lisa's beautiful.'

'She doesn't look smug.' Julia took the picture from him. 'She looks sweet.'

'It wasn't an insult, Jules. It was a comment.'

'Just don't say anything,' she said. 'Please.'

Paul sighed, then nodded. 'It's good,' he'd told the celebrant. 'Use that picture. Mum was happy with it, anyway.'

What else had Goldie been through that she'd never let slip to her daughter? Julia was certain she'd been an adult when she'd last balanced a phone on her shoulder to ask, *How's Pam Weir?* Certain that over in Perth, her mother had said, *Oh, she's fine*. Everything was always fine.

- ☾ -

Evie rides that bus again but doesn't see the man, though she checks. Walking the aisle, she glances at each row, the inclined faces, but none are his. Listens out as men talk to the driver in their deep, confident voices, but not his voice. Feels a hot squirl behind the sternum, disappointment and relief.

The bus can be a dangerous place. Parents deliver lectures before boarding, checklists afterwards. Did anyone sit too close? Try to touch you? Make sure to sit up front near the driver, keep your hand on the bell. Ask to be dropped off closer to your house, between stops; they'll do it for an underage girl.

Stranger danger, she's heard all about it. But the man is not a stranger.

Hey, *he said.* We know each other.

Something must have been shared between them. An adult is never wrong.

— ELEVEN —

From story time at the library, Julia and Davina had gone on to school, walking behind their mothers with Lou and baby Paul in prams. They sat together in class and stood arm-in-arm during the fruit break, each anxious if they weren't touching the other. Julia, who'd been both excited and terrified to go to big school, found the transition easier when attached to Davina. At rest time, the girls' mat was in a coveted position under the window, so they could look up through the blinds and see the sky. 'It's *ours*,' Davina squawked if anyone rolled across the line. 'Best friends *only*. Get your own!' She reached for Julia's hand in the dim room and held it so tight it hurt, but that was okay. There was plenty of quiet time at home.

But the next year, to their horror, the girls weren't in the same class. They hadn't considered it was possible; even their mothers were stunned. They met at McDonald's for a fortifying coffee, letting the older Weir girls loose in the play centre. Julia and Davina sat at one end of the table with a packet of animal cookies, colouring a roaring lion to win a Happy Meal.

'I guess it'll be good for them,' Goldie said doubtfully, jogging a grizzling Paul against her chest. 'Make new friends.'

'I bet it was Tina,' Pamela snarled, referring to their previous teacher. 'That bitch.'

Goldie looked at the girls in case they'd heard. Julia's ears were on stalks, but she kept her gaze on the paper. 'They'll see each other at play time, still.'

Pamela didn't believe in playing with children's emotions to prove their resilience. Davina was her most sensitive child, and it was easier to let her have things the way she wanted. The problem was, she mooned, she'd already gone to the principal, but apparently changes were out of the question. She snatched a cookie off the girls' tray and bit into it angrily.

Back home, Goldie told Don she was worried about Julia. She could barely name anyone in her previous class, aside from Davina.

Don, of course, thought this was bullshit. 'Give the child credit,' he grumbled. 'She'll be fine.'

In Mr Goh's class, Julia was put next to Kimmie Wessels, who spoke English in a fascinating accent. 'In my old house,' Kimmie told her that first morning, 'you can see a mountain from one window and the sea from the other.'

'Wow,' Julia breathed. From her bedroom she could see a fence; from the windows on the other side of the house she could see a different fence. 'What else was there?'

'Lots of animals. Every animal you can imagine.'

Julia gasped. 'In the city?'

'Not the city,' Kimmie admitted. 'But we could drive out and see a zebra any time we liked.'

They were decorating name-cards for their desks. Julia found herself picking up every pencil Kimmie set down. 'I saw a zebra at the zoo.'

'Not zoos. Outside. You look at them from your car.'

When the class broke up for little lunch, Julia told Kimmie to find her after she went to the toilet; she had someone for her to meet. 'Okay,' Kimmie shrugged. Like she didn't mind either way if she made friends or not!

Julia brought the news to Davina like a present. 'She's seen zebras before,' she reported. 'Up close, not at the zoo.'

Davina squinted. 'So?'

'Zebras,' Julia had repeated. 'Out in the open?'

Davina shrugged. 'That's where they live.'

The new girl came down from the bathroom block. 'This is Kimmie,' Julia announced, waving her closer. 'She's from southern Africa.'

Kimmie was drying her hands on her skirt. Davina crossed her arms. 'Don't they have paper towels in southern Africa?'

For the first time all morning, Kimmie looked uncertain. Wrinkling her freckled forehead, she hooked her elbow through Julia's, the way Davina usually did. The contact felt all wrong: Kimmie was a different height, her flesh was harder. She smelled sharp and slightly lemony, like grass.

'Hello,' she said. 'It's nice to meet you.'

With her free hand, Julia pointed. 'This is Davina.'

'Your voice is funny,' Davina said.

Julia gasped quietly.

'What's funny?' Kimmie asked, the muscles of her upper arm tightening against Julia's.

'Your voice,' Davina repeated.

'She means your accent,' Julia explained. 'Since you're from southern Africa.'

'South Africa.'

'Wherever.' Davina stared down at the linked elbows. 'Come over here for a minute, Julia. I want to tell you something private.'

'Secrets are rude.' Kimmie's *r*'s rolled prettily.

'It's *private*, not a secret. Privacy is allowed.'

Smiling in apology, Julia had untangled herself from Kimmie and allowed Davina to take her over to a large tree, the branches drooping down to shield them from view. There was a cold knot in her stomach. Davina was about to say mean things about Kimmie Wessels, she was sure.

Davina leaned close. 'I have tuna for lunch.'

'What?'

'A tuna sandwich. Gross. Do you want it?'

'Oh,' Julia said. 'Maybe.'

'I took some money from the girls' room,' Davina said, referring to her older sisters. 'I'm going to get a meat pie instead. You can—'

Kimmie's red sandshoes appeared below the curtain of leaves. 'Excuse me,' she called, pulling some aside. Her chin was very pointy, Julia noticed with sympathy. 'Mr Goh said you'd show me around the school.'

Julia was going to tell her they could do it at big lunch

while Davina queued for her pie, but Davina spoke first. 'You already know the toilets. That's the most important thing.'

Kimmie looked at Julia. 'I don't know where the office is, or where to buy my lunch.' She took a five-dollar note from the pocket of her dress. 'I'll buy you something too.'

'No thanks,' Davina sang.

The worst thing in Julia's life so far was the slow drop of Kimmie's shoulders as she walked away. It made her feel sick, but also powerful. From the flash in Davina's eyes, she knew her friend felt the power, too.

The next afternoon, for the first time since Julia had been back, there was a knock at the door.

Don's chair was only a few feet away, but she knew better than to expect him to answer. Besides, he'd dozed off, the television on low. The dog got up to follow Julia.

She knew who it was from the shadow against the decorative glass. For a moment Julia considered freezing, pretending no one was home until she went away, but Biscuit stretched up his front legs and scratched the door handle.

'Hello?' Davina called, her voice distinguishable even through the wood.

Julia pulled the main door open, but left the flyscreen shut. Davina looked stricken. 'Where's your dad?' she asked.

'Asleep,' Julia whispered.

Lowering her voice to match, Davina said, 'Can you talk?'

Julia unlatched the wire door and Biscuit slipped around to sniff the visitor, nuzzling his snout into the crooks of her knees. Julia followed him outside and closed the door.

'So this is the dog,' Davina said with delight. 'What a gorgeous animal.'

Julia watched her stroke him for a while, then said, 'What's up?'

'I feel bad about the other day,' Davina said. 'After dinner.'

Her eyes did look shadowed, her lips bloodless. Julia pinned her shoulders back. 'Oh.'

'I shouldn't have let you walk home. Or should've checked you made it okay.'

Julia stared.

'I know I was too tipsy to drop you back,' she continued, 'but Billie has her P-plates. Or we could've got an Uber.'

'It was a ten-minute walk. It's fine.'

'I just kept picturing you getting hit by a car or tripping and breaking your ankle.' Davina laughed, her *ha!* soft and thoughtful this time. 'I got spooked.'

'It's all right,' Julia relented. 'No harm, no foul.'

The shadows on Davina's face slipped away. 'Thank goodness,' she said. When she smiled her lips were pink again. Julia couldn't help but be flattered at how much Davina had worried about her, even if she'd focused on entirely the wrong thing. All the stuff about babies hadn't been mentioned. Maybe it was better if it stayed that way.

'So, what are you doing this weekend?' Davina asked.

'More of the same, I guess.'

'Let's have a girls' night,' Davina suggested. 'Head into Northbridge, have dinner and a drink. What do you think?' Seeing Julia's hesitation, she continued, 'Bill and Jax will be

at their dad's. It's been ages since I had some adult time.'
She pouted comically. 'Come on, say yes. You must be going
crazy in here.'

'All right,' Julia relented. She could do with a break.

'Legend!' Davina beamed. 'It'll be good for both of us.
Shake off a few cobwebs. Have some stupid cocktails.' Julia
nodded, warming to the idea. 'We'll get an Uber, so I don't
obsess over you getting kidnapped this time.'

When she went back inside her father wasn't in the lounge.
Biscuit had slipped away when the two women stopped paying
him attention, and man and dog were in the backyard, Don
sitting on a dusty plastic chair while Biscuit sniffed around
the yellow stalks of grass, occasionally dousing them with
piss. Julia stepped out. 'All right, Dad?'

He grunted assent.

'That was Davina. We're going out for dinner on Saturday.'

Don said something she didn't catch, so she stepped closer
and waited for him to repeat it. 'Aren't there any other people
for you to hang out with?'

'I don't know.' Julia shrugged lightly. 'Davina's keen. I like
her.'

'I thought you were here for a reason.'

She felt a quick pulse of anger. 'I'm allowed to do other
things.'

'You should go back to your husband.' Her father stared at
the back fence, refusing to meet her eye. 'I can sort things out
here.'

She couldn't believe him. The house was full of threats.
A large pot could tumble down from a high shelf, a loose

rug could pitch him headfirst into a pane of glass. He could slowly decompose under a pile of his own history. Even the negative spaces presented a hazard: their depths, their widths. It wasn't impossible for him to one day expire halfway to the kitchen, an Arctic explorer stranded on the tundra. 'No, you can't, Dad. You haven't in seven years. That's why I'm here.'

Without waiting for a response, Julia went back inside and shut herself in the guestroom to call Paul. She wanted to catch him before the evening rush.

'Hello?' His voice was stronger and clearer than she'd felt in days. 'Jules? Everything okay?'

She was sobbing already, her rage and discomfort and sadness spilling into snot and saltwater. Paul waited for her to gather herself, murmuring that he was there, that it would be okay. Paul was a good person in a crisis, she thought as she wiped her face with the hem of her top, tears finally subsiding. 'Sorry. Sorry.'

'Is it Dad?' He was grave. 'Did something happen?'

'Nothing like that,' she said quickly. If Paul had ever phoned her from Perth and burst into tears, she would've thought the exact same thing. The same thing as when she'd come back from Davina's the night before to see Don silent and motionless in his chair. 'He's fine. He's just being an arsehole.'

Paul let out a breath. 'Let me guess. He thinks he doesn't need your help.'

'Got it in one.'

'You know he does.'

'I know. I just want him to acknowledge it.' She sniffed back a second wave of tears. 'It's a fucking hard job.'

'I'm sure.'

'I'm away from Rowan, I'm away from Evie. I've taken time off work.'

'I appreciate it, Jules,' her brother said formally. 'I couldn't do what you're doing.'

Julia had wanted someone to say that, but as soon as he did, it didn't sit right. 'Yes, you could. You just couldn't get the time off.'

'I couldn't do the hard slog. I certainly couldn't live with him for weeks.' After a pause, Paul continued, 'Anyway, I told Dad I'd never come back to that house.'

Julia sat up. 'What do you mean?'

'I let him know the only way I'd see him again was if he saw sense and moved somewhere smaller, with help. Otherwise, I wasn't coming back to Perth.'

She sucked in air. 'You didn't.'

'He was a living skeleton, Jules.' Her brother's voice didn't rise, didn't speed up. The disconnect between his words and his tone made her dizzy. 'He was living in his own filth. I wasn't going to entertain it.'

'So, you'd just leave him here?' Julia's own voice was small. 'To die?'

'I didn't have to. He agreed to go.'

Though he couldn't see her, she shook her head. 'Paul.'

'I told him my feelings. I know it's a big fucking surprise in this family, but I told him how I felt, and I told him the truth.'

Paul sounded so composed. She imagined him clicking coolly through spreadsheets in the bar's back office, selecting a tie to greet the first customers of the evening. Just another day, to him.

'You should give it a try sometime, Julia,' he continued, ready to sign off and get on with his real life. 'You might find it's very effective.'

- ☾ -

Heading again for the bus stop, Evie slows to a dawdle, letting her shoes catch on the ground. Stops when she hears the engine in the distance, watches dispassionately as the vehicle passes her by.

What's the point, if he isn't going to be there?

Turns instead, heads in a different direction.

Down to the river.

– TWELVE –

Evie called the following day. Julia's hands shook as she answered, filled with the nervous remnants of the new dream: her stepdaughter letting the bus go by and setting off in search of the man. Oblivious to the dangers that go along with being a woman, and young.

'Evie!' she shouted, as if the connection was already bad. 'Are you all right?'

'Of course.' It was so good to hear her stepdaughter's blunt, slightly sceptical tone. 'Why wouldn't I be?'

'I don't know. I had a bad dream.'

'Dreams are meaningless,' Evie said cheerily. 'Just the mind digesting its experiences.'

'Did you learn that at school?'

'I just know things. It's not hard.'

She was walking along and chewing something. 'Where are you?' Julia asked, imagining the path away from the bus stop, towards the river. Even though it wasn't real.

'Just finished school.'

'You'll go straight home?'

'Why wouldn't I?'

Julia had been going through the guestroom's wardrobe when her mobile rang. Now she slid down the doors to sit on the carpet. 'You left your dad's last night.'

'Yup.'

'Had a good week?'

'I guess. It was weird without you there.'

'I'm sorry.'

'It's okay, you have to do it.' Evie swallowed whatever she'd been eating. 'How's Grandpa Don?'

'He got a dog.'

'Really?'

'I was just as surprised as you.'

'Has he ever had a dog before?'

'Not to my knowledge.'

'Yeah,' Evie said slowly. 'It makes sense. What's the dog like?'

'I'll send you a picture.'

The sounds of South Yarra swirled in the background: the beep of pedestrian crossing signals, the hum of vehicles. The suburb where her father lived was silent, and Julia felt a brief ache for home.

'Can we get a dog?' Evie asked.

'You'd have to ask your father.'

'We can't have one in the flat.' Evie sighed. 'That'd be cruel.'

To change the subject, Julia said, 'Give me the update. What have I missed?'

Evie was more than happy to dive in. Unlike Davina, she didn't hover at the perimeter of the stories she shared, but put herself right in the centre. She was quitting ballet, she told Julia, because she realised one of the girls had an eating disorder, and though Evie had tried to talk to both the teacher and sufferer about it, no one was taking action. Her interest in ballet was waning anyway: she'd long since stopped ooh-ing and aah-ing over the blisters and bruises that patterned their teacher's feet or the old pink bloodstains in the lining of her shoes. She'd decided to do hip-hop next term, because it was for fun and expression and exercise: you didn't have to prove yourself with pain.

The topic moved to school. There was a prac teacher in maths who, while the supervising teacher was out of the room, wrote on the board with permanent marker. Worse, the number was 69. The class lost their shit. Evie didn't mind the laughter, but when the teasing began, she'd put a stop to it. 'You're so immature,' she told the loudest boy. 'Stop, seriously. You're making us all look bad.'

Finally, leisure. Evie and some friends went shopping at Melbourne Central on the weekend, and there was a homeless man with a cardboard sign near the entrance. Her friends hadn't acknowledged him, though not out of malice. 'They didn't say anything rude,' Evie defended, in case Julia thought otherwise. 'I guess their parents would do the same, so that's what they did.' Julia and Rowan didn't go up to all the unhoused people they saw, so Evie hadn't learned it from them. 'I mean, he did look kind of pissed off. But it makes sense.'

As her friends went ahead, Evie approached the man, gave him a dollar coin, asked how his day was going. The weather was warmer than he'd expected, so she opened her backpack and took out a bottle of spring water, warm and plasticky from days of storage, but unopened. She asked if he wanted it, but he said no, so she wished him a good day and hurried to catch up with her friends. One claimed the water bottle and thirstily drank it down.

Julia was amazed. Her stepdaughter had never been afraid to wade into the lives of those she saw floundering and lift them above the waterline, calling to others to come and assist. Evie always seemed certain that no one else would act properly until she made them, and she was often right. In all of Evie's stories, Julia would've been part of the crowd: overlooking the starving ballerina, ignoring the homeless man, laughing at the student teacher's mistake. Knowing it was wrong but forgiving herself because she hadn't started it.

'So that's probably everything,' Evie summarised. 'Crazy week, huh.'

Julia realised that none of her stepdaughter's news was about Rowan and wondered if this was on purpose. She couldn't ask, couldn't put Evie in the middle.

'Well,' she said, 'all I've done this week is clean and tidy.'

'Have you found a place for him to stay?'

Julia had not. She was putting off this vital part of the process and she knew it. Better to take on the labour she understood. 'Not yet.'

'Jules. You have to.'

'It's just hard to imagine him somewhere else.' She gazed up at the ceiling. 'He's been in this house for so long. It's going to be a massive change.'

'It's for his own good,' Evie said, parroting Julia's own argument. 'Being in a big house all by himself isn't safe.'

'He is while I'm here.'

'Yeah,' Evie said patiently, 'but you can't be there forever, can you? You have a life.'

On Saturday Julia woke up and thought, *Fuck this.*

She kicked her way out of the damp sheets and headed for the bathroom she'd cleaned over and over again. Stamping out of pyjama bottoms: *Fuck this.* Lining up the tricky taps so the shower was a survivable temperature: *Fuck this.* Dragging her towel from the rail: *Fuck this.*

Drying herself, she heard the shuffle-*teck* of her father making his way to the kitchen. He claimed he could look after himself; well, he could start by making his own breakfast. When the hallway echoed with the snap of the kettle switching off, she slid out of the bathroom and into her old bedroom. She hadn't gone in there since she arrived from the airport and her father sent her to the guestroom, with its new sheets and furniture. Now there were things she needed.

The bedroom was the same as she'd left it fifteen years ago: a narrow bed draped in a unicorn-patterned quilt, white dressing table with sparkly resin handles, a full-length mirror hanging behind the door, encased in a fuzzy blue frame. The childishness of the decorations pained her: she'd slept here into her twenties. She wondered if she'd ever asked her parents for new furnishings and been refused because there was nothing wrong with the old ones. Surely this hadn't been her taste.

In all the rooms she'd tackled so far there had been a sense of hesitation based on what she was afraid to find. The kitchen and TV room had only been tedious, the bathroom off-putting; but even now, after two weeks, she couldn't get it together to move on to the bedrooms, the dining room, her father's precious lounge. Today was the first time she'd felt the desire to hunt something down.

When she opened the cupboard, Julia let out a long whistle of appreciation. A dozen dresses hung from the rod. They were decades old, but she was sure she'd find something that wasn't too dated. And if it was, she thought, taking the hangers down, then so what? It was a girls' night. *Fuck this*, she told herself, gleefully this time. She put the desk chair under the doorknob in case her father came searching, then shucked her robe.

One good thing about her body was that it hadn't changed since puberty – narrow and flat then, narrow and flat now. The dresses still fit. They were all hideous sweatshop rubbish, scratchy polyester with bad stitching, but had seemed so glamorous in the windows of the cheap boutiques. Thirty dollars was a lot of money in those days, to a fifteen-year-old. The fabric of each one had either clung, pinched under her arms or pulled to one side, but she'd felt like a vixen with her matchstick legs and elegant shoulders. She put her face to the necklines and smelled old perfumes seared into the lining.

The one she liked best was pale blue, gathered at the breasts and with a circle skirt that made her want to spin. Its spaghetti straps looked as if they untied but really the bows were stitched to the neckline. It had been kept in a cupboard for two decades and that was exactly how it smelled, but Julia knew if she hung it in the bathroom or from the patio rafters the air would get through it and make it presentable.

With her robe back on, Julia kneeled to look under the bed, where she'd kept her party shoes. She could see some in a clear plastic tub, so she took the handle and dragged it out.

The container had been packed past its limits, the lid swelling and a long crack tracing along one corner. The shoes were at the bottom, packed in beneath a pile of other stuff, all Julia's. There was no order to any of it: a dried pasta art project from primary school sat on top of a year nine maths exam; a birthday party invitation slipped out of a program for a school Christmas concert. Julia searched for her name, finding it alongside Kimmie Wessels under Angels Who Are Heard on High, Act Three. Davina's came much later, a sheep in the stable when baby Jesus was born. Julia could picture her costume: a fluffy white bath mat taped around her waist, black socks on her feet and hands. Julia and Kimmie had wire coat hangers wound with tinsel for halos, their mouths and cheeks coloured with lipstick. Backstage, Davina said they looked like clowns.

It was the year Julia and Davina were in different classes. Their mothers sat together in the audience, Pamela's big hand clutching Goldie's smaller one. It was a bit weird for grown women to do that, but it wasn't too bad, and Julia had liked the twitch of pleasure on Goldie's face. Paul sat on the other side of her, quietened by the miracle of sound and colour, and next to him was Don, his arms folded, hair wilted from the crowd of bodies. At the end of the show he'd applauded loud and fast with his hands over his head, circles of sweat printed in his armpits.

Davina's father hadn't come. He worked away a lot of the time, so the Weir girls didn't see him much. Their house was violently female as a result, the four sisters bouncing off the walls, pulling each other's hair, yanking limbs off dolls and putting them in the microwave. The house was long and thin, all its big windows facing the street, and being there felt like performing onstage. Julia found it both exhilarating and frightening, the way the rooms seemed to echo with old shrieks, the tension of hairclips snapping shut, clouds of body spray at eye-watering strength. Some fundamental balance seemed to be thrown off, like the agitator in a washing machine tipping and clanking as the spin cycle ratcheted up. She knew it was sexist, but Julia was convinced that more masculine energy would have helped to even things out, the way her own father's did. The Lambett household may have been dull, but at least it was calm.

Goldie and Julia had gone back to the Weirs' after the concert; Paul fell asleep, so Don took him home. The mothers went to the kitchen for champagne, or whatever champagne-like drink had been cheapest at the bottle shop, and Davina shut herself and Julia in the small bedroom, ignoring Lou's outraged screams. They lay on their stomachs on Davina's bed, dressed only in the base layers of their costumes: white undershirts and skin-coloured tights, Davina's feet still in her black ankle socks. *Hooves*, Julia thought, kicking her lower legs so her heels bounced off her bottom. She was skittery with elation.

Davina frowned. 'Lipstick.'

Touching her face, Julia felt the grease. Earlier she'd wiped a handful of tissues against her lips but forgot the circle of colour on her cheekbones. 'Whoops.'

'Here.' Davina stuck out her tongue and licked her palm from wrist to fingertips, then reached for Julia's cheek. Julia froze, not sure if her friend was joking, but she wasn't. The hand was sticky as it touched her skin.

Davina was talking, and at first Julia couldn't concentrate. The sour scent of Davina's saliva hung in her nostrils. Something about a person on the top floor of a building. The person was walking around, doing something maybe, or just wandering. Julia didn't want to ask any questions that would show she hadn't been listening.

'So she's all dressed up, you know. It's a very elegant occasion.' Davina was scratching the skin around her fingernails, digging out threads of black cotton left by the hand socks. 'Long silky gown, silver high heels with pointy toes.'

'Wow.'

'It's cold, so over the top she's wearing this beautiful fur coat with a really long train.' Wincing, she held up a shred of skin, then showed the red dot where the bleeding had started. Julia gave her a sympathetic look. 'She's got her hands in the pockets to keep warm, and she starts to walk down the stairs.'

Julia closed her eyes, remembering the sensation of the wet palm tugging at her cheek. Davina kept talking. 'The very first step, her shoes catch the edge of her coat and she flies forward, all the way from the top of the staircase to the bottom.'

Julia's eyes snapped open. 'What?'

'In one go.' Davina used her torn hands to demonstrate: a body is at the top of a very high incline, then arcs through the air above it. The bottom is extremely far away.

'Why didn't —' Julia began. She didn't know how she was going to finish the question.

'Her hands were caught in her pockets so she couldn't get them out. Her face went *smash* into the very last step.' Davina shrugged, shoulders lifting high around her ears. 'Nothing to break her fall.'

Soon after that her mother came in to take Julia home. Because of the two glasses of sparkling wine, Goldie didn't seem to notice Julia's silence on the walk back, her mind going around and around what had happened that evening: the high-pitched singing, the swipe of spit along her cheek, the woman in the fur coat falling headfirst, unable to make it stop.

– THIRTEEN –

It was years since Julia had been out in Northbridge. When she'd turned eighteen it was the place to go, getting tipsy at a bar before crossing the street to one of the nightclubs, the entry stamp on her wrist going unwashed so everyone could see how she'd spent her weekend. Waiting for Davina at the agreed spot, she watched young women starting their nights the same way she used to, the heels of their stilettos clomping on the pavement as they hurried along the footpath, voices loud with exhilaration.

Davina rounded the corner a few minutes late, wearing black leather pants and a silky maroon shirt cut into a deep V at her cleavage. Her skin looked shockingly white against it. When she drew Julia in for a hug there was a faint alcohol scent to her, perfume and pre-drinks. 'Ready to eat?' she asked, gesturing towards the signage for a steak restaurant. 'I'm starving.'

It wasn't what Julia expected from a girls' night, being

led between low leather armchairs to a corner table made from heavy wood, the smell of meat and whisky heavy in the air. Despite it being evening, she'd thought of cupcakes and champagne, high teas with layered sandwiches. The pale blue of her flouncy dress seemed inappropriate in this cave of crimson and mahogany.

The bread came out and Julia watched Davina tear off a hunk with her fingers, then press it into the dishes of oil and balsamic. 'It's so good,' she said, her tongue dark red behind neat teeth. She ate with a relish that was almost sexual, groaning and rolling her dark-lined eyes to the ceiling. A trickle of vinegar ran from her mouth like blood.

'I've never been here,' Julia said, pressing butter into her sourdough. 'Is it new?'

'My friends and I come here all the time,' Davina said. She hadn't swallowed her most recent mouthful and it hid, oil-soaked, in the pocket of her cheek. 'The steaks are amazing. The mushroom sauce ...' She trailed off with a theatrical smack of her lips. 'There's nothing like meat and wine, don't you think?'

As if cued, a slender European waiter bent over their table to pour from the bottle of red Davina had ordered. She tasted it and nodded, so he filled both their glasses and withdrew. Davina lifted one by the stem and ran her finger over the swollen glass, the liquid inside purplish under the low lighting of the restaurant.

'Those wide champagne glasses are meant to resemble Marie Antoinette's tits,' she said thoughtfully, 'but mine are shaped more like this.'

She took a deep swallow, then grinned at Julia's surprised expression. 'I'm only joking.' Davina lowered her eyes to Julia's chest. 'I guess you're more of a Marie Antoinette, though.'

'Jeez,' Julia said. The other woman fired her shotgun laugh. 'I haven't had enough wine for that.'

'Fine,' Davina said. 'Maybe later.' She leaned over the table and rested her chin in her hands, the line of her cleavage puckering as her upper arms pressed her breasts together. 'Tell me about your husband, then.'

'I thought I did.'

'You barely scratched the surface!' Davina objected, pouting. 'Come on. I told you I'm a sad single lady. Give me the juice.'

Julia sipped her wine. It was strong and deep and her cheeks warmed instantly. 'Like what?'

'How'd you meet?'

'I was working for a lawyer. Rowan came in for advice.'

'About what?' Davina coaxed. 'Did he commit a crime?'

Julia laughed. 'It was a commercial lawyer. Ro was starting a business.'

'The physio clinic.' Julia had told Davina that part earlier. To her credit, she did listen. 'So, you fell in love immediately?'

Julia took another sip. 'I don't know about *immediately*.'

'Tell me!'

'You want to hear the whole thing?'

Davina nodded. 'Every word. It's girls' night.'

Julia talked. All the way through the server coming with

their meals, pouring the sauces over their steaks, refilling their wine, Julia talked. She spoke with food in her mouth, shielding the sight with a limp hand, hooked on Davina's wide eyes and supportive nods. She talked until they finished their mains and the plates were collected and a second bottle of wine brought out and the dessert menu placed in front of them and they ordered and the menus were whisked away and replaced with a third bottle, Julia's wineglass filling and emptying and filling and emptying as it had at Davina's the other night; the way she rarely ever did at home.

She'd met Rowan during a period of indecision, she told Davina. She'd been in Melbourne for a year and wasn't really settling in. Her life consisted of going from her studio flat in Richmond to work and back. On the weekends she took long, aimless walks until her feet were so blistered she had to wear thongs under her office desk. By the time they'd healed it was the big empty weekend again.

Though she was unhappy, she didn't want to go back to Perth. Paul had just moved to Sydney and she would have joined him if it didn't make her seem pathetic. Nowhere else was appealing; a stint overseas was too hard. She didn't have any friends. She didn't have any in Perth, either, but it'd been easier to hide there, with her parents and brother.

The law firm was very small, she explained to Davina. She was the receptionist, secretary, paralegal and PA. The lawyer was old and slowing down. He hadn't taken on a new client in years, but he'd done work for the Chengs before, and the space Rowan wanted to lease was only a hundred metres further down Toorak Road. He called the lawyer 'uncle' and hugged him hard when they met. That was the first spark, for Julia. His openness. His sense of family.

For his second appointment the lawyer was running late, so Julia made Rowan a coffee and led him into the meeting room. She'd meant to leave him there, but he'd started talking about his business, his feet tapping against the carpet. His enthusiasm was contagious. The atmosphere at the law firm was pleasant, but not inspiring; the only other colleague was an associate who'd worked there for donkey's years and just wanted to be home by the time her kids got back from school. Rowan envisioned a chain of clinics, branding, value additions like classes and personal training. He was planning something big.

The next time Rowan came in was to sign documents. Julia was the witness; the lawyer had left at lunchtime. She wore her most flattering clothes and left her hair down, so it swept lightly over the pages when she leaned over. Rowan noticed. He asked if she wanted to help him celebrate with a drink.

'Did you get it on?' Davina asked.

'It took a few dates.'

Davina pressed her hands together in prayer. 'What a gentleman.'

What Julia kept to herself was how, when she went to walk him back to the lobby, Rowan had seen her step into her court shoes and wince. How he'd knelt in front of her in a way that was almost reverent to inspect her ripped feet. How he could tell from the pattern of blisters that she had an uneven gait. 'You need to strengthen this muscle,' he said, brushing the outside of her hip. 'I'll give you some exercises.' After two weeks the blisters were gone, and she didn't need to fill her weekends with walking anymore. She was seeing Rowan.

'What did you think about him having a kid?' Davina asked.

'I didn't really mind.'

That was an understatement. Actually, when Rowan showed her the picture of Evie, she'd felt a thrill. Rowan had such a life already: a flat of his own, a new business, a child. Julia had nothing. She was hoping he'd share.

As the only physio at the clinic, needing to be available for walk-ins, Rowan's days became long and static. Julia brought him food on her lunchbreak, collected his mail, found cheap, inoffensive art at garage sales to hang in the treatment rooms. She met Evie and Samara and won their approval. Her sense of purpose was strengthening, stabilising; she no longer imagined moving to Sydney or home to Perth.

Things picked up slowly. Rowan had rented a space that was expensive but highly visible, and he was photogenic on the advertising materials, with his good haircut and expensive watch. They marketed to ex-sportspeople and those who thought of themselves that way: cyclists, joggers, golfers, treating them for aches and pains from sitting at desks or carrying kids or getting older. While he massaged and strapped and needled, Rowan talked about nutrition and exercise, the benefits of wakeboarding, the gut as a second brain, the ideal supplements for smooth joints. He made them feel like Olympians on hiatus.

Julia did Rowan's books and manned the reception desk on Saturdays, which were their busiest days. Her lease in

Richmond ran out and she moved into the South Yarra flat. They got a joint account, engaged, married. The business made money. Julia trained her replacement at the law practice and became Rowan's full-time office manager. She could leave work in the middle of the afternoon to collect Evie, then set her up in a beanbag in the corner of the office while she finished her tasks. When Julia's mother died, she was shocked beyond belief, but her husband helped her through it.

The crème brûlées came out, pink quenelles of ice cream nestled against the ramekins. Julia felt lightheaded from talking. She had a mouthful of wine to lubricate her throat.

'I'm sorry about Goldie,' Davina said. 'I didn't know if you wanted to talk about it.'

'There's not much to say.' Julia hit the dessert with her spoon, enjoying the sharp crack through the glossy surface. 'She got the flu, had complications. Random chance.'

'Terrible,' Davina said. She hadn't touched her cutlery. 'Awful. I couldn't believe it when I found out.'

'I saw you at the funeral,' Julia fibbed.

'I wanted to pay my respects. Goldie was lovely.'

'She was.'

They finished and Davina called for the bill, then started rummaging in her purse. Julia shook her head. 'I'm paying.'

'Don't be silly, it was my idea.'

'You made dinner for me,' Julia argued. She didn't mention Billie's irritation at how much her mother had spent. 'It's my turn to treat.'

'We can at least go halves. Look at what I ordered.' Davina gestured to the list of items. 'I don't want to take advantage.'

'You're not.' Julia slid her credit card into the billfold. 'I haven't had to pay for a thing since I got here. I'm living high on the hog at Don's.'

They moved from the restaurant to a bar. Julia ordered while Davina went to the bathroom, but she took a while and Julia's glass emptied quickly. She was halfway through her second when Davina reappeared, eyelids heavy and top twisted so that one breast was barer than the other. Or maybe it was just Julia seeing things off-kilter again; all the wine seemed to be hitting at once. She held onto the tabletop for balance.

Davina's gaze locked on her again. By now Julia knew what was coming. She closed her eyes against the onslaught. 'And after your mum died?'

'What do you mean?'

'What happened next? You didn't finish your story.'

Julia tried to laugh. 'What story was that?'

'You and Rowan.'

'There's not much more to tell.'

Davina looked incredulous. 'Nothing's happened since then? What was it, ten years ago?'

Julia rested her forehead against her arms, but Davina pinched her wrist. 'If they think you're drunk, they'll kick you out.'

'I am drunk,' she argued.

'No, you're not. You don't drink much alcohol, so it's made you tired.' Julia was surprised at the accuracy. 'Now come on. Keep going with the story.'

'What makes you think there's more?'

Davina stared coolly, knowing who'd give in first.

'The baby thing again.' Julia took a ragged breath. 'Why are you so ...'

'I can tell it bothers you.'

You're not my friend, Julia thought, but wasn't drunk enough to say. She was drunk enough to say the rest of it, things she usually kept to herself, though first she finished her wine and pretended not to notice when Davina nodded to the bartender for another.

What happened next was that Julia turned thirty. Her mother's sudden death was still raw and aching, but not so much that she couldn't think about other things. She saw that the business was going well and the three of them – she, Rowan and Evie – were getting older. They wanted more children in the family, and there seemed no better time to try.

That was six years ago.

'What happened?' Davina asked softly, though this time she didn't need to push. Julia was going to tell her.

There was so much momentum in the first five years of their relationship. From meeting at the lawyer's office, they'd built a thriving business, they were partners, they'd made life-changing decisions. Then, almost at the same time they made this final one, to try and have a baby of their own, everything else seemed to run aground. The practice's growth flatlined. Until there was a baby, there was no reason to sell the flat and move. Evie went into year four, year five, year six, then brought home the high school's straw hat and blazer.

They took holidays: a week in Thailand, skiing in New Zealand. Julia stood at the base of the run and watched people tumble over, groaning and laughing. Her period was late, and she held her abdomen protectively. 'What if I'm pregnant?' she asked, but Rowan just shrugged. After two days of gentle lessons and superstitiously avoiding liquor at the lodge, she'd gone to the toilet and found a circle of brown blood.

'When was that?' Davina asked. Someone had brought over their new drinks, and she rubbed her finger against the glass to make it squeak.

'A couple of years ago.'

'Did you go to a doctor?'

'Because of my period?'

'Because of what it meant.'

'We're not—' Julia had a statement for this; she just had to locate it. 'We're not interested in intervention. Either we have a baby, or we don't. We have Evie. We're not childless.'

'*You* are.'

Julia's face flamed. She sucked down her wine. 'Just because I didn't give birth to her.'

'No, because she's Samantha's.'

'Samara.'

'Samara's. She's yours as well, but it's not the same.'

'I don't think of it like that,' Julia muttered.

Davina shrugged. 'Yes, you do. I can tell by your face.'

You're not my friend, Julia thought again. But no one else was either. 'I'm not going to spend a bunch of money because my body won't.' She shook her head and stared into the clarity of the glass.

'Might not be your problem,' Davina said. 'Might be Rowan.'

'He had Evie. There's nothing wrong with him.'

'That was fourteen years ago. Sperm can die.'

'He's the healthiest person you've ever seen.'

'So are you.'

The table was strewn with empty glasses; Julia hung off her stool, dress pooling heavily between her thighs.

'Even if you can't have a baby yourself, there's other ways.'

'Yeah, I know,' Julia bared her teeth. '*Just adopt.*'

'Not adoption. Surrogacy.'

Julia's sudden laughter brought wine to the back of her throat. She sat up straight and put her hand to her mouth. 'I think I'm done for the evening.'

'I had two babies,' Davina continued. 'Complication-free. Fell pregnant at the drop of a hat. And I'm available.'

Julia drifted to the side again. 'So?'

'I could carry a baby for you.' Davina reached out suddenly, staring into Julia's eyes. Davina was a bit drunk too, surely. 'I could be your surrogate, if you wanted.'

'Wow,' Julia murmured.

A burly man in a black T-shirt ambled over from the bar. 'Ladies. Might be time to call it a night.'

'Okay, okay,' Davina said, holding Julia's hand as they made the treacherous journey down from their chairs. 'We're going.'

It was cold outside, with a fine misty rain. Davina ordered an Uber and they walked around to the pickup location, the chill breeze startling Julia sober. She hadn't brought a jacket.

Their driver was a few minutes away when accepting the ride, and they waited without speaking. 'That's it,' Davina announced, pointing to an approaching sedan. She jostled

Julia's hand, their fingers still linked. 'I'm serious about my offer, you know.'

'I know,' Julia said. 'Just let me think.'

The two women gazed at one another. In that second Julia felt a swoop of the old excitement, the sense of promise and possibility that used to come with seeing Davina. The only others she'd ever felt that for were Rowan and Evie.

- ☾ -

Now Evie's down at the river, long grass and thick mud where a tributary used to be, shopping trolleys buried in the muck. Low hum from some nearby highway. Mosquitoes and bees, the odd stray dog. Stories of someone finding a sealed bag of kittens along here once. Various versions of whether they were alive or dead.

She rides slowly, helmet full of sweat. A pink plastic flower on the front of the basket. Jogging feet pat along the bitumen behind her, and she dips the handlebars so the bike veers left.

At their loudest the footsteps slow and do not overtake. She turns to see what's going on, arm above the eyes to block out the sun. The figure is familiar: short brown hair, ears crackled with sunburn. No denim jacket or boots today. A grey circle of sweat at the neck of his shirt.

I thought it was you, he grins. Jogging on the spot, the big hand reaches for her shoulder, then lifts away at the last moment. How's it going?

The bike wobbles and she pulls back on it like a bridle. Yeah, good. It's hot, though.

Very hot. *His big thumb loosens his sticky collar; chest hair sparkles in the sun.* What are you doing down here by yourself?

She shrugs. Don't know. Something to do.

Well. *The big hands go briefly to his waist.* Don't stay past dark. *Leans in close, eyes teasing, the smell of sweat and old aftershave.* You never know who you'll run into.

– FOURTEEN –

When school went back after the Christmas break, the three girls were all in the same class. Julia's stomach had gone hot and sloshy when she found out. It could either go really well, or be really, really bad.

It turned out to be both.

The teacher, Mr Andrews, would not allow students to choose their seats, instead waiting for everyone to arrive before assigning them a spot. It would be in alphabetical order, he told them, and Julia had reached out and squeezed Kimmie's arm. K came after J.

Starting at the desk closest to the door, Mr Andrews moved along the rows, reading out names. 'Zhang,' he called. 'Williams. Wessels. Weir.' Kimmie wrinkled her nose as she went to join Davina, who twisted around to stare at Julia as if everything was her fault.

Julia ended up in the middle row, directly behind Davina and Kimmie and between two boys. She craned to see. Was

Davina whispering in Kimmie's ear? Was Kimmie – *laughing*?

'Miss Lambett,' Mr Andrews called. He was old and sarcastic, with deep round nostrils like the insides of shells. 'Something we can help you with?'

'No,' she muttered. 'Sorry.'

Davina and Kimmie glanced over their shoulders. Their smiles were sympathetic, but also sharp, hiding scalpel teeth.

They became an uneasy trio. Each week one girl would find herself on the periphery, ejected by the others, who were now best friends forever. On Mondays, the unlucky girl would learn her fate, arriving at the classroom to find the other two engaged in such close conversation their lips almost touched, stopping exaggeratedly when she appeared. The chill feeling settled in the stomach at that moment, the realisation you were about to be excluded in a minor but devastating way: the others whispering and giggling, eyes sliding in your direction. If you said anything about it, the denial was instant. *We're not talking about you! Don't freak out. You're always like this.*

The first half of the week was spent crawling back into the others' good graces. Behaving yourself, trying not to complain. Bringing back two extra doughnuts from the canteen even though you knew they'd been talking about you while you were gone. Laughing on the edge of jokes you didn't understand. Waiting for the tide to turn.

By Thursday, the work had paid off. You were allowed back in, even centred. The others bracketed you with admiration and love. They stroked your hair and included you in whispers. Strength ran through you. It was over. By Friday, all three were on the verge of tears at the thought of a weekend's separation.

Then, if you were lucky, Monday found you on the inside.

The conversation turned, lazily, towards the missing third. *She does this all the time*, you'd hedge, and the other girl would nod. Say something mild about the missing one's hair or some stupid thing she'd said, how she never shared the good stuff in her pencil case. The other girl's arm found yours, wound around it like a snake, leaving you breathless. You bent your heads together and the other one said, *Why are we even friends with her?*

Turn your heads as the last girl finally arrived, already devastated. Nod coolly, touch your forehead to the other chosen one's. Close everyone else out. Feel bad, but mostly thrilled. Powerful.

More often than not, Davina was one of the pair. Julia could count on her fingers the number of times it was her and Kimmie. Even when they managed it, equilibrium was usually achieved by Wednesday, maybe even Tuesday. There just wasn't as much to say without Davina.

There was a necklace set from the bargain shop, two silver-coloured chains, each with a pendant that formed half a broken heart. One pendant said *Best Friends* and the other *Forever.* The set was Davina's, and she wore the *Forever* side. On Mondays she handed the other to her new confidant, then later claimed it back, saying it wasn't fair, they were all best friends. After that, Davina was always in the twosome; it didn't work without the necklace. It was a relief, in a way: excluding Davina was more stressful than being excluded.

For the Christmas holidays that year Kimmie went to South Africa and Davina's family stayed with relatives in Esperance. Julia spent the summer at the dentist; she'd begun to grind her teeth.

They saw the Weirs the day before school went back. Davina had grown taller over the six weeks and developed her single, hooting laugh.

'You know we're all in the same class again?' she announced. Her hair was longer, and she flicked her thick braid back and forth over her shoulder until Julia noticed her bare throat.

'What happened to the necklace?'

'Oh, that. My sister broke it.' Davina shrugged. 'I don't care, it was dumb.'

Julia felt her jaw relax. 'Yeah.'

'We can all be best friends at the same time,' Davina said. 'Can't we?'

'I hope so.'

'Yes,' Davina insisted. 'Yes. We are.'

Julia woke with a pinching headache and sandy mouth, joints throbbing like the red wine had crystallised in them. She lay prone on the mattress for as long as she could before giving in and staggering to the toilet. The urine stream was hot and endless, and she dozed off for a second with her chin on her fist, waking when she swayed towards the ground.

The kitchen smelled of burned toast. It was eight o'clock, early for a Sunday morning but late for Don, who'd apparently grown tired of waiting and made his own breakfast. Well, good. Through cracked eyelids Julia pushed three slices into the toaster for herself, drinking lukewarm tap water while she waited. When the bread popped, she slathered it with butter and ate standing over the sink, staring out into the overgrown yard.

She remembered everything from the night before. The

good steaks and Davina's attention. Holding herself up by the elbows at the pub as Davina insisted that there was nothing wrong with Julia, and that she could be a surrogate for Julia and Rowan's baby.

Both of those things couldn't be true at the same time. One, maybe even both, had to be wrong.

Julia had taken care, over the long years of trying, not to imagine herself pregnant. When online shopping, she clicked away from maternity clothes; she put her head down as they passed baby stores on Toorak Road. Maybe she'd jinxed it. But she could see Davina with a swollen belly cradled in her hands and a look of cool pride on her face.

Had Davina woken this morning with the same perfect recall? Did she know what she'd offered and, if so, did she now regret it, the way she'd regretted letting Julia walk the perfectly safe streets home the other night?

When she'd finished her toast, Julia filled the kettle and switched it on. The water had eased her aching throat, and now she needed caffeine to knock the edge off her headache. All the mugs Julia had kept were in the cupboard, meaning her father hadn't made himself anything to drink. She took two down and spooned in coffee and sugar.

The kettle was beginning to rattle when Biscuit trotted down the hall and stood in the doorway. 'Hey, boy,' she called, and he came over for a pat and a couple of rounds of tricks. Since she'd found out what he could do, Julia had been practising with him, making sure he didn't lose the skills someone had worked so hard to develop.

Don was in his armchair, a crumby plate on the table beside

him. She used it as a saucer for the mug. 'Good morning.'

'Yes,' he said grimly, waiting until she'd sat on the sofa to peer into her offering. 'Thank you.'

He didn't ask about her night and she didn't tell him. Holding her mug in both hands, she sipped gratefully, feeling the sharpness of the coffee push through her, waking her up.

The pile of things Julia had gathered for Don's inspection had grown so high some had tipped off the chair and onto the carpet. Trying to claim his usual space, Biscuit lay half on top of some embroidered towels Julia had found in the guestroom. The dog huffed out air and a stiff handkerchief fluttered. 'If you set yourself, say, ten items a day,' she said, trying to sound patient, 'you'd get through that stuff pretty quickly.'

Don glanced at the pile in distaste, then had a mouthful of coffee.

'I'd just chuck it all out if I wasn't afraid of losing something important. I'm making as many decisions as I can, but I don't know the stories behind it all.'

'Not everything has a story.'

'No, I know not *everything*. Just this stuff.' She swallowed her anger. 'If you saw the amount of stuff I *have* got rid of, you'd know this is barely a dent.' Maybe she should be storing the full bin bags in her father's bedroom between trips to the tip. Maybe he should face the enormity of the job and realise that a few dozen objects stacked on a chair was fuck all, in the grand scheme of things.

'Just get rid of it,' Don muttered. 'What do they say? When in doubt, chuck it out.'

Her headache rebounded, slapping her right across the browbone. If he was so cavalier about his possessions, if everything meant nothing to him, then why had he held onto it for forty years? Riding the surge of irritation, she decided to call his bluff. 'Okay, well, good. I'll get through it a lot quicker this way. But in that case, we'll have to get moving on finding you somewhere else to stay.' She was careful not to say *live*; it felt too confrontational.

'Not while I have Biscuit,' he said.

'What?'

'Not while I have Biscuit.'

'What do you mean?' Julia asked, her heart sliding down the wall of her chest.

'Exactly what I said.'

'You're not moving without Biscuit.'

'I'm not moving Biscuit at all. He can't take more upheaval.'

Julia looked at the dog, lying half on top of her father's junk. His tail knocked a carved wooden box, sending it skidding to the floor. 'You're joking.'

'No.'

'Dad.'

He took a measured sip of coffee.

'Dad,' she said again. Her annoyance had drained away; now her body was filling with panic. 'Dad. We've talked about this.' Julia shook her head, realising that she and her father had never actually discussed it. 'You talked to Paul,' she corrected.

'The dog needs to be taken into consideration. He's a living being.'

'You never even said you had a dog.'

Don held himself stiffly, the coffee mug in one claw, the other pressed against the armrest. He was trying to look relaxed. He knew exactly what he was doing.

'I'm sure we can find somewhere that that will take Biscuit,' she said. 'There must be places that cater for—'

'I'm not making Biscuit move again. It's cruel.'

'You mean it's cruel to make *you* move.'

Don looked into her eyes for the first time since she'd entered the room; maybe the first time in days. His were a clear, glassy blue, the soft rims of his eyelids turned out and sore-looking. 'I'm going to stay here while I have Biscuit.'

The dog was eight, the man was ninety-two. Paul had threatened not to come back if their father stayed in the house; maybe Don would do it out of sheer bloody-mindedness and take Biscuit down with him. The pair of them getting thinner, weaker, less able to fend for themselves, until they were two skeletons lolling against the kitchen cupboards. 'I can't believe you,' Julia whispered, her throat parched again.

Don shrugged. 'I have my reasons.'

'So this has all been a big waste of time.'

'It wasn't my idea.'

She stood up from the sofa and hurried out of the room, wanting to rage and kick and smash all the ugly brown glass in the fucking house. She'd never been so angry, had never felt so powerless.

Because her father, after all, was right.

− FIFTEEN −

She gave in and called Rowan.

He answered almost before the ringtone started. 'For God's sake, Jules.'

The reaction made her defensive. 'What?'

'It's been two weeks.'

'We said we were going to give it time.'

'That was total bullshit.'

She was glad he couldn't see her burning face. 'Well, you didn't call me either.'

'I was giving you space.'

The silence lengthened between them. There was a faint buzzing on the line. 'Are you there?' Julia asked.

'Of course I am.'

'Dad won't leave.'

'What?'

She exhaled heavily. 'I've packed up half the fucking

house, I'm about to look into nursing homes, and then he turns around and tells me he's staying here.'

'What the fuck?' Julia was pleased Rowan sounded as frustrated as she felt. 'Why not?'

'He got a dog.'

'Right. Paul told me.'

She was surprised. 'You spoke to Paul?'

'I needed intel from somewhere.'

Julia decided to park this revelation for the time being. 'The dog's a mystery. He didn't have it when Paul was here, as far as I know. He's never had a dog in his goddamn life, and now he's so bonded to the thing he won't leave the house without it.'

'Right.' Rowan paused. 'Well, I'm sure there are places that would accept —'

'I suggested that, but he reckons he's not scarring the dog further by moving him to a new environment.'

'Jesus Christ,' he groaned. 'It's a fucking dog.'

Julia felt bad to be talking about Biscuit that way. She was sure he'd happily go anywhere as long as he was with Don, and that the line about not unsettling him was a bunch of bull. It was Don who felt unsettled, Don who didn't want his environment to change. Don who'd agreed to this, or had seemed to, until the last minute.

'How old's the dog?' Rowan asked.

Julia knew what he was thinking. 'Eight. He's a good, healthy dog. He could still be around when Dad turns a hundred.'

There was the ticking sound of Rowan sucking his lip, the way he did when he was thinking hard. 'What are you going to do?'

'I'm not sure.'

'Is there someone else who could take the dog?'

'I don't want him left with the ranger or anything,' Julia said. 'It's not his fault.'

'No, I know.' The ticking sound again. 'Do you want me to book you a flight home?'

She did want that, wanted it so much it was a physical pulling in her chest, but she knew she couldn't leave yet. 'I'm going to talk to Dad again. He's got to realise this is for the best.'

'I'll google some places for you,' he suggested. 'See what's around that allows pets.'

Emotion welled in her throat. To have help, even in that tiny way, after a fortnight on her own. 'Thanks.' She coughed and wiped her eyes. 'What's going on over there? I spoke to Evie the other day.'

'I know, she told me.' Before Julia could ask, he explained, 'More intel.'

She smiled into the receiver.

'We're okay. We had an okay week. I managed to put together some protein and veggies before midnight most nights. Asked if she'd done her homework five minutes before she left for the tram.'

'I'm sure you were fine.'

'It's pretty awful here without you, Jules.'

'Oh,' she whispered.

'Not speaking to you ...' He took a deep breath. 'I fucking hate it. I *hate* it.'

'I know. I hate it too.'

But this wasn't the full truth. It wasn't that she'd enjoyed the past two weeks; more that she hadn't thought about her husband as much as she'd imagined she would. The separation had been a constant lack rather than a raw, deep need, and that feeling could be pushed to the background easily enough. There was so much to deal with here: Don, Biscuit, the house, even Davina.

'From now on, can we talk, please?' Rowan asked. 'Even if it's just once a week.'

'All right.'

'It's embarrassing to have to ask your brother what's going on. Not to mention Evie.'

'Okay. Once a week.'

He sighed. 'Good.'

She asked about work and Rowan told her how Sruthi was performing as office manager. 'She likes stickers,' Rowan said. Over the past two weeks stickers had appeared all over their documentation, *sign here* and *please file* and *attention*. 'I need my own roll of stickers that say *will do,*' he joked. 'You think they've got that at Officeworks?' His other complaint was Sruthi's habit of leaving Rowan's paperwork lying lengthways across his keyboard to make sure he saw it. 'There's an in-tray ten centimetres away! Maybe I should put a sticker on it to get her to notice.'

Julia shook her head and smiled. Things were running fine if these were the only gripes he had.

'Bit of gossip,' he continued lightly. 'Bethany's pregnant.'

'Bethany? Seriously?'

'She offered to show us a sonogram, but I told her we don't need photographic evidence.'

'Did you really?'

'No,' Rowan admitted. 'But I didn't look at it either.'

'Who's the father?'

'She didn't share that part.' He sounded uncomfortable.

'Right. Well, congratulations, I guess.'

'Sruthi got her a card with petty cash.'

'That's good.'

She had the urge to tell him about Davina's wild offer from the night before, but didn't think it would go down well over the phone. There was the whole history to explain, as well. How would she feel if Rowan got in touch after two weeks of silence and told her that someone he'd been to school with had volunteered to be their sperm donor? She didn't think he'd even heard of the Weirs.

Julia tried to look on the bright side. She might be on the other side of the country sorting through the belongings of an ungrateful semi-hoarder, but at least she'd avoided having to hear Bethany Taylor announce her pregnancy.

Later, Julia sat cross-legged on the floor of her old room and retrieved the plastic tub from under the bed. She'd taken out a pair of sandals to wear for the girls' night, but it felt no lighter, the wheels jammed by dust. The Christmas concert program was on top and she put it straight in the rubbish bag, determined to be as ruthless with her own possessions as she'd threatened to be with Don's. The pasta art and maths exam followed, then Julia came to the party invitation. DAVINA was printed across the top. At first Julia thought there'd been a mix-up, but reading on, she realised the birthday girl's name had taken pride of place, rather than who she was inviting. DAVINA IS TURNING TEN! PLEASE JOIN US FOR A FUN PIZZA PARTY AND SLEEPOVER! The date and time followed in bright pink pen. HOPE TO C U THERE!!! In the corners were drawings of things the attendees would enjoy: Pizza triangles with wheels of pepperoni and worms of green capsicum, cloud-shaped yellow popcorn, a multi-layered cake topped with ten red candles.

Julia had helped to decorate the invitations, sitting alongside Davina and Kimmie at the Weirs' kitchen table. The party was a massive coup: the first big birthday sleepover, a promise of proper Pizza Hut delivery, and a cake from a bakery, not the boring old *Woman's Weekly* cookbook, like Goldie made. The girls at school fought to be invited. Pamela measured the lounge room and declared it would fit eleven girls if they bunched up tight, but there were only twelve girls in their class, and it seemed mean – even to them – to leave out just one. In the end Davina decided to have seven guests, and Kimmie and Julia got to help pick the lucky five who'd join them. Julia had that stretchy, powerful feeling again for the first time since the best friends necklace broke.

On the day of the party, Julia and Kimmie arrived early. Davina stationed them in front of the big window in the living room so they could report what was happening on the street while she applied body glitter in her older sisters' room down the hall. By three o'clock all the girls were there, sleeping bags rolled tight under their arms, feet tapping with excitement. Julia and Kimmie stood on either side of Davina and nodded knowingly as she walked the others through the small house, calling hello to Tahlia and Christie when they stalked past to prove how comfortable they already were. When Davina opened her presents, Julia and Kimmie binned the torn wrapping paper and collected the cards, and they were the ones who carried the bowls of chips and popcorn from the kitchen when Mrs Weir asked for helpers. They played all the good games at the party: the one where you dress in a hat and gloves and have to cut into chocolate with a knife and fork; the one where you wrap bandanas around your wrists and eyes and try to eat a doughnut hanging from a string.

At ten p.m., after they'd stuffed themselves with the promised pizza and cake, the girls sat in a circle on the lounge room floor with Kimmie lying in the centre and Davina standing at her feet. They were doing Light as a Feather, Stiff as a Board. Julia was so excited she thought she'd burst. She'd read about the game in novels, and seven was a lucky number, a witchy number. Anyway, Kimmie was pretty small. Julia wanted to slide her fingers under the other girl's arm and watch her float up, hair streaming. *Rise, rise, light as a feather, fly, fly, stiff as a board.* She wanted the others to step away one by one until they realised only Julia's fingertips were still touching; that she was the one in control.

'Ready?' Davina intoned. Her face was sombre and shadowed; the only light came from a floor lamp. 'On my count, we—'

She stopped and let out a choked cough, like some unseen entity was strangling her.

The girls by Kimmie's head looked at one another, suspicious that they were being tricked. Kimmie lifted herself on her elbows, blinking. Julia followed everyone else's gaze and groaned when she saw what loomed out at them.

Julia recognised Mr Weir right away. He looked half-asleep, hair matted to one side, but the worst thing was that he was wearing boxer shorts and nothing else. The lamplight revealed his hairy, golden abdomen and bare, knuckly feet. Julia swallowed back her horror.

'*Dad!*' Davina hissed. 'What are you *doing*?'

Mr Weir was sheepish, one hand hovering at his waistband as if to cover his shame. 'I just had a craving for those marshmallow things.'

'Are you *serious*?' Davina seethed.

He shrugged, helpless.

Julia went to the coffee table, hoping there were a few chocolate marshmallows left in the bag. 'How are you girls going,' Mr Weir said to the others. 'Having fun?'

'*Dad.*'

'No marshmallows, Mr Weir,' Julia reported. 'There's some pretzels, though.' She held out the bowl.

His eyes found hers with less urgency than Julia expected, given how angry Davina was. Her heart pounded.

'That'll have to do,' he said easily, taking the pretzels. 'Thank you, Julia. You girls have a lovely night.'

Finally, he left.

They all looked at their ankles in embarrassment and Kimmie stroked the carpet, unwilling to lie down again. Though Julia had her back to the window, she felt as if crowds had gathered outside and were peering in, like at a museum display.

'I'm kind of tired,' she said. It felt like she was shouting.

Within minutes all the sleeping bags were unrolled. Julia and Kimmie lay on either side of Davina, blocking her from the other girls' whispers. 'I'm so embarrassed,' Davina moaned, face in her pillow. 'I told him to keep out of sight.'

'It's not your fault,' Kimmie said. 'Dads do stuff like that.'

Julia closed her eyes, pretending to sleep. She thought both girls were wrong: Davina to be embarrassed by Mr Weir, Kimmie to say it was just the way fathers were. To Julia, it was the girls who should be ashamed of their behaviour, of what Davina's father had stumbled on. *Light as a feather, stiff as a board.* They weren't powerful or magic, they were stupid. They were just lucky Mr Weir was the only one who'd really seen.

That Mr Weir would never say anything about it made it worse. If Don Lambett had walked into a room to find eight girls pretending to be witches, he'd tell them they were being silly and to cut it out. Then they'd have an outlet to defend themselves: *It's not silly! We'll show him!* But Mr Weir hadn't commented, and it left them with no release. The shame rattled around inside them.

In all ways, Mr Weir was a different father than Don. To see the two men together could be deceptive. Alec Weir was younger, better looking, and worked a manly job with long stints away. Surely Don, a generation older, who came home every night and seemed to have no close friends, was the more sensitive of the two. But Don Lambett was hard and dry where Mr Weir was as collapsible as a sponge full of water. Whenever Julia saw him, Davina's father always seemed wracked with emotion, hands crossed at his chest in an approximation of a hug, or some holy symbol. 'You kids,' he said, shaking his head. 'How did I get so lucky?' Julia had never heard her father ask such a question: not even of Goldie, the source of all his luck.

At the dinner table, if Julia stayed over with the Weirs and he was home, Mr Weir addressed each of them in turn, his wife and daughters and their guests, and asked how they were, what was new, how they felt. His eye contact was steady and his nods were deep, serious. This attention was only offered to females, Julia noticed: Mr Weir was not the same with boys. He was nice when Paul was around, but he didn't overflow with the same emotion he had with his daughters and their female friends. In fact, Davina's father seemed stiff and awkward around boys, his voice rising and becoming self-conscious. 'How you doing, sport?' he said to Paul, like they were in some American sitcom. 'How you travelling?' He pretended to give a friendly biff on the arm. It made Julia doubt Davina's theory that her father was desperate for a son.

The questions made Julia squirm, but it wasn't as bad as seeing his focus shift to a daughter who had nothing but disdain for it, who rolled her eyes and muttered monosyllables and kicked her sisters under the table. Once they started, Pamela was the only one who could get them to stop.

'Girls,' she said, once her husband had been cut down enough, 'come on.'

In deference, the four sent anger into their gestures rather than their words: they sliced their meat with fury, they formed fists so tight their fingers blanched white.

What Julia didn't understand was why Mr Weir kept going when he always got the same response. Was he a slow learner, or just optimistic? Julia was careful to record reactions to her behaviour for future guidance. She watched kids at school act up in class and be told off, act up again and be ordered out to the corridor, act up a third time and get sent to the principal. The pattern was so easy to spot. When they complained, Julia wanted to ask what they thought was going to happen. The rules were clear, they were consistent. Fairness had nothing to do with it. That preservation instinct was why, though she died inside for Mr Weir, she never spoke over Davina or her sisters to answer his dinnertime questions. She knew what would come from doing that; she wasn't a glutton for punishment, like him.

It was only later, as an adult, that Julia found a third reason he might have been unable to stop himself. She was on the floor with Evie, poring through a box of dress-ups. Evie was so fascinated with the wigs and oversized glasses she'd ignored Julia's mundane comments: *This is nice, isn't it? Wow, that's so blue! Do you think I look good in a feather boa?* After a while Julia assembled an outfit that was, she thought, particularly hilarious. 'Evie. Evie-bear. Look at this. Look, look, look.'

Finally, the child glanced up. Julia held a plastic crown in one hand and pulled a necklace of fake pearls away from her neck with the other. 'Hel-*looooooo*, I'm the queen, hello hel-*looooo!*'

The assertion struck something deep in Evie, and she dropped what she was holding and reached out. 'No, *I'm* the queen!'

Julia ducked her head. 'I am! I'm wearing the crown.'

'No, Jules, no!' Julia was surprised at the force of Evie's voice, the increase in pitch. She couldn't tell if the little girl was delighted or enraged: it seemed like both. '*I'm* the queen, *I'm the queen!*'

'Oh, really?' Julia took off the crown and held it out just of reach.

The little girl's eyes flashed with thrilled fury.

'So this is yours, then?'

'Yes!' Evie waved her arms. 'Yes, yes, yes!'

When Julia at last handed her the crown, Evie jammed it down on her own head. The tension in her voice and body eased a little, but not all the way. As they kept playing, Julia would see Evie glancing at sidelong at her, suspicious of the next provocation.

At the time Julia thought Mr Weir was deluded, trying to get his daughters to respond in ways they obviously never would, but maybe he'd known exactly what he was doing. To get Evie's attention, Julia had resorted to winding her up, and it worked. Like a rat tapping a button that would deliver an electric shock straight to the pleasure centre of its brain,

Mr Weir took the path most likely to get what he wanted: a reaction from his daughters. So what if they scowled and called him names? At least they were looking. At least they knew he existed.

– SIXTEEN –

That evening, while the chops and potatoes baked in the oven, Julia took a spray bottle and cloth into the dining room and wiped the dust from the table. When the food was done, she set two places and slid a flower from a neighbour's verge into a slim vase. 'Dinner's ready,' she called. 'In here.'

Her father looked suspicious as he shuffled in, propping himself on the walking stick. 'What's the occasion?'

'The furniture's going soon. Might as well make the most out of it.'

The table was octagonal with a bevelled edge, and the eight matching chairs had a fleur de lis set into each backrest. This was the Christmas lunch furniture, barely used. Julia put thick placemats down so Don couldn't complain about it being destroyed.

Bracing against the stick's handle, her father got himself up the step to enter the room and paused for a moment before sitting down. He nodded at the stubby of light beer in her hand and Julia unscrewed the top, pouring the contents into an oversized German beer stein. She'd scrubbed an inch of dust and crud out of the bottom of it for the occasion. 'Heavy,' Don commented, his wrist wobbling with the effort of holding it aloft.

'Is that why you never use it?' she asked, ladling peas onto his plate.

'You've made your point.'

Julia sat down. 'Have I?'

'I told you, I'm happy to go. Once I don't have Biscuit to worry about.'

'The dog will be fine, I promise.'

Don's tone was amiable as he said, 'No.'

They ate, cutlery tinkling against the plates. Don pulled at the lamb with his fork until the fascia came away from the circle of bone, then picked it up to suck out the marrow. When it was hollow the pink point of his tongue poked through. His eyes crinkled cheekily.

Julia pushed out her own marrow with the tines of her fork. 'You have to move. You promised Paul.'

'Under different circumstances.'

She wasn't sure what he meant: if the circumstances were different when he'd agreed to move, or if he'd agreed to move under different circumstances. Trying to pin it down would only lead them away from the matter at hand. 'We're worried about you.'

'Parents worry about their children,' he said. Now he was

mashing the potato with the back of his fork, shredding the skin and mixing it in. 'Sometimes children worry about their parents.'

'But you could fix our worries easily.'

'I'm worried about the dog.'

No, you're not. 'The dog will be fine,' Julia repeated.

'You don't know that.'

'This isn't a safe environment for a dog either, you know.' She needed to stay calm, to change her father's mind through facts and not emotions, but she'd lost her appetite. She put down her cutlery. 'He doesn't get walks or stimulation, he doesn't get taken to the vet.'

'I'm looking after him.'

'That's what I'm saying, though. You're not.'

Her father shovelled up potato and pushed it between his lips.

'You can't look after him.' She was trying to be gentle, even if he didn't think so. 'You can't look after yourself. You've cancelled the groceries and the house cleaners now. You're going to end up like you were when Paul was here.'

In her mind, she dared him to ask, *Like what?* Then she could say, *Like a skeleton. Paul said you were like a skeleton living in its own shit.*

Instead, Don shrugged at his potatoes, as if they were observing the conversation. 'It's a simple matter, hiring them back.'

'You cancelled them because you were ready to go.'

'I'll go, Julia,' he snapped. 'Just not yet.'

'*We – are – scared – for – you,*' she seethed. 'I don't want to leave here without knowing you're somewhere safe. *And* the dog,' she added.

'So, wait.'

'For what?' A hot, sudden anger forced her to her feet. Hands shaking, she lifted her half-finished plate and reached for her father's, but he yanked it away from her. He'd mashed most of his peas into the potato as well, so it looked like a toddler had been at it. 'I have a life in Melbourne, remember. I put it on hold to help you.'

'Then go,' he said. His sneer was as childish as his food.

'What if I took Biscuit with me?' she asked, desperate. 'You know I'd look after him.'

'He'd have to go on a plane.'

'I could drive.' Rowan would murder her. They'd have to move. But at least Don would have no reason to stay in the house.

'He's my responsibility.'

Julia went to the kitchen, trying to calm her breathing. Her father was resigning himself to death in this house, with her supervision or without it, *all for a bloody dog*. She let her plate crash into the sink without bothering to scrape off the remains of her food. On her way back up the hallway she ducked into the guestroom for her purse and phone.

Her father was finishing the last lumps of vegetables as if nothing had happened, Biscuit watching at his elbow.

'I'm going out for the night,' she said. They looked at her with placid expressions. 'I need to think about this.'

Don picked up a strip of fat he'd cut from his lamb and gave it to the dog. 'Where are you going?'

'Davina's.'

For the first time all evening, Don seemed concerned. She'd called his bluff. 'That's a bit dramatic.'

'You want it to be just you and Biscuit,' she said. The food fought in her throat; she had to leave soon, or she'd be sick. 'I'll have my phone on. I'll be a few blocks away.'

'All right,' he said. 'If you must.'

Biscuit followed her out of the room, and she scratched his head and told him to sit. His bum went straight to the floor and stayed there while she stepped out and closed the door behind her.

Davina got her settled on the sofa and went to find a bottle of wine.

'I shouldn't,' Julia groaned, remembering their other two nights on the piss, then shrugged. 'Go on. I need it.'

Davina filled a glass and passed it over, then poured a slightly smaller one for herself. When the bottle was capped, she crossed her legs and leaned forward, that same searching look on her face. 'What happened?'

'Dad.'

Davina's eyebrows rose. She'd probably thought it was something with Rowan, Julia realised. The two of them hadn't spoken since Don started getting difficult. She shook her head: it had only been that morning. The day seemed both too long and too short. 'He's being a pain about finding a place. We don't have to go into it.'

'You sure?'

'It'll just make me angry.' Julia bounced the bottom of her fist against a cushion. 'He's so stubborn. Are your parents like that?'

Davina sipped her drink. 'Like what?'

'Stubborn.'

'They're not as old as Don.'

'No, I know,' Julia said. 'I feel like parents turn into completely different people when you're an adult. You know more, you can see their flaws.'

After a pause, Davina said, 'Whose parents?'

'Anyone's. I mean, your point of view changes.' Julia took a fortifying swallow. 'My mother was wonderful, I really believe that, but now I think she didn't have much of a life.'

Davina looked uneasy. Of course, it was difficult to criticise someone else's parent, especially a dead one. 'Do you want to talk about your dad, or not?'

'I don't.'

'So, what else is going on?'

Julia thought back through her mess of a day. 'I talked to Rowan.'

'Oh, yeah?' Davina seemed unimpressed.

'Just about the usual,' she added, remembering that she hadn't said anything to Davina about their two-week silence. 'Work and stuff. I guess they're getting by fine without me.'

'I'm sure they're not.'

Julia told her about Sruthi's stickers, the passive-aggressive placement of paperwork, and Davina laughed. 'See? It's a basket case.'

'I guess,' Julia said, feeling oddly comforted. She allowed the warmth of the wine to go through her. It had been the right idea to leave her father's house, give the two of them space. She checked her phone, but Don hadn't been in touch.

'Tell me about work, maybe,' Davina suggested. 'Your own business. That's amazing.'

'It's Ro's business.'

'Are you serious?'

Taking another mouthful of wine, Julia realised she was. 'I don't know. I guess it's always felt like his. It *is* his, obviously. He's the physio. I wouldn't have had anything to do with it if we weren't together.'

'But you were there from the beginning.'

'Yeah,' Julia said. 'Still.'

Davina's eyes fixed on her, pinned her down. 'You don't give yourself much credit, do you?'

Not sure how else to respond, Julia laughed.

Again, Davina brought her out of her shell with a mixture of wine and attention, asking her to describe the clinic, the patients, the co-workers. 'Fitness nuts, are they?' she asked with sympathy, taking a deep swig. 'I don't want to be rude' – there was that phrase again, signposting the rudeness to come – 'but I always find them so stiff and un-fun. I mean, they never lie around like this, do they?' She tilted her glass in Julia's direction. 'They don't relax. They don't enjoy themselves. I don't mean Rowan,' she hurried to add.

'I didn't marry him because he's fun and relaxing.'

'Why did you marry him then?' Davina joked.

'Our staff can be kind of ...' Julia reconsidered. 'We don't always have a lot in common, let's put it that way.'

She used Bethany as an example. She was their newest hire, a part-time women's health physio. During the interview, Bethany seemed so much like Samara that Julia had trouble remembering her real name. Later, Julia had mentioned the likeness, sure that Rowan would agree, but he'd claimed not to see it. 'I don't mean physically,' Julia said. 'Her bearing. Her manner.'

'If you say so.'

Maybe because of her resemblance to Samara or maybe in an effort not to be biased against it, Julia had been the one to propose her for the role. Rowan preferred another woman, a recent graduate of his own university. 'I think having someone more mature will reassure people,' Julia said. 'Someone with experience.'

'Their qualifications are basically the same,' Rowan said, flicking between the CVs.

'But Bethany's were over a longer period of time. It gives the knowledge a chance to … to set.'

Rowan grinned. 'That's a weird way to put it.'

In the end, Julia had managed to sway him based on the fact that Bethany already had a second job as a continence specialist with a nursing home chain, while the more recent grad wanted full-time work. She'd said she was happy with a half-time position, but Julia convinced Rowan she'd leave as soon as she got a better offer.

When Bethany started with them, Julia couldn't see how she'd ever been reminded of Samara. Rowan's ex-wife was sleek Melbourne money, her skin creamy, clothes tailored, travelling in a cloud of tasteful perfume. Bethany could have been a swimsuit model with her muscular calves and hairless forearms. She had a high, bouncing ponytail and her fake tan was a shade too dark. In the morning, as Julia unlocked the building, Bethany's sudden hellos were so sharp and perky she often dropped her keys.

Julia was used to the distance between her and their employees. The physios completed marathons in barefoot running shoes and the receptionists went clubbing every weekend. She knew they saw her as Rowan's wife first and their manager second. If she disciplined them – only ever gently, educationally – there was disbelief in their eyes; she knew they wanted to say, *You're not my boss.* The chat in the tearoom died when she walked in, but for Rowan they came alive. He was one of them.

Well, fine. Julia didn't need the staff to be her friends; she just wanted to be taken seriously. She didn't think that was too much to ask. They may have looked doubtful when she asked them to do a task or reprimanded them for leaving the treatment rooms in a state, but at least they never said anything.

Bethany did.

Julia hadn't even pulled her up: Bethany's behaviour, like her appearance, was perfect. She left notes about rubber gloves running low, she kept her pigeonhole clear, she put her towels through the wash. She was there on Thursdays and Fridays at seven, standing behind Julia and surprising the shit out of her, and she didn't leave a nanosecond before she was scheduled even if she didn't have a patient. In some ways, Bethany was like Julia: she tidied the tearoom, pledged for everyone's City to Surf, brought in spinach and feta muffins to share. The receptionists and juniors idolised her, and she was so popular with clients she'd be booked out weeks in advance. The woman's presence filled a room, attracting people like some sort of pheromone. Twenty seconds of her photocopying in the main office was long enough for someone else to drift in.

'Bethany,' they said as she tapped the edge of her papers against the desk. 'Ah, Bethany. I had a question for you. Just let me think …'

Julia was the only one with the opposite reaction: Bethany walked past, and Julia began chewing her cheek like an animal gnawing at a trapped limb.

'Hello!' Bethany greeted as she always did, just that notch too loud. 'How's it going with you?'

The irony, Julia thought later, was that the way she responded to Bethany was exactly how the staff responded to her: dumb, faintly cold. Julia figured Bethany could tell she was just awkward. Bethany was a nice person, fundamentally.

She gave Davina a potted version of this history, colouring Bethany's tan an even darker shade, making her breasts a little more artificial, her lip gloss pearlier in sheen. When Davina began rolling her eyes, Julia knew it was working. Her version of Bethany's voice was more nasal, and she nodded with each word: 'Hi, Julia! How's it going, Julia? How's your day been?'

'She sounds painful,' Davina said.

The fake Bethany *was* painful, and the fake Julia was serious and quiet, focused. This Bethany scared this Julia out of important work by towering over her. (Bethany was statuesque, but for Davina she became lanky and clownish, stalking the office in search of Julia.) The rest of the staff shrank, made stupid by their fascination with the ungainly woman.

'Actually,' she interrupted herself, jaw loose and floppy with alcohol, 'Bethany's pregnant.'

'Oh yeah?'

'Not sure who the father is, either.'

A spark of a smile lit Davina's face. 'Really?'

Sorry, Bethany, Julia thought grimly. After everything Bethany had done for her.

Davina shook her head and stood up. They needed more wine. 'There's always a Bethany, fucking up your jam.' She went through to the kitchen.

Julia checked her phone, but there was still nothing from Don. She felt swimmy and stretched her legs out, wiggled her toes. The house was quiet but for the steps and scrapes of Davina. Billie and Jax must have been out. When Julia got there, she'd assumed the closed doors meant homework or privacy, but it had been hours and still hadn't seen them. It must disappoint Davina, to have them leave so soon after coming back from their father's.

Davina came in brandishing a bottle. 'Mind a switch to white? It's nice and cold.'

Julia held out her glass, not caring about the streaky remains of her shiraz. When she got it back there were chains of pink floating in it like drops of blood. She sipped and sucked back her lips at the tartness. 'It's good.'

Davina resumed her place at the opposite end of the sofa. 'So, what happened?'

What happened was that Bethany had been proactive. Her whole job was about not settling for things as they were: she strengthened weak spots, improved on damage. To that end, she'd gone to Rowan and explained how Julia made her feel.

Later that same day, Julia and Rowan went to the tearoom before closing up. They only discussed work at work, to make sure they didn't bring problems home. As he made himself a coffee, Rowan insisted that Bethany's complaint hadn't been bitchy. To the contrary, she'd actually been kind.

'Kind about what?' Julia asked. So far, Rowan had only complimented Bethany. Her handling of the situation was exemplary, apparently. Whatever the situation was.

'You can imagine the position she was in. Having to talk to the husband.' In case she didn't understand, Rowan thumbed his solar plexus: 'Me.'

'She spoke to *her boss* about a work issue,' Julia argued. 'Isn't that what we expect?' Yes, it was. Julia had written the document in Bethany's onboarding pack about fairness, honesty, professionalism. She'd used an extended sports metaphor and put a graphic of a soccer ball at the bottom of the page. *Let's work together to score every goal!* 'But I don't know what the issue *is*.'

Rowan sighed, making Julia feel like a child. 'You're not pleasant to her, Jules.'

'What do you mean?'

'She didn't say hostile, but I got the impression it's verging on it.'

'Me?' Julia had been genuinely stunned. 'Hostile?' She spread her arms, wanting to remind Rowan who they were talking about. Julia, who was three years younger and eight inches shorter than Bethany; Julia, who was pale, who was not a popular health professional, who absorbed and destroyed good cheer wherever she went. 'I'm awkward, I know I'm really awkward around her, but never hostile.'

'She tries to engage you in conversation, but you refuse.' Rowan looked sympathetic, though to her or Bethany, Julia wasn't sure.

'She says hello to me,' she said. 'She always says hello. But I say it back.'

'It's affecting her work performance.' Rowan sucked his lower lip between his teeth. 'It's affecting her mental health, apparently.'

'She said I *depress* her?'

'The *situation* depresses her. Think about it from her point of view,' he argued when she shook her head. 'She's got this boss she keeps trying to engage with, but she just keeps getting blanked. It'd eat at you, wouldn't it? It'd make you doubt yourself. Don't you think?'

Yes, Julia wanted to say. She knew from experience. 'I'll try harder,' she said.

He drained his coffee. 'I don't want to be a sexist old fucker,' he began, 'but is it possible you're a bit jealous?'

She shrugged. 'Oh, I'm sure I am.'

'Yeah.' Rowan looked pensive, like he didn't think they'd really got to the heart of the issue. Julia collected his dirty mug, wanting the conversation to be over. She'd never been so embarrassed in her life.

'Do you maybe,' he continued, 'have a little bit of a crush on her, or something? Platonically,' he said hurriedly, 'like you idealise her or—'

'Jesus Christ, Ro.'

'It's a question.'

'This isn't an issue of *Playboy*.'

'Platonic,' he argued. 'I said *platonic*.'

Julia stood at the door with her purse until he took the hint. They were silent as they locked the office. For the first time since she'd started working for them, Julia wondered what Rowan thought of Bethany; *really* thought of her.

Davina seemed to be flagging, her head lolling against the arm of the couch. Their feet met on the middle cushion, and when Davina shifted, their toes brushed together. Julia sat up with a jolt. 'Can I tell you something?'

'Sure,' she murmured.

'It's about Rowan.'

Davina opened her eyes. 'I'm listening.'

— SEVENTEEN —

'Hello, Bethany,' Julia had practised. 'Hi, Bethany. Bethany, *hi!*'

It was no good; the artificiality Bethany had complained to Rowan about was baked in. Julia smiled at herself in the mirror, trying to make the expression seem natural and warm. 'Good *morning*, Bethany.' It just got worse. She closed her eyes and tried to superimpose the face of a different staff member onto Bethany's. 'Hey. Hi.' Maybe that was acceptable?

The next morning Julia waited under the awning, facing the street so Bethany didn't sneak up on her. That might be the core of it, how she associated Bethany with always being startled. Seeing the other woman step down off a tram, Julia hooked a smile onto her face. 'Hi, Bethany.'

'Julia.' Bethany seemed her normal self. Her skin shone. 'Good morning.'

'Did you have a nice evening?'

'I did.'

'I'm so glad.'

Worried that this was laying it on too thick, Julia unlocked the door, the Christmas wreath bouncing against the glass. The decorations had just gone up, lending an artificial cheer. Julia stepped aside. 'After you.'

Just when Julia thought it had gone as well as could be expected, Bethany stopped in the doorway. 'Do you have a few minutes to chat?'

Oh, God. It was too little, too late; Bethany was going to quit. Rowan hadn't even had the chance to talk to her yet, to pass on Julia's earnest promises about making her feel welcome and safe. 'Are you sure you don't want to wait and see Rowan?' she asked nervously.

'Oh, no,' Bethany said, shaking her ponytail. 'It's actually about Rowan.'

Stunned, Julia followed Bethany. Yesterday she'd asked for a meeting with Rowan to complain about Julia. Was she now wanting a chat with Julia to complain about Rowan?

They went into the office and Julia put the sign on the door. Taking a seat, she indicated to Bethany to do the same, but the physio opted to stand. When they were closed in the small room together, there was nothing but Bethany's perfume, the happy evenness of her teeth. It was a little sample of what everyone else felt, maybe. 'What's up?' Julia asked, trying to seem relaxed.

'Do you know Zoe Bantham?'

'No.'

'She's a physio, too. Rowan's friend?'

Julia shook her head. 'I've never heard of her.'

Sighing, Bethany sat in the chair beside Julia. 'I'm very uncomfortable doing this.'

'I'm sorry,' Julia said automatically.

Bethany woke up the office PC and typed something into the web browser. An email account opened; webmail, not work. Julia was bewildered. 'She does women's health in the western suburbs,' Bethany explained. 'I see her at conferences and training quite a bit.'

'Right.' Julia felt certain she didn't know where this was going. Still, her hands clamped the edges of her seat, sweating into the fabric.

'She was at that Hilton one a couple of months ago. The one we all went to.'

Bethany meant all the physiotherapists. Julia remembered it: a quiet day in the office, no appointments. For her lunchbreak she lay down on a treatment table and ate a packet of chips from the vending machine in the lobby.

'I introduced her to the team. She's got her feelers out for more work. A day a week, I think.'

'If we wanted to fill another day, we'd ask you,' Julia said.

Bethany smiled, distracted. 'I know. Thank you. But I thought it couldn't hurt, just in case I ever move on. And Rowan might hear on the grapevine about other opportunities.'

'Don't move on,' Julia said, wanting to reach out and still Bethany's hand on the mouse.

'I'm not,' Bethany said. 'At least, I hope not.'

She double-clicked on an email. The sender said 'Zoe', the subject line 'More ...'

'I don't feel good about this,' Bethany murmured as she turned the screen to Julia.

In telling Davina about it, Julia didn't quote exactly what she'd read, though she could remember it all. It was too painful, and at the same time, felt so silly: The words were powerless out of context. *He's weirdly hot* and *We just keep messaging each other* and *No joke, it's the best relationship I've ever had* and *I do feel guilty about him being married.* In her emails Zoe paraphrased what she and Rowan had apparently texted one another, and there didn't seem to be anything explicit; they hadn't even seen each other since the Hilton. *It's like in high school when you had a crush and you could think about them forever and nothing happened. That's what makes it so delicious.*

Julia had swallowed down whatever she was feeling and pushed her chair away from the screen. 'Okay.'

'I told her to stop,' Bethany said quietly. That was true; it was all through the replies. 'It's not appropriate.'

Julia guessed that this Zoe actually liked being told she was doing the wrong thing. It made it naughtier. *It's not really that bad*, she'd objected, when Bethany told her she shouldn't. Julia had no idea what Zoe looked like, but she saw a wicked smile hanging disembodied in the air, like the Cheshire Cat's. Saw the tongue run sly along the curving lips. *Is it?*

'Have you mentioned this to Rowan?' Julia asked, though she was sure the answer was no. He'd given no hint of Bethany having dirt on him the day before; he'd stuck up for her too much. 'Told him what Zoe's told you?'

'No, I know,' Bethany said. 'I just thought – between

women. I could have asked him to tell you himself, but then I wouldn't be sure that he'd ...' She pressed her lips together.

'Thank you,' Julia said. She reached out and patted Bethany's arm, surprising them both. 'I am grateful.'

Bethany logged out of her email and closed the browser window. 'If it were me, I'd want to know. That's all it is.'

'We'll leave it there,' Julia said. 'If that's okay.'

'Of course. And I didn't say anything to anyone else.' Bethany stood. 'I really prefer to stay out of it.'

At the other end of the sofa, Davina's eyes were glassy with wonder and alcohol. 'Stay out of it? She's trying to fuck up your marriage.'

'No, no.' This wasn't going the way Julia wanted. 'She was looking out for me. She really was arguing back in those emails.'

Looking dubious, Davina raised her glass, but it was empty again. She scrabbled for the bottle, which had rolled across the carpet.

'It wasn't terrible or ... or slutty or whatever.' Julia was too tipsy to find her words. She felt tired and full of regret that she'd brought this up, given Davina this impression of Rowan that so closely followed a caricature of Bethany. No wonder Davina couldn't follow who was meant to be the hero and who was the villain. 'It was just stuff you don't want a woman to say to your husband. Or your husband to read without telling you about it.'

'What was he saying?' The bottle in one hand and her glass in the other, Davina shuffled on her knees back to the sofa. 'Was he chatting her up? Was he being a dirty boy?' She held out the wine, but Julia shook her head. 'There's only a bit left. Let's finish what we started.'

'I'm okay.'

'Whatever.' Davina tipped the last of the bottle into her mouth, then bowled it back across the room without the cap on, the neck dripping as it spun.

'It wasn't that bad. I mean, it wasn't great. It made me uncomfortable. I wouldn't do it to him.'

'Did you guys fight?'

Julia shook her head. She never fought with Rowan, not in the way Davina would have meant: screaming, smashing shit, ugly words you can't take back. 'We talked about it. I don't know. It's all a bunch of nothing. I shouldn't have—'

'Talked about it?' Davina repeated. There was something sharp and nasty in her eyes. Julia pressed herself back against the cushions. 'Don't take this the wrong way, Jules, but you can be such a doormat.'

Julia cleared her throat, but there was nothing to say.

'I'm not tryna be mean.' Davina's words melted into one another. 'I want you to stick up for yourself. You were like this when we were kids. You let Kimmie bully you.'

'I let—'

'You should get mad,' Davina continued. 'It's all bullshit. Men! My ex fucked a nineteen-year-old. He said it wasn't about her age, it was about her as a *person*.' It took Julia a moment to realise that, for the first time, Davina was talking about herself. 'He said he loved her. I'm like, is that s'posed to make me feel better? I had your baby, that's why I look like this. The fucker.' She went to sip from her glass, then scowled when she realised there was nothing in it. 'You shouldn't have a kid with someone who treats you this way. Believe me.'

It was too late and Julia was too drunk to explain how different the two situations were. 'I think we should try and sleep,' she suggested. 'Think about it in the morning, maybe.'

Groaning, Davina hoisted herself off the couch. 'All right then. Come on.'

Julia followed her, feeling even more off-balance and sick now that she was upright. The room Davina entered had an unmade queen bed, the floor around the wardrobe piled with clothes and dented tissue boxes. She reached under some loose pillows and pulled out something silky, then lifted the hem of her shirt. Before Julia could react, Davina's breasts appeared, soft and heavy-looking. Her nipples were dark brown against her white skin, and in the dimness of the room they were like two unblinking eyes.

Too late, Julia turned away to give Davina privacy. 'Do you have a spare blanket?'

'What?' Davina's voice was muffled through the fabric.

'I can just use the sofa cushions, that's fine, but if you've got something I can cover myself with?'

'You can sleep in here.'

Julia glanced back. Davina had pulled the silky thing down so her chest was covered, but she'd missed one strap, which caught under her arm. 'The couch is fine.'

'It's a big bed.' Davina stepped out of her jeans and crawled across the mattress. The negligee pulled up at the back to show her underwear: a girly pink, saggy in the seat. 'Don't be crazy.'

Julia felt stuck, unable to communicate how badly she didn't want to get between Davina's unmade bedsheets. It wasn't a sexual thing; she didn't think Davina would make a move or anything. It was the closeness, knowing the other woman's hangover breath would be in her face, their warm legs brushing together. 'I didn't bring pyjamas,' she said.

'Get something off the floor to wear.' Davina raised her head from a pillow. 'Shut that door. It's too bright.'

Julia grabbed something made of white cotton from the pile. It was an oversized T-shirt with branding she didn't recognise, smelling faintly of BO and men's deodorant. It hung from her fingers as she debated which was worse: putting on this thing that Davina, or maybe even Jax, had worn, or picking through the rest for a better option. Deciding she'd rather sleep in her clothes, she dropped it back onto the floor.

There was a light gurgling sound from Davina's side of the bed. She was asleep.

Julia closed the door and tiptoed through the dark house back to the sofa. A nearby streetlight cut through the thin curtains, leaving the room a limp grey. She pushed her face against a cushion to block it out, the corded fabric smelling damp and intimate, and tried to breathe through her mouth.

Sleep pulled at her limbs, but the effects of the wine were retreating, leaving a sobriety that felt as stark and unavoidable as the fluorescent light outside. A cold drip of regret in the pit of her belly. Why the hell had she told Davina all that? To impress her? She exhaled, her moist breath carrying the sharp scent of wine. What kind of person shared the tiny tragedies of their marriage in order to amuse someone they didn't really know? Davina was right, Julia was a doormat.

But then, what kind of person was entertained by that stuff? Who *was* Davina, really? If she was ever questioned about Davina's life, all Julia could say for sure was where she lived and the names of her kids. She wasn't very tidy, she was flirtatious, she liked wine. Millions could be described the same way.

Was it Davina's closed-off nature that made Julia want to talk? She usually wore awkward silences longer than anyone. But there hadn't been any with Davina: just questions, interest. Was a little bit of attention all that was required to crack Julia open? She thought of Davina's father's questions at the dinner table when she'd stayed there as a kid, how desperately she'd wanted to answer. It wasn't only to ease his discomfort; she was stunned and flattered that an adult would inquire after her thoughts and feelings. She hadn't even known she had any until he asked. Maybe she should've been glad for the Weir girls' bitchiness at the dinner table, their refusal to let their father indulge himself. God knows what Julia might have told them if they'd given her the chance.

- ☾ -

School assembly. Bare thighs stick to the floor, the smell of wet armpits and wood polish, hunger for the chips and fruit waiting in the bags at the back of the hall. Torpor tugs like weights.

A girl was flashed on the way home. Her name isn't given but everyone knows. She's off sick today.

That's a total scab, *voices murmur.* You don't need a day in bed just cos you saw some guy's dick.

The teacher in charge doesn't give details. Her words are formal, intangible: Exposed. Indecent. Distressing. *The man didn't try to touch the girl and she was able to run to safety.*

There are rules for safety, in games anyway. If a chaser gets too close, just yell, Stuck in the mud! *and squat in place. But then you're trapped until someone comes to your rescue.*

Imagine the girl – you know who – running from the flasher until she's around the corner, then ducking down. Staying there until a policeman comes.

Where did you learn what is flashed by flashers? No one thinks the shiny black coat might contain a really bright torch, or a firework. But the condition of the flashed penis is never specified. Is it soft, or excited? Surely the second one, though maybe it requires pulling the coat akimbo and feeling the breeze to get that way.

You can't ask anyone this, of course. They'd think, psychopath.

Dying for a banana, softening and browning with every passing second. The sun cuts through the high windows at the perfect angle to burn the backs of fifty necks. Can the bell ring, can the teacher shut up. Flashers are losers, everyone knows. They've got tiny dicks like snails.

We urge you, *the teacher says — that wasn't a good verb, people are sniggering —* to be aware of your surroundings when outside the school grounds. Even as you get older, strangers still present a threat.

Strangers. Not anyone you know. A scientific hypothesis, then: if you know them, then they are safe.

– EIGHTEEN –

First light cracked through the curtains. Julia rolled over with a groan, heavy and sweaty from her night on the sofa. There was a knitted blanket draped over her.

The sound of a kettle boiling from the kitchen. She sat up groggily and checked her watch. Half-past six and Davina was awake? Unless it was one of the kids, locked quiet as mice in their rooms all night. Julia stood up, bells ringing in her head.

Davina was on the other side of the breakfast bar, drying her hands on a tea towel. She smiled brightly when Julia entered. 'Morning, sleepyhead!'

The scene gave Julia déjà vu. Despite the extra inches of height and dark brown hair, it was her own mother who flashed into Julia's vision: that sunny-morning attitude.

Davina poured hot water into mugs. 'Milk? Sugar? I thought I remembered, but it's gone right out of my head.'

'Milk, please.' Julia gave a wan smile. 'Two sugars. This morning, anyway.'

'Feeling the effects?'

'I am,' Julia admitted. 'Aren't you?'

Spooning the sparkling granules into the mug closest to Julia, Davina shrugged lightly.

'I had this dream we were back at school,' Julia said, sliding onto a stool. 'We were getting a lecture about stranger danger. Some girl had been flashed.'

'Oh yeah.' Davina sounded uninterested.

'It felt so real. Now that I'm awake it feels like it did happen, but I can't quite get a hold of when. Do you remember?'

'We went to different high schools.'

'Really?' Julia was embarrassed. 'I must have forgot.'

Davina topped both mugs with milk and pushed the one with sugar across the breakfast bar. 'Want something to eat?' She opened the fridge. 'We've got eggs, some bacon – that might not be in date anymore, let me check – tomatoes, I could maybe do some mushrooms –'

Julia shook her head, the list of foods making her nauseated. 'Just toast, if that's okay.'

Davina raised an eyebrow but made it for her, spreading butter on each slice and sprinkling over a little salt. Julia bit down and it was heavenly. After a few mouthfuls the leaden feeling left, with just a mild sourness hanging in its wake. 'That's so good.'

'A little trick I learned from an ex.' Davina put the bread and butter away without making herself any, then dragged a stool around to her side of the bench so they were facing one another. 'You've got a bit of colour back now. It hit you hard!'

Julia shrugged and sipped her coffee. Surely Davina felt

similar, having drunk just as much. But her skin and eyes looked clearer than Julia's felt, her posture was good. On five hours' sleep, as well.

'The things I said last night, about Rowan,' Julia began. 'Can we keep it between us? I was a bit – indiscreet.'

Davina put down her mug. 'Seems like Rowan was the one being indiscreet.'

'No, I know.' She shifted on her stool. 'It's just very personal. I don't really want to talk about it, or have other people talk about it.'

'I wouldn't do that.'

Julia had to hold back a snort. She sought refuge in her coffee, swallowing the last of it, then said, 'I'd really appreciate it.'

Davina put a finger to her lips. 'You have my word.'

'Thanks.' Julia put the mug onto her plate and stood up. 'I'd better get back.'

Davina stayed where she was. Her eyes glimmered. 'The offer still stands, by the way.'

'Offer?'

'You remember.' When Julia didn't react, Davina nodded down at her stomach, circling it with her hands.

The gesture made Julia's nausea resurface. 'Oh.'

'Many women have babies by themselves these days, as well.' She was still holding her belly as if there was something in it beyond coffee and wine, and Julia wished she'd stop. 'Have you thought about that? It can be extremely rewarding.'

There was something in the phrasing that made Julia think of monetary rewards rather than emotional ones. She knew very little about surrogacy, but she did know it could only be done altruistically; no money was allowed to change hands unless it reimbursed a cost. Not that she thought Davina was hinting at some kind of payment, and not that Julia would ever do that. Still, the way she said *extremely rewarding* was unsettling.

'It's all a bit much for me right now. So much to think about.' Julia moved towards the door, but Davina stayed where she was, as if the conversation hadn't finished. At least now her hands were resting on her thighs.

'I feel like I'm closer to Bill and Jax than I would have been if I was still with their dad.'

'I'm sure.'

'I'm just saying. There are options.'

Julia tapped the wall with her knuckles. 'I'd better get back. Thanks for the hospitality.'

Davina stood up to hug her goodbye. Julia breathed in her unwashed odour with its traces of wine and knew she smelled exactly the same.

'Just at least think about it,' Davina said softly, her warm breath making Julia's ear tickle as if there was a bug deep inside, writhing to get out. 'Take care of yourself.'

Julia unlocked her father's door. The scent of lamb chops hung in the air from the night before and she was surprised at how much had happened in so little time: twenty-four hours ago, her father seemed ready to leave; twenty-four hours ago, she was yet to speak to Rowan.

She looked into the living room, but Don's chair was

vacant, the television switched off. It was seven-thirty; he was usually up by now. His bedroom door was wedged open as it always was overnight, so Biscuit could get in and out. Julia peered in, chest tight, afraid of what she might find, but the room seemed empty. Don had straightened his sheets and propped his pillow against the bedhead, and the doors to the wardrobe and en-suite were closed.

Julia projected her voice: 'Dad? I'm back.'

From the bathroom came a scratching sound, followed by the dog's whine. Did he let Biscuit follow him into the loo?

'Dad!' she called, louder. 'Is everything okay?'

When she got no response, Julia entered the bedroom. From the new angle she could see Biscuit lying against the bathroom door, his nose touching the edge where it met the wall. Feeling her footsteps on the carpet, he looked around and whimpered.

Julia bent to pat him, then tugged him back by the collar. She knocked against the wood. 'Dad?'

Don's voice was sudden and forceful: 'Don't open that door!'

Relief washed through her at the sound of his voice. 'All right,' she said. 'Are you okay? Is it ...' She couldn't bring herself to say *diarrhoea* or *constipation*. 'Is it your stomach?'

'Don't open the door!' he shouted again, voice thinning with distress.

'Dad, I won't. I won't open the door.' She gave him a moment to relax. 'Are you sick?'

'I'm stuck.'

'Stuck?' She looked at the dog as if for an explanation. 'On the toilet?'

'On the floor,' Don said. 'Behind the door. If you push it open, I'll ...' He trailed off in a grunt.

Julia put her ear to the sliver of space between the door and the frame and heard a scratchy, shuffling sound. 'Are you trying to stand up?'

'I'm trying to get away from the – *bloody* – door.' Her father was out of breath. 'Just a – look.'

'What's happening?'

'I've moved back a bit.'

'Can I open the door?'

'Gently. Not all the way.'

Before trying, Julia tapped Biscuit on the skull and told him to sit. Hesitant, he lowered his front half like the Sphinx, shoulders rigid with anxiety. 'Good boy. Stay. Just stay there a minute.' She turned the doorknob and pushed it very lightly, until it met new resistance. 'All right, Dad?'

'Be careful,' he said. 'My knee.'

The gap was a few centimetres wide, enough for her to see in but not enter. In the far corner of the room, the shower door was open, crystals of glass piled on the plastic non-slip mat at its base. Alarmed, Julia looked at the opposite wall, sure the mirrored cabinet must have fallen on the tiles and shattered, but it was intact. In its reflection she could see Don on the floor between the shower and toilet, legs gathered in front of him. To clear space, he'd dragged himself so close to the wall that a towel hanging from the rail above gathered shroud-like over his shoulders. His face was long and grey with shock.

'Are you hurt?' she asked. 'Or just shaken?'

'Both.'

'What happened?'

'I fell,' he said, looking down at his lap.

Following his gaze, Julia was glad to see his pyjama bottoms pulled up over his dignity. 'Do you think you can stand?'

'No.'

She tested the door, but it hit his foot before the opening was wide enough for her to get through. 'If you give yourself a minute to catch your breath, you might be able to shift your weight—'

'I've tried. I don't have the strength.'

'Are you sure?' she asked, dismayed. 'Do you want to have another go?'

'Can't you take the door off?'

Julia looked at the hinges, older than she was and embedded deep into the wood. 'I'm scared I'd drop it,' she said, picturing the heavy door slipping from her grip and crashing down on her father's fragile skull.

He closed his eyes and let his head drop back into the softness of the towel, the bright red material covering his face. 'I'm awake,' he said, before she could panic. 'I'm just tired.'

'I'll have to ring for the doctor,' she said. 'Do you think?'

Without opening his eyes, he murmured, 'Ambulance. Please.'

Julia did as he asked, going into the kitchen to make the call so he couldn't hear. When the call-taker said she could hang up, she filled a plastic cup with water, took two Arrowroots from the open packet and returned to the bedroom. Biscuit had poked his head through the opening and was touching Don's foot with his snout. Her father smiled down at the dog, eyes moist.

'Here,' she said, threading her arm around with the water and food one at a time to make sure he had hold of them. Before he took the second Arrowroot, Don squeezed her fingers in thanks and she could feel how weak he was, how he trembled with effort and fear.

'That glass—' she began.

'The shower door.'

Looking at it again, she understood. The previously sturdy door was not propped open, as she'd thought, but had smashed onto the floor around the shower stall. 'Be careful,' she said unnecessarily. Her father didn't respond.

The paramedics were bright and efficient, only a ten-minute wait on a weekday morning. Julia stood by to help as they set up, but they kindly ordered her out of the way.

'Why don't you take the dog outside?' the female one said, grinning as she lifted her chin from Biscuit's desperate licks. 'We'll sort your dad out and call you right back.'

She lingered. 'Will you take the door off?'

'Don't worry.' The paramedic nodded towards the hallway. 'Won't take us long.'

Biscuit followed her out to the backyard without complaint. On the patio, Julia dropped her knees to the bricks and put her face against the dog's neck. He was patient while she wept, touching his damp nose to her cheek as she pulled away. In the pantry she found a long-lasting dog chew, the biggest in the pack, and tossed it into the overgrown grass for him to find and devour.

They allowed her back into the room once Don was strapped onto a wheeled stretcher, some colour back in his face. He frowned as the male paramedic asked questions, entering the answers into a tablet. Julia knew her father only wanted an ambulance because he was trapped; he'd be wishing his daughter could be trusted to unscrew a pin, so he didn't have to go through this humiliation.

The female paramedic took her aside. 'Your dad's pretty shaken up, no surprises there. Query broken hip because of his age, query wrist, query coccyx. He's come down heavily on tiles, not pleasant. Good news is that there's no sign of head injury, and he hasn't cut himself on the tempered glass.'

'But why did he fall?' Julia asked. 'Did he pass out?' She tried to keep her tone curious rather than desperate. 'Was it a stroke?'

'He says he slipped getting off the commode. Rogue bath mat. It's wadded up in a corner.' The paramedic clucked her tongue. 'His slippers have zero grip, so they're pretty much rollerskates in contact with those tiles. Plus, he was sitting there for a while. Might have a touch of hypothermia.'

Julia's cheeks burned. 'I only just got home. I shouldn't have—'

'Don't blame yourself. Do not.' The woman ducked her chin, eyes searching until she was sure she had Julia's attention. 'Older people, I've seen it a million times. They want to be independent. In the end, you've got to let them. A bung arm and a few days in the hospital is no more miserable than not being able to live your life.'

Julia was speechless.

Behind them, her father's questioning finished, and the male paramedic folded the tablet away.

'I'm very sorry about all this,' Don said formally. He was trying to be a cool customer, but Julia heard the fray in his voice.

'Don't apologise,' the woman said, wagging a finger. 'It's our job. Keeps us out of mischief.'

Julia followed them outside, the male paramedic wheeling the stretcher while his partner carried the equipment. The ambulance was parked in the driveway, bright white and attention-grabbing, but to her surprise there were no neighbours standing around having a gawk.

She stood back as her father's stretcher was pushed into the ambulance, the legs collapsing underneath as it slid into place.

'Will I come with you?' she asked. 'Or follow in the car?'

'Don't leave Bickie by himself,' Don ordered, his voice stronger now.

The female paramedic stood beside Julia on the driveway. 'You may be waiting for the doctors a while, Mr Lambett. I think you'll need your daughter's company more than the dog will.'

'Biscuit will be fine,' Julia told her father.

'He won't,' Don snapped. 'He's never alone.'

It was true: the dog was either with her father or walking

with her. Though she'd gone out a few times since she arrived, her father hadn't left the house once.

'I have to come see you,' she said. 'I'll find someone to keep an eye on Biscuit.'

'Who?'

'We're about to head off,' the male paramedic interrupted. 'If you want to say a quick goodbye.'

Julia stepped up into the ambulance. Her father was spindly in the narrow bed, thick blue belts holding him in. She reached for his hand and felt the quick, frightened squeeze he'd given from the bathroom floor. 'I'll see you soon. Don't worry.'

Don nodded, grimacing. 'The dog.'

'I know.'

He closed his eyes. 'Just look after him, please.'

Julia bent and brushed her lips against his dry, cool forehead. The paramedic smiled reassuringly at her, then gave a loaded glance towards the house. She stepped back onto the driveway and the vehicle's rear doors shut.

She waited on the verge with Biscuit until the engine started and the ambulance slowly took her father away.

– NINETEEN –

Julia had always been shy about entering her parents' domain. When they were kids, she and Paul were not allowed inside without permission, even to use the toilet. With her father gone, she could do what she wanted, but still she felt an almost physical resistance as she followed Biscuit into the bedroom, as if the ghosts of Don and Goldie were pushing her back.

A plasticky smell of medical equipment hung in the air, along with the chemical tang of her father's anxiety. The paramedics had used the bed as a staging area for their things, leaving the doona rumpled like two people had been sleeping on top of it. Julia straightened it out again before checking the en suite. The door hung half-open and looked scuffed, though that could have been Julia's imagination. Inside she found the bath mat, crumpled and kicked up against the shards of shower door. The toilet seat had a crack in the plastic and the towel hung skewiff on the rail. There was no blood.

She tidied quickly, hanging the bath mat over the edge of

the vanity and sweeping the tiles clean. Lifting the toilet seat, she peered into the bowl and sniffed. The water was dark and smelled of ammonia, so Julia gave a quick squirt of bleach under the rim and pressed the flush.

Sitting next to his master's bed, Biscuit watched her work. It might have been wishful thinking, but to Julia he looked mournful.

'Good boy,' she said, scratching his head. His tail slapped the floor in melancholy. 'Come on, Bickie. You're going on an adventure.'

He walked purposefully on the lead, seeming to know the direction he was being taken. Her stomach felt hot and unsettled, but there was nowhere else she could think to go.

Davina answered the door wearing thin leather leggings and an eggplant-coloured top. Her hair had been restyled from earlier in the morning, but there was something about her that seemed unwashed, despite being dressed up. 'Julia!' she cried, as if they hadn't just seen one another. Biscuit's tail moved uncertainly.

She explained the situation quickly, appreciating the concern on Davina's face, the way she twisted and bit her lips. 'Is your dad *okay*?' she asked, hands clasped to her chest.

'That's what I need to find out,' Julia said. 'He forbade me from leaving the dog alone, and I don't want to make him any more upset than he is already. Don, that is,' she went on, 'not Biscuit. I really think he'd be fine for a few hours.'

'Probably.' After a pause, Davina squatted as much as the tight leggings would allow and patted Biscuit's neck. 'He seems sweet.'

'He's great. He's no problem. Look.' Julia took Biscuit through his commands, ending with him lying on his stomach with his chin between his paws. Davina smiled faintly. 'Is it okay to leave him here for a bit? Even if he just stays out the back, or in the laundry? Will you be home?'

'I guess,' Davina said. Her body still blocked the doorway. 'Yeah, I guess.'

'I really think he'll be fine.'

'I mean,' Davina began, 'you could just *tell* your dad you left him with me.'

Julia was confused. 'Are you going out?'

'No, it's okay.' She laughed, though her expression stayed flat. 'All I mean is, how would Don know if you did leave the dog by himself? But yeah, he can stay here.'

Julia bent down and scratched Biscuit vigorously between the ears. 'Okay. Thanks.'

At last, Davina stepped aside. The dog got to his feet and trotted into the house. 'Bye, Biscuit,' Julia said weakly. 'Be good.'

Biscuit regarded her from behind the wire door as Davina pulled it closed. His eyes were wide and droopy, like he'd known all along there would be a betrayal.

When Julia got to the hospital, her father had already been admitted to his own room. Don was knobbly and small in his loose gown, and the rough and tumble of the morning had started to show: his face was pale, his neck blotchy, arms red and blue with bruises. Some effect of static on the pillow made wisps of his hair stand up. His eyes were half-closed, but opened at the sight of her. 'You're here.'

She turned a chair so she could sit facing him. 'What's the verdict?'

'They did some X-rays and sent me up here. They're going to give me a scan.'

'What kind?'

His brow folded. 'Some big machine.'

She took her phone from her pocket. Don frowned. 'What are you doing?'

'Telling Paul.' Seeing the shadow in her father's eyes, she said, 'He needs to know.'

'Just wait, can you. Until we know the full story.'

She sighed.

'Otherwise you'll be sending him messages every hour. *Dad's had a fall. Dad's in the hospital. Dad's having a scan.* Just wait till you can tell him something useful.'

She hesitated, then put her phone back. Her father was right. Paul would be about to start work, anyway, and while the situation was unsettling and inconvenient, it wasn't critical. Besides, Julia reminded herself, that's what she was there for: to see that her father was safe. Too bad she'd been derelict in her duties that morning, of all mornings.

'Was Biscuit okay?'

'Fine. I took him for a walk.'

'Is he all right?'

'He's being looked after.'

Don didn't ask who she'd found to watch the dog. Julia had the feeling he could guess.

After a couple of hours an older man in scrubs came to

take her father for a CT scan. Julia followed until they got to a door that didn't admit visitors, so she squeezed his shoulder and wished him luck. His eyelids were fluttering from the painkillers, and she was relieved he might at least sleep through the procedure.

Once the assistant had taken Don through, Julia called Rowan. Her phone wobbled against her ear and the syrupy sweat of her relief sucked at the screen. He'd be seeing patients, she realised, but didn't hang up.

He answered after half a dozen rings, sounding out of breath. 'Jules?'

'Were you working?'

'It was Mr Carmichael.' Carmichael was a long-term patient, twinges shifting around his body like gremlins: an achy shoulder, a sore knee, a clicky ankle. He wouldn't mind Rowan nipping out for an urgent call. 'What's up?'

'Dad had a fall,' she said. 'He's in hospital.'

'Oh, shit.'

'He's fine. Conscious, irritable. Might've broken his wrist, I think they said.'

'Not worst-case scenario, then.'

'Luckily not.'

'Are you okay?'

'I was out.' Julia gave a shuddering sigh. 'I came home, and he was on the bathroom floor. I couldn't get the door open wide enough to help him up.'

'So what did you do?'

'The ambos came out. They must have squeezed him through.'

'Jeez.'

'I guess Dad was more embarrassed than anything.'

'Must have been scary.'

Tears bit at her eyes. 'I shouldn't have gone out. If I'd been there ...'

'He would've fallen anyway. You don't go into the toilet with him, do you?'

'No,' she admitted. 'Still.'

'Do you want me to come across?'

Julia looked over her shoulder, as if he might be there already. 'To Perth? No, it's all right.'

'Are you sure?'

'No. Thanks, though. You'd better get back to work.'

'Thanks for calling me, Jules,' he said before saying goodbye. 'Thank you for thinking of me.'

Julia wanted to say her first instinct was to tell Paul, but she knew this wasn't what Rowan meant. 'It's okay.'

'I love you.'

'Me too,' she murmured, closing her eyes to say it.

Midafternoon, a doctor came to see Don, wheeling a computer on a stand in behind him. He had curly hair and long earlobes and seemed younger than Julia. It made her feel ancient, for a person to be able to get all the way through medical school and graduate without having lived as long as her.

Despite bringing up Don's notes on the device, the doctor seemed to have everything memorised, his strong gaze shifting between Julia and her father as he spoke. Mr Lambett had a sprained right wrist and a bruised coccyx. His head and brain appeared uninjured, as did his hip. But.

'We'd like to look further into some of the results. Conduct a few more tests, while Mr Lambett is here.'

'What results?' Julia asked. Her father was silent.

'The CT showed Mr Lambett's lymph nodes appear to be enlarged.' Despite referring to him in the third person, the doctor looked Don in the eye. 'It might be benign, it might be the accident, but it may be something that needs investigation. We'll run a few blood tests.'

Julia waited for her father to speak. 'What are you looking for?' she asked the doctor, when Don didn't. 'Cancer?'

'There's a range of considerations,' the doctor said. His forefinger hovered in front of the computer screen. 'Has Mr Lambett seen any specialists recently?'

'Dad?'

'No,' he murmured.

'When did you last see your GP?'

Don shrugged.

Looking disappointed, the doctor lowered his hands to the rod that connected the screen of the computer to the wheels.

'We'll get in touch with them,' he said. 'They'll have records.' He told them someone would be along to bandage Mr Lambett's arm and take blood, then left the room.

Julia waited until the squeaks of his rubber soles against the floor had died away before asking, 'How long since you've been to the doctor?'

He rubbed his forearm.

'Dad?'

'I'm not one of those people that's off to the doctor every second bloody day.'

'So, you don't know anything about the lymph nodes?'

'Why would I?'

'Are they sore?' she asked, brushing her fingers against his neck. He flinched. 'Do they feel swollen?'

'I'm sore and swollen everywhere.'

The nurse who came was younger still, in his mid-twenties, dark hair buzzed close to his rosy scalp. He introduced himself as Colin, said he was there to torture Mr Lambett for a while. After dressing Don's wrist, Colin scooted to the other side of the bed, where he'd left a kidney dish of phlebotomy gear.

'How are we with needles, Mr Lambett? Brave, I bet?'

'He's very resilient, aren't you, Dad?' Julia said, but Don ignored them both.

Colin prepared the instruments swiftly. 'Count down from twenty, Mr Lambett, out loud if you'd like. Twenty – nineteen – eighteen –' The needle slipped into the vein and cherry-red blood rushed into the first tube. Colin's fingers rolled like a magician's, popping new collection tubes on and off until half a dozen lay in the kidney dish. 'Four – three – two – *won*derful effort, Mr Lambett, and we're done!'

Pressing a square of gauze to the inside of Don's elbow, the nurse nodded crisply at Julia. 'If you could hold this for a minute, please, Miss Lambett.'

Her father's skin was thin, the colours of the veins and

sinew and fat showing as if through glass. After a couple of minutes, Colin took over again, whipping away the pad and replacing it with a rose-coloured plaster.

'You'd better go,' Don said to Julia when the procedure was finished and Colin had carried the dish away, whistling. 'Fetch Biscuit. He'll be stressed.'

'I guess.' Though she knew the results wouldn't be back until the next day at least, Julia felt reluctant to leave. 'Are you going to be all right?'

'I'm in a hospital, Julia.'

There was nothing she could rightly say to that.

She called Paul from the car park and it went to voicemail. She decided a text message would be less alarming, so she typed quickly: *Nothing to worry about, but Dad had MINOR fall this AM and is currently resting in hospital. ALL FINE. Call when you can.* She hesitated before the sign-off, remembering Paul's admonition about people in the family sharing their feelings. *Love you*, she added, then hit 'send' before she could second-guess it.

Back at the house, Julia left the Commodore in the driveway and walked the short distance to Stewart Avenue. The sun was beginning to set, the sky the orange-pink of peach flesh, and the breeze was sharp on her face.

Davina was in the same clothes from earlier, her makeup slightly smudged from the day, feet bare. Biscuit barrelled past as soon as the door opened and leapt up at Julia, panting with joy.

'Everything go okay?' she asked Davina.

'Oh, fine.' Davina yawned. 'You were right, I barely noticed him.'

'Great.' She massaged the dog's head and his eyes closed in ecstasy. 'Thanks for doing that.'

'How's Don?'

Julia gave the report from the doctor, minus the concern about Don's lymph nodes. It felt oddly personal, and besides, Paul was yet to hear any of this. She felt like he should know first.

Davina looked distant while Julia was talking, like she wasn't really listening, but at the end she said, 'You must feel pretty guilty.'

'Why?'

'Well.' She gave an exaggerated shrug and Julia felt a poisoned spear of anger. 'If you'd been there this morning, he might not have fallen down.'

'I don't go into the bathroom with him.'

'Oh,' Davina said mildly, like it didn't matter. That made Julia angrier: if it was such a non-issue, why had she brought it up?

'This is the whole point,' Julia continued. 'He's not safe in that house. He needs to be someplace where help is available to him. If he can be taken to hospital just because he slipped —' She took a breath. Biscuit pressed his head into her thigh, and she relaxed down to pat him. 'It's not my fault,' she finished.

'I didn't say it was your fault.' Julia felt Davina's eyes on her, trying to pin her again. 'We can feel guilty about things that aren't our fault.'

Davina went to get Biscuit's lead and Julia was struck by how quiet the house seemed. She'd thought Jax at least would be interested in the dog, since he didn't have one of his own. Maybe he was afraid of them, or just uninterested, shut in his room playing video games like the night Julia met him. When Davina returned, she asked, 'Are the kids home?'

'Both out.' She bent to snap the lead onto the dog's collar, then gave his ears a quick rub. 'Bye, doggo.'

Biscuit pulled all the way back to the house, a faint whine curdling in his throat. Julia wondered if he remembered the morning's upheaval and was desperate to see Don, or whether he just wanted to be back where things were familiar. Maybe her father wasn't being paranoid. Maybe if she had left him alone all day, she would've returned to the house torn apart, piss all over the walls, the big space a prison without the master there.

When they arrived Biscuit burst straight into Don's bedroom, standing on his hind legs to sniff the bedcovers before curling up where Don had fallen in the bathroom. He let out a long sigh.

'He's all right, Bickie,' Julia said, rubbing the dog's belly. He licked mournfully at her wrist, then lay back to endure it, the way Don had when the nurse drew tubes of his blood. 'I promise. He's okay.'

She stood and walked back to the entryway, but the dog stayed where he was, sad eyes gazing up at the ceiling.

- ☾ -

Down by the river, the man appears as if invented. Swing one leg off the bike and glide to a stop, riding side-saddle like a lady in a movie. Meet by a desiccated old tree trunk that was picked out in advance.

He offers his water bottle. Say no by instinct, regret it afterwards. The sun is sharp. Almost summer holidays. He asks what she'd like for Christmas, eyebrow arched. Unsure of his meaning, she shrugs and gazes at the water. Think of the long white line of a neck, the tendrils of hair flickering over it like fingers. If not for sticky armpits and the wasps droning overhead, this could still be a movie.

— TWENTY —

The hospital where they'd taken Don hadn't existed when Julia last lived there. It was now the tertiary facility for the southern suburbs, a sombre grey building like Lego blocks beside the freeway. Julia weaved the Commodore towards it, stunned by the amount of traffic at nine o'clock on a Tuesday morning. Only weeks out of the cycle of regular life and she was already perplexed by such things as peak hour. Where were all these people going?

She hunched over the wheel as the speed dropped for a school zone. Teenage girls in uniform flooded the footpaths, their knee-high socks and heavy skirts reminding her achingly of Evie. She'd had another dream about her stepdaughter just the night before. This time Evie was arranging to meet with the older man in the sweat-soaked shirt, his wedge of Adam's apple bounding in his throat. They were still down by the waterway that Julia knew her subconscious had mixed with the river near her father's house. The symbolism was easy to unpick: rivers as being pulled along, losing control, natural forces; the shrouding of the man's face as mystery, exoticism, unveiling. The hot weather and sweat were clearly sexual.

Julia was sure the dream she'd had at Davina's was part of the whole thing. In that one she'd been herself, not Evie. The smell of floor wax, rows of girls with their sharp knees touching, the teacher wringing her hands; those had all been from Julia's own teenage years, but they'd come to her because Evie was under threat. The thought Julia had before waking on Davina's couch – that if you knew a person, then they couldn't be dangerous – was about Evie. The man she was meeting was a person they knew.

But there was no man, Julia reminded herself. She wasn't psychic, she was stressed.

Five minutes from the hospital she turned off the highway and weaved along several local roads, listening closely to Siri's instructions. Not wanting to ask Davina for another favour, she'd gone online and found a doggy day-care near the medical precinct that took drop-ins for an exorbitant price. Julia watched as Biscuit was led into the playroom with the other pups and one of the owners gave her a sympathetic smile. 'Like our kids' first day of school, isn't it? You kind of want them to miss you.'

Julia had had that feeling, with Evie, but didn't like the assumption. 'I don't have children,' she said stonily.

The woman was unperturbed. 'You know what I mean.'

It was a kilometre from the dog minders to the hospital. After two wrong turns on the footpath and a needless trip up and down in the lift, Julia got her bearings and found the ward where she'd seen her father the day before. As she entered the corridor a woman in a dress shirt was coming the other way, a takeaway coffee cup in her hand, the smell briefly covering the antiseptic odour of the hospital. It was so delightful after a fortnight of cleaning sprays and dust and instant coffee that Julia paused, wondering if she should order a flat white of her own before she went in to sit with Don.

The woman stopped walking too. 'Julia?'

The ID tag on her lapel had flipped around, but her outfit and posture made Julia guess she was a social worker. A cool fear ran through her. 'Yes?'

The woman's smile revealed square, white teeth. Julia noticed how short she was and the neat cluster of freckles on her forehead at the exact moment the woman said, 'It's Kimmie.'

Realising she was shaking her head, Julia forced herself to stop. 'Kimmie,' she repeated cautiously. 'Hi.'

Kimmie Wessels didn't try to hug or touch her, the way Davina had at the supermarket.

'I just dropped in on your dad,' she said. 'How *are* you?'

'I'm okay.' She took in the second old ghost. Kimmie's hair, which had always been styled in thick braids when they were kids, was cut very short, and she wore chunky, red-framed glasses. A row of gold hoops climbed the outside of each ear. Beneath her buttoned shirt and black slacks her physique was like Julia's: narrow as a rod. *Light as a Feather, Stiff as a Board,* Julia thought. 'What a coincidence.'

'Well.' Kimmie made an apologetic face. 'Not exactly. I work at the pharmacy and I saw your dad's name on a list for meds yesterday. I thought I'd peep in on him before work, but he's sleeping.'

'He had a fall.' Julia wasn't sure if Kimmie needed this explained, or if the information might accompany his prescription. She described the previous morning: Don knocking the shower on the way down so the tempered glass burst, her inability to get to him, the call for the ambulance. 'He sprained his wrist and coccyx. It's lucky it wasn't worse. They're keeping him in for—' Julia decided not to say *tests*, suspecting Kimmie would have a special understanding of that word. She didn't want to go into it. 'Observation. He's ninety-two.'

'Amazing,' Kimmie said. 'Wow.'

Her fascination could easily be read as insincere, but it didn't feel that way to Julia. There was something comforting about Kimmie's easy sympathy. 'It's a good thing I was there to find him,' Julia continued. 'I'm just over from Melbourne for a while.'

Kimmie clucked her tongue. 'How lucky. You hear terrible stories about older people and falls.'

'That's why I came. He's going to move into a home soon.' Don's obstinate expression swam into her consciousness, but she banished it. 'It's all getting a bit much for him.'

'He still lives in the family home?'

'The same one.'

'Wow,' Kimmie repeated. She shook her head slowly. 'What a remarkable effort.'

A man in a polo shirt with the hospital's insignia pushed a trolley of breakfast trays towards them, and the women broke apart to let him through. When he was gone, Julia said, 'How about you? When did you get back from Cape Town?'

Kimmie looked pleasantly puzzled. 'What do you mean?'

'I heard you went back to South Africa.'

'No,' she said, amused. 'Only for holidays still. Why, who told you that?'

'Davina Weir.'

The lightness shifted from Kimmie's face. 'You're still friends with Davina?'

'I don't know about friends,' Julia said, feeling uneasy. 'I've seen her a few times since I've been back, that's all.'

She was disappointed when Kimmie switched her coffee cup to her other hand and made a show of checking her watch. 'I'd better go. I start at half past.'

'Thanks for taking the time to see my father. That's really kind of you.'

'Oh, you're welcome.' Smiling wistfully, Kimmie brushed her fingers against Julia's upper arm. 'Take care of yourself, okay? And Don.'

'I will.'

Julia hovered in the corridor, watching Kimmie walk to the end of the ward and press the elevator call button. When the lift didn't come after a few moments Julia headed for her father's room, knowing it would be too awkward to stand and wait with Kimmie after they'd already said goodbye. She'd have to get coffee later; maybe her father would want one too.

Sometime after Davina's sleepover birthday party, the one where the girls had tried to play Light as a Feather, Stiff as a Board, the Weirs had come into money. Julia didn't know what happened exactly, but Mr Weir was home more often, and the family got a new van and a table-tennis table and a pool. She, Kimmie and Davina had watched from the window as the bright yellow Caterpillar zipped around the side of the house, carrying earth and piling it on the front lawn. It seemed to take forever, until one day the hole was deep enough that they could imagine the springy board, the inflatable rafts floating in the breeze. Mr Weir rigged up chicken wire to stop Lou tumbling over the edge, saying, 'Not long now, girls.' The dirt and sweat formed an orange paint on his skin, and his daughters shrank away. 'It's so close you can almost taste it.'

But it still took weeks and weeks, to the very end of the summer holidays. Lou tried to fill the hole with bowls of water from the kitchen and was caught by Pamela tracking brown mud into the house like dog shit.

Finally, a few days before school went back, a truck sat at the end of the road with an enormous fibreglass bowl swinging from its hoist. The Weir and Lambett children cheered.

'What did I tell you?' Mr Weir kept saying. The smile on his face was so wide it looked painful. 'What did I tell you, hey?'

Once it was bedded in, the pool took twenty-four hours to fill with water, and then the chemicals had to be added. By then, only Lou and Julia were hanging around. Julia sat on the lip of the pool with her lower legs submerged, watching as Mr Weir tossed in salts and solutions. As he worked, he told Julia about the existence of a little bug, microscopic or smaller, that lived in warm standing water. If you dived into it or even just dunked your head, it could shoot right up your nose. From there, it was mere centimetres to the brain, and your brain, Mr Weir said cheerily, was its favourite food.

'It eats your *brain*?' Julia whispered, trying not to let Lou overhear. She was only little.

'There's no cure. It's called amoebic meningitis. Nasty little so-and-so.' He gave a charming smile, the one his daughters hated most. 'But chlorine and salt kill it dead, promise.'

Julia looked into the water. Everything Mr Weir had tossed in there had disappeared without a trace.

Finally, when it was almost too chilly to swim, Mr Weir had pronounced the pool ready to go. Lou somersaulted in, determined to be first, and Davina and her two older sisters came out to dip their toes and complain.

'Julia doesn't think it's too cold,' Mr Weir said. 'Right, Julia?'

She'd shaken her head, but the others were right, it was freezing. Besides, she was scared of the water now, even if it was clear enough to see to the bottom. The meningitis amoebas lived in droplets, as specks within specks. Julia swam an awkward doggy paddle, keeping her head up, while the older three threw their towels around their shoulders and returned to the house.

Julia was shivering when she got out, embarrassed by her bare white thighs and the hard bumps on her chest that showed through her bathers. Her cheeks were windburned and her neck ached.

Mr Weir watched as she took her own towel down from the pool fence. 'Did you have fun, Julia?'

'Oh, yes.' She nodded. 'Thank you.'

'You can put your head under, you know.' His eyes were regretful. 'I didn't mean to scare you.'

'That's okay.' She touched her scalp. 'I don't like getting my hair wet anyway.'

'You do have lovely hair,' he said.

'Thanks,' Julia said, pulling her towel hard around her shoulders, enjoying how the stiff fibres scratched against her skin.

Lou was under the water, seeing how many laps she could do on one breath. It made Julia feel dizzy.

'I'll watch her,' Mr Weir offered gently. 'You have a nice hot shower.'

She liked the Weirs' bathroom; it was the only room in the house that didn't have massive windows, making you feel like you were on display. The thumping water from the showerhead pasted her bathers to her skin, and there was a sucking sound as she pulled them away, letting the loose fabric fill like she had a big pregnant tummy. When she was warmed through, she peeled the leg-holes away from her hips so the heavy sack of water emptied out, pulling her bathers down to her waist with the force of it.

In the plastic box under her childhood bed, Julia had found a picture of herself, Paul and Kimmie with the Weir girls, posing in front of the pool the summer after it was put in, the water flat and reflective behind them. Thinking Davina would get a kick out of it, she'd snapped it with the camera on her mobile phone but hadn't got around to showing her. Now, entering her father's hospital room to find him still asleep,

Julia sat on the chair by the bed and found the digital copy of the photograph.

Kimmie Wessels stood at one end of the line of children, scowling into the sun, or maybe because the Weirs had been teasing her. Her swimsuit was strawberry red with big white spots and a white bow between her non-existent breasts. Beside her were Tahlia and Christie, who were barely teenagers but still seemed so glamorous, with dark hair down to their waists, their eyes hooded, lips full. They had women's bodies, or what Julia understood at ten years old to be women's bodies: they wore string bikinis, they had sharp white hipbones. Beside them, Julia was dressed in a short-sleeved rash vest and board shorts, the wet clothing hanging from her shapeless frame. Tahlia had told her she looked just like Paul.

'Like a little *boy*,' Christie explained, as if she didn't know what they meant.

The phone buzzed in Julia's hand, jolting her. Samara's name and headshot came up on the screen. *Evie*, she thought, stepping out into the corridor. 'Hello?'

Samara didn't contact Julia often, but when she did it was always by video call. She spent so much time on her appearance that it made sense she wouldn't want to waste it. The camera connected and Samara appeared in an emerald silk shirt buttoned to the neck, faint touches of green in her eye makeup to complement the deep shade. 'Jules,' she exhaled.

Switching on her own camera, Julia was surprised by the sudden flash of her face, round and pale as a plate, before it was sucked down into the corner of the screen. She held the phone further away. 'Is everything okay? How's Evie?'

'Is everything okay with *you*?' her husband's ex-wife countered. Julia thought that if she looked like Samara, her attention would constantly be shifting to the little picture of herself, but her eye contact was impeccable. 'Ro told me about your dad.'

'Oh. Thanks. Yeah, he'll be okay. Just a bit knocked around.'

Samara's *mm-hmm* of acknowledgement was full and luscious. 'And how are you? It must have been scary.'

'It was.' Julia smiled weakly. 'But he's all right now.'

'Lucky you were there. It could have been so much worse.'

First Kimmie, and now Samara: the sympathy was too intense. Julia shifted to self-flagellation. 'I wasn't home,' she confessed. 'I don't know how long he was on the floor.'

'Don't blame yourself,' Samara admonished.

Like that, the guilt fluttered up off Julia's shoulders. It hung just overhead, threatening to drop back at any moment, but at least there was room for breath now. She took a deep cleansing one, sucking the bleach-and-boiled-vegetable air of the hospital into her lungs. 'How's Evie?' she asked again.

'Worried about you.'

'Don't say I'm just—' a disembodied voice argued.

Samara looked off-screen and smiled. 'Do you want to speak to her?' she asked Julia.

Her heart thundered. 'Yes, please.'

The screen blurred and then it was centred on Evie's face, her young brow furrowed with concern. It was probably all in Julia's mind, but she seemed older already, like years had passed, rather than weeks.

'Are you okay?' Evie asked. 'And Grandpa Don?'

'We're fine,' Julia assured her. 'He's a bit sore, but he's fine.'

Something glinted in the image and Julia bent closer. It was the fine shimmer of tears in Evie's eyes. 'I don't want something bad to happen and you to be there all alone.'

'Oh, thank you, sweetheart,' Julia said. 'But Grandpa and I are here together.'

Too late she realised what Evie had meant, that the 'something bad' she'd imagined was the same 'something bad' that hovered in Julia's mind each time she entered the house to her father's stillness, his silence.

Samara re-entered the frame, touching her cheekbone to her daughter's. 'Evie had an idea.'

The girl blushed. 'I don't know.'

'Don't be silly,' Samara said gently.

'What is it, Eves?' Julia asked.

'We thought – we thought –' She looked to her mother for help.

'It's school holidays after this week,' Samara explained, 'and Evie thought a productive use of her time might be to come to Perth for a few days and help you out.'

Julia was stunned. 'Really?'

'Rowan has appointments,' Samara continued, 'but I'd be happy to bring her over.'

'We can stay in a hotel,' Evie hurried. 'So we don't stress out Grandpa Don.'

'That's ...' Julia couldn't think of what to say. The urge to cry, which had been rising and dissipating regularly over the past day and a half, or two and a half weeks, or five years, peaked. She shook her head, trying to get the words out, and

Evie's face fell for a moment. 'That's fantastic,' she said hoarsely. 'That would be amazing.'

'Excellent,' Samara said. 'I'll suss it out and send you the details. You don't have to worry about a thing.'

The power of Samara, Julia thought as she hung up the phone, was that you could believe in every single thing she said. She would bring Evie to Julia's side, and all her worries would slip away.

— TWENTY-ONE —

After Bethany had shown her the emails the other physio sent about Rowan, the first thing Julia did was search the internet for a picture. Zoe Bantham was easy to find: on the website for an Altona clinic; in game summaries for Newport weeknight netball; on Facebook, on Twitter, on Instagram. She had her own blog called 'The V Diaries' where she posted about common post-birth issues, advising readers at the end of every entry to come see her for a friendly face and warm hands. Julia gritted her teeth at the implication.

She'd closed out of Twitter quickly – she wanted to see the woman, not hear her stupid thoughts. On all the other sites, Julia was rewarded or punished with Zoe's face over and over again. Clear-skinned in her work uniform. Red and sweaty after netball training. Painted and preened for a night out with the girls. Julia clicked and clicked and clicked. Either Zoe had chosen some specific privacy settings for her Facebook page, or all she posted was pictures of herself. She mugged at the camera, she smiled brightly into the faces of friends, she turned her back to take in a mountaintop view. *Turn around*, Julia thought. *Look at me when I'm talking to you, goddamn it.*

The faces of Zoe Bantham piled on top of one another, they weighed her down. Julia felt foggy and lethargic. She needed to purge. She shut all the browser windows, went out to the balcony and breathed deeply.

The next day she did it again.

And the next.

The photos became so familiar she saw Zoe in her dreams. In the daylight, she looked at Rowan and there was Zoe, the two of them giggling like high school crushes.

But at the same time, Julia couldn't see Zoe at all. Had no idea of her facial features, would've been unable to pick her out of a line-up. She clicked through the images. What did Zoe look like? Not like Julia, at least. And blessedly, not like Samara or Bethany, either.

A few days after she learned about Zoe, Julia found a post about the physiotherapy conference. After the last session the attendees had taken a group photo, dozens of them huddled to fit the frame, kneeling in the front or peeking their heads through at the back. Despite her blindness to Zoe's appearance, Julia zoomed in on her immediately. Bethany was on her right, and Rowan on the left. Zoe had an arm slung around each of their necks.

We need to talk, Julia kept thinking. She was practising the line to say to Rowan, the same way she'd practised engaging with Bethany. *We need to talk.* Waking up beside him, in the tearoom at the clinic, sitting down to dinner. Like being in a dream, needing to scream for help but being muted. *Ro, we need to talk.* It had taken her too long to say.

Energised by the news that Evie and Samara were coming, that afternoon Julia finished purging her childhood bedroom in one frenzied effort. Afterwards, caked in dust and dirt, she took a long shower, opening the medicine cupboard when she emerged so the mirror faced away. She never liked to see herself step out of a shower, flushed and wet, the steam rising off her. It made her feel vulnerable, like that scene from *Psycho*: an attacker coming around the curtain, ready to strike.

She'd slept terribly the previous night, not just because of the Evie dream. Wind had come in from somewhere, moaning dully, and the settling of the foundations seemed amplified. It was the first time she'd ever slept in the house alone, Julia realised; she'd never had to do it before, not even as a teenager.

For her second night by herself, she pulled the pillow and blankets from the guest bed and padded up the hallway to her parents' room. There she wrapped the yellow doona around herself and lay on the far side of the bed. Her mother's side. 'Come on, Bickie,' she called. 'Come next to me.'

The dog jumped up, tracked a circle onto the mattress and bent to sniff. Catching Don's scent, he relaxed onto his master's spot, facing Julia. She rubbed under his chin and he yawned, long tongue flopping out.

'Good boy,' she said. Reaching for his paw, she held it like a hand. 'Goodnight.'

The next afternoon, Don was discharged. When Julia arrived to collect him, he was in his dressing-gown in the visitor's chair, so freshly washed that water dripped from his hair and down the curves of his ears. Julia handed him a clean shirt and pants and watched him shuffle into the bathroom, thinking how ironic it would be if he fell in there, too.

On the table by his recently vacated bed there was a small box of chocolates from the gift shop, a card wedged under one corner. Julia squinted, trying to read the note without touching it. She thought she could see the words *love to see you* and wondered what other patient had struck up such a friendship with her father. He hadn't mentioned anyone.

The door clicked and he came out. He couldn't bend his wrist to work buttons, so the shirt flapped open, and he had to hold up his trousers with his good hand. 'Julia,' he said, face clenched. 'Help me with this, would you.'

She pulled out the waist of his pants to zip and button them, then buckled his belt to keep them in place. With his shirt she left the neck loose, so he had air. When she was done her father sat down heavily on the edge of the bed, and she winced at how it must have jarred his bruised tailbone.

Once he seemed calmer, she reached for the chocolate box. 'What's this?'

'Girl from the pharmacy came by. Said she was a friend of yours.'

'Kimmie?'

'Rings a bell.'

Julia shifted the box so she could read the card. *Dear Jules, Crazy bumping into you yesterday! I feel like we should catch up properly before you go back. Give me a call, I'd love to see you.* Her mobile phone number followed, along with a row of X's and O's. 'But the chocolates are for you, right?'

'I certainly hope so,' Don said. 'I ate several already.'

There was a knock at the door and a middle-aged woman wearing red lipstick and brightly coloured sneakers entered the room, followed by four adults with shiny young faces. Julia hadn't seen any of them before, but Don grinned as they formed a semi-circle around him.

The lipsticked woman looked Julia's father in the eye. 'Mr Lambett! Ready to go?'

'More than ready.'

'You don't like our hospitality?' she joked, then gestured at the others. 'Do you mind if the medical students-?'

'No, no, fine,' Don said, smoothing down the thighs of his trousers with his left hand. 'Hello, everybody.'

A couple of the students nodded, mouthed hello. One stepped forward, pre-chosen, and read from his notes. 'Mr Donald Lambett, ninety-two. Brought into the emergency department Monday morning after falling onto a tiled floor and becoming stuck.' Julia blushed and looked at her father, but he just gazed out the window, lips curled at the corners. 'X-rays revealed no fracture, however he has suffered a grade-two sprain of the right wrist and bruising to the coccyx. A CT scan showed incidental enlarged lymph nodes. Further testing revealed borderline anaemia and thrombocytopaenia, though there was no apparent bleeding. Mr Lambett was admitted for observation and further testing.'

'Borderline anaemia and what?' Julia repeated.

The doctor nodded to the student. 'Low haemoglobin,' he explained, 'and low platelets. Basically, human blood is made up of—'

'I know what they are,' she said, remembering to add, 'thank you. What does that mean though, low haemoglobin and platelets? What happened?'

Now the medical student looked to the doctor, who pressed her painted lips together. 'We're not entirely sure.'

'I'm a mystery!' Don boomed, kicking his feet with delight.

'It might have been a response to the fall,' the doctor told Julia, 'or it might have been the cause of the fall. The numbers were just on the cusp, you know. It's possibly related to age, or maybe just how Mr Lambett is.' She delivered an exaggerated frown to Don, who chuckled. 'If he saw his own doctor more regularly, we might have something to compare it to.'

Her father winked. 'You're the only one allowed to stick a needle in me, Dr Fong.'

The medical students exchange amused looks.

Dr Fong wagged her finger. 'Mr Lambett is being discharged with the promise that he will follow up with a GP for further blood tests.'

'I keep my promises, don't I, Jules?' Don asked.

Julia wasn't interested in her elderly father's flirtations. 'So, it isn't cancer,' she said to Dr Fong.

She stopped making faces and set earnest eyes on Julia. 'I know you must have been very worried about your father,' she said. 'No, we don't believe cancer was the cause. Though he must get in contact with a GP.' She looked at Don again. His reaction reminded Julia of Biscuit; if Don had a tail, he'd wag it. '*Must*, do you hear me?'

He saluted with his good arm. 'Yes, ma'am!'

Dr Fong reached for his hand, pressing it with both of hers. 'You take care of yourself,' she said. 'We don't want to see you ever again.'

The students smiled at this final line, then followed their mentor out of the room.

With the charming doctor gone, Don's cheery expression slackened. The pinkness in his cheeks faded back to white.

'Are you okay, Dad?' she asked, squatting in front of him.

'Just get me home.'

'You don't want to stay here? See if Dr Fong is interested in a date?'

He tipped his chin to his chest. 'We were just having a little fun.'

An orderly appeared and helped Don get settled in a wheelchair, then pushed him towards the exit while Julia carried his things. Though they were accompanied, Julia couldn't help expecting some kind of alarm to go off as they passed through the automatic doors to the car park. It seemed oddly easy to dress her father in day clothes and abscond with him. The box of chocolates Kimmie delivered were on his lap, and as they went down the footpath towards the Commodore, he pulled off the lid to reveal what was left.

'Truffle?' he asked the orderly, popping one into his mouth.

There was no wheelchair to use when they got to the house, and Julia saw firsthand how much her father had needed it.

She stood by the car door with her arm held out, so he had something to grab. The force from his left hand was weak, but he made it to his feet. The dozen or so steps seemed to take an age.

'We'll have to find somewhere for you now, Dad,' she said, letting him brace against her as she found the key in her bag.

He shook his head.

Biscuit was waiting when the door opened, his tail arcing through the air.

'Bickie!' Don called, and the dog bounded over the threshold and pushed his head between his master's knees. 'Bickie, Bickie boy, I missed you,' he crooned, bending a little so the dog could reach up for him. 'You left him by himself,' he grumbled to Julia.

'It was a couple of hours.'

'If he's fretted and made a mess, you're cleaning it.'

Julia didn't point out to her father that he'd be incapable of doing it anyway. Carefully, she manoeuvred him down the step to the front room, Biscuit hanging back until Don's buttocks were safe in the chair before diving for him again. 'Bickie, oh Bickie, I missed you too, mate, I missed you too.'

While the pair had their joyful reunion, Julia performed a quick check of the house, but everything was as she'd left it. As she'd guessed, Biscuit had been fine. If her father was wrong about that, she thought, going into the kitchen to make tea, then he could also be wrong about moving the dog.

'Oh, thanks, love,' Don said when she placed the mug by his chair. 'I'm gasping.'

From the couch, Julia watched her father drink. His left

hand quivered, but not badly. Probably it always had. The bottom of the mug was loud against the side table when he put it down, but he was also tired. She wouldn't mention aged care again today; she was beginning to think it wasn't his decision, anyway.

'Evie and Samara want to visit you,' she said instead. She'd saved the news for when she knew he'd be coming home.

Don's features lifted the way they had for Dr Fong. 'Really?'

'This weekend, actually. A whirlwind trip.'

'You're kidding,' he said. 'Evie and Ro?'

'Evie and Samara. Evie's mum,' she explained, sure that Don knew who she meant but not wanting to take the risk. 'It's school holidays and Evie's really keen to come, so they're taking a few days. Ro's busy.'

'They'll stay here.'

'They're going to get a hotel, since you're only just out of hospital.'

'No.' Don's voice was firm. 'They'll stay here.'

'Oh,' she said. 'Well, I'll tell Samara. She might have made a booking.'

'Bookings can be cancelled.'

Don's tea was finished, so she stood to take away the dirty cup. Her father reached out and held her arm. 'You have a lovely family, Julia.'

'I know, Dad.'

His grip was weak, but steady. 'I consider Evie my grandchild.'

'And you're her granddad,' Julia confirmed.

Don nodded deeply, as if something had been settled.

'I might have a little sleep,' he told her, feeling for the recliner's lever, which was, luckily, on the left. As soon as the leg-rest was deployed, Biscuit stretched out underneath it. 'When are they coming?'

'Friday,' she said. 'Two days away.'

He nodded and closed his eyes. 'Good-oh.'

Julia took the mug down to the kitchen, leaving man and dog to sleep.

On Thursday, prompted by the gift Kimmie left for her father, Julia walked Biscuit to the shopping centre and bought a flower arrangement. As they continued on to Stewart Avenue, she considered the significance of what she'd chosen: flowers as gratitude, flowers for honour, flowers to say goodbye. She recalled her father's description of the bouquet Pamela Weir sent after Goldie died, like the plumage of a peacock. Julia's selection was much smaller, a few blooms in yellow and orange, their stems tied with red ribbon.

She had the quiet hope that Davina would be out, so she could leave the gift on the doormat, but when she rang the bell there were sounds in the house. When, if ever, did Davina go to work? Julia shook off her irritation; anyone could ask the same thing of her.

Davina opened the door wearing a robe made from lilac-coloured silk, vines embroidered along the sleeves. It was short and showed her thighs.

'Jules,' she said, then saw the dog. 'Again?'

'Oh no, no.' Julia shook her head emphatically. 'No, it's fine, Dad's back from hospital. We just wanted to say thanks for watching Biscuit the other day.' She held up the flowers.

Davina's face creased. 'For me?'

'To say thank you.'

'You didn't have to do that,' Davina said, reaching for them. Though it was a common thing to say, her tone was blunt. She frowned.

Julia wondered for a moment if she'd remembered to remove the price tag. 'It's just a token of my appreciation,' she said limply. The dog stared up at them.

'I don't mean to be rude,' Davina began, and Julia steeled herself for the blow, 'but it's a bit over the top, don't you think? I mean, it was just a small favour. Between friends.' She narrowed her eyes. 'Would you babysit Jax for me, if I needed you to?'

'Of course,' Julia said, thinking, *Please don't ask for that.* Maybe this was why she'd really bought the flowers; so as not to owe Davina anything.

'So you don't have to be all sucking up just because I watched the dog.'

'Right,' Julia said. 'Sorry.'

Davina rolled her eyes. 'Don't *apologise.*'

Julia's chest tightened. What the fuck did Davina want her to do? Not say thank you, not apologise. Act like they'd been best friends all their lives; more than that, act like sisters. Julia remembered the Weir girls storming around, screaming at each other one minute and eating off each other's plates the next. The intimacy was unbearable.

'Anyway.' Davina shifted her weight. She hadn't invited Julia inside. 'Have you talked to Rowan yet?' She rested the fingertips of one hand against the knot of silk at her abdomen.

The gesture caused something to stir and turn over in Julia's pelvis. 'I will,' she murmured, not yet sure if this was a lie.

'It's a lot, I know.' Davina's voice was beatific. 'Take your time. I'll be here.'

The house was quiet again. It was likely Jax was at school and Billie at TAFE or work, but the air felt emptier than that. Like the only real occupants since Julia left on Monday morning had been Davina and the dog. 'Have you talked it over with the kids?'

'What do you mean?'

'The idea of their mum being pregnant, but it not being their brother or sister.' Julia imagined Evie in the same position, seeing Samara's belly grow and shrink without receiving a sibling. Or the opposite situation, the one Davina had offered, of having a sibling come to life on the other side of the country and then, what? Get brought over by plane, like freight? 'They might have some feelings about that.'

'They're adults,' Davina said. 'Or almost adults. They can deal with it.'

But Jax was only eleven, Julia thought. Surely that wasn't old enough to just accept it. 'There's a lot of moving parts,' she murmured.

Davina stepped back into the house. 'Think about it some more,' she said coolly. 'Thanks for the flowers.'

- ☾ -

On the footpath by the river, idly dragging a branch in the water. Watch for fish, but disturb only flies and jumping insects. Nothing lives down here.

He's coming down the path again, but now it's different. He is walking quickly. His expression is stiff.

Pause, alert to everything. For a second, only the whine of bugs. A rich earthy smell: the river ripe, on the turn.

The man stops very close. His voice is low, cold. What did you do?

Tight gnarl in the gut. Look down at his bare legs, dirt etching frowns into the faces of his knees. Say nothing.

Your father came over. *Wormy fingers touch her chin, tilting it up. His eyes are bright, forehead seared red.* Seems convinced something's going on. *His hand falls away.* What'd you tell him?

Count breaths. They are small and tight, but will sustain her.

There's nothing … *He trails off, gnawing his lip.* You want to get me into trouble again. Do you think it's funny?

Shakes her head desperately. Of course it's not funny. It's deadly serious.

He steps back. I thought we were mates. I didn't blame you the first time, but this. Where does it end?

Weak, forced voice: It wasn't me. I didn't say anything.

It doesn't matter. *His lip curls.* There's too many problems. I thought you were the mature one. Not crying to daddy.

Wants to cry now, so badly. I didn't.

But he is past you now, dodging your shoulder like a stranger, hurrying away. He doesn't turn back.

He is gone.

- TWENTY-TWO -

Julia parked the Commodore at the Qantas terminal and waited for Samara and Evie by the baggage carousels. It was late evening, stars printed across the navy sky. Earlier, Evie had called from the departure lounge in Melbourne, excited that her parents had picked her up from school with her luggage and a fresh set of clothes for the plane. She'd gone into the closest bathroom to change, other girls watching with envy. Rowan dropped her and Samara off at the airport in plenty of time for their six p.m. flight.

It was a faint ache, almost the memory of a pain, to imagine the nuclear family travelling up the freeway, singing along to the radio or arguing good-naturedly. Any other person in the drop-off bay would have seen the attractive parents emerge with their stunning daughter and believed they were a unit, the father staying behind while his wife and child went somewhere. Maybe the parents' goodbye was a little stiff, a little unromantic. Julia could only hope.

Tears tickled her eyes when she saw them coming down the escalator. It took Evie a moment to find her in the crowd, but when she did, Julia was rewarded with the sight of pure joy flooding her face. Samara was a few steps behind, gazing down like a queen on a balcony. She raised her hand to Julia and smiled.

Evie's hug was so tight it was breathtaking. She was weeping lightly, but laughing at the same time.

'Evie, Evie, Evie!' Julia cried. 'I missed you, baby, I missed you!'

At last they parted and Julia turned to Samara. There was a brief pause as the women made eye contact, each assessing what the other expected, then they hugged tightly, too. Samara's neck was long and smooth, the perfect cradle for Julia's forehead. She allowed herself to rest it there for a moment.

Samara went to stake out a spot by the carousel and Evie attached herself to Julia again. 'Why have you been gone so lo-ong,' she hummed, then shook her head. 'No, it's okay, I know. Poor Grandpa Don.'

'He's all right. He's home safe.'

Evie gave her a grave look. 'Has he learned from the experience?'

Julia laughed. 'Of course not. Why would he?'

As they drove to the house, Julia recalled her own taxi ride a few weeks before, the stunning unfamiliarity of the streetscapes. Now it felt as if she took this route every day. In the back, Evie pressed herself to the window, commenting on things they passed, comparing them to Melbourne. Samara, in the passenger seat, bent her head to check emails on her phone, but looked up every few minutes to give Julia a warm smile. The kind of luck she'd had, to be welcomed into this family, Julia realised. As if reading her thoughts, Samara patted her knee.

Don was waiting with the television turned off.

'Grandpa Don!' Evie called, sweeping down the step. He snapped his armchair upright. 'How's your arm, does it hurt, are you okay?'

Biscuit leapt up in greeting and Evie squealed gleefully. 'Oh my God, he's so gorgeous, hello!'

Samara followed her into the room. 'Hi, Don.'

'Samara.' His good hand fluttered at the armrest as if about to push himself up. 'How lovely to see you.'

He and Samara had met a few times, and only in Melbourne, but the pair always got along. They had tightly confined natures and moral certainty in common, along with their dry humour.

'Don't get up,' Samara ordered, and Don slumped back. She rewarded his obedience by adding, 'You're looking well, considering.'

'Not enfeebled?'

Samara smiled. 'No more than usual.'

Julia had changed the sheets in the guestroom so Samara could sleep there. Evie was in Julia's old room, where she usually stayed, and Julia moved to Paul's childhood bunk bed. As she slid between the sheets, she wondered what Samara thought of the house: its size, its age, its piles of old familial crap. Her expression when taking in Goldie's precious vegetable-patterned tiles had been stoic. It would have been a long time since she'd been presented with such out-of-date décor.

Lying in the dark, Julia couldn't shake the feeling that Rowan was back in the top bunk, his comforting weight where it belonged. She went to sleep easily, as if she was on Melbourne time as well, and woke early. Through the wall she heard Samara and Evie whispering, a sound as gentle and reassuring as the running of a far-off stream.

Around midmorning, Samara said to Julia, 'Walk with me.'

Earlier, Evie had followed Don to the front room and stood by the pile of things on Goldie's chair. 'What's this?' she asked, and Julia gave her father a meaningful look. The pair had been going through the items since then, Don telling Evie the story behind each one. Once its origins and meaning had been shared with his step-granddaughter, it was easier to make a decision about whether to keep an object or not.

Julia held Biscuit's leash loosely. It was a bright day, but cool, and they walked quickly to stay warm.

'So, how are you going?' Samara asked when they reached the end of the street, as if the question had to be saved until Don's house was out of sight.

Julia admitted, 'I didn't know such mind-numbing tasks could be so stressful.'

'Rowan said your dad's making noises about not going.'

She nodded. 'He says he doesn't want to disrupt the dog. It's bullshit.'

'Has the fall made him change his mind?'

'I brought it up a couple of times, but he's gone quiet.'

'It must be difficult.'

Julia didn't know whose situation Samara was referring to, her own or Don's. Probably both. 'Paul told him he was never coming to this house again. That he'd only visit if Dad moved somewhere safer.' Samara clucked her tongue. 'It's just crazy. He's got to go. He broke his arse on a bath mat, for Christ's sake.'

'There's still things to sort through, though.'

'I've got to keep the momentum up.' They crossed a main road, Biscuit pulling slightly. They were following the usual route, down to the river. 'I can't just give in to him. If I can't get him to actually move, he can at least be in a less cluttered environment.'

'He'll always need a bath mat,' Samara pointed out, her voice soft. 'You can't protect him from everything.'

They took the next corner in silence.

'Have you had a chance to do anything else?' Samara asked after a while. 'Other than pack up boxes?'

'I bumped into a couple of people I knew when I was a kid. I've been hanging out with one of them.' Julia described Davina as they passed the riverside café, struck again by how little there was to tell. When she tried to talk about their childhood instead, she became embarrassed by the young Julia who watched in silence as four girls bullied their own father, who felt an electric shudder of glee at taking power from others. Who let a friend wipe saliva down her face and tell her stories of people falling headfirst off staircases and smashing their skulls on the ground. She moved on to Davina's birthday party and the aborted attempt at Light as a Feather, Stiff as a Board.

'Did you ever play that game?' she asked Samara.

'I don't think so. But we did seances and stuff. Scared the crap out of each other on purpose.' She shook her head. 'Teenage girls are psychos.'

They had reached the river. 'What's Davina like now?' Samara asked as they joined the flow of walkers on the bitumen.

'She's a bit—' Julia used the first word that came to mind, 'intense.' It felt right. When Samara nodded, she continued, 'She watched the dog for me the other day.' Julia wanted to give Samara evidence without going into the things she now regretted telling Davina: Rowan's contact with Zoe Bantham, their inability to have a baby, how long it had all been going on. 'So as a thank you, I took over some flowers. She seemed actively pissed off.'

'Did she say why?'

'She's decided we're such good friends that we don't need to thank one another. Like love means never having to say you're sorry.'

'And you don't want that kind of relationship with her.'

Of course Samara was able to crystallise it, make it sound almost unbearably simple.

They got to the bench where Julia and Biscuit sometimes rested before turning around, and the dog lay down and bared his belly for pats. While Samara leaned over to scratch him, Julia looked out at the water and saw a big, white branch, half-submerged in the muck. Her dream came back to her.

'I've been having nightmares, too,' she murmured, telling herself that if Samara didn't hear, she'd let it go. 'About Evie.'

Samara took her hand from the dog's stomach and sat up straight. She fixed her eyes on a boat puttering down the waterway. 'Have you?'

'I know it's a bunch of stuff, stress and being away and worrying about her. But you know how something happens in your dream and you wake up with a feeling? It's been every two or three nights since I got here.'

Samara asked for details. Julia's stomach chilled as she began to explain. 'At first she's on a bus and someone reaches out and says they know her. In that kind of creepy, threatening-but-not-threatening way, you know?'

'Who was it?'

'An older man. Kind of middle-aged.'

A tightness went out of Samara's shoulders. 'Okay.'

'Then I dreamed she was back on the bus looking for him, but he didn't show up. Then, and I know it's all mixed up, but it switches to Evie here, down at this river, and she's meeting the guy on purpose. Like something's happening between them.' Samara turned to face her and Julia, becoming flustered, shook her head. 'Nothing happened in the dream, but it felt bad, to me. Then in my last one, the other night, the guy said Rowan had talked to him. He was pissed. Evie was upset. I got the feeling ...' Julia brushed the soles of her shoes over the bitumen. 'I don't know. It felt so real.'

Samara smiled faintly. 'I don't think meeting with an older man is one of Evie's problems, luckily.'

Julia's stomach rolled at the phrasing. 'But she is having problems?'

'Some of the girls at school.'

'Evie's so popular, though.'

Samara's mouth tightened. 'Not this month, apparently.' They got to their feet and retraced their steps.

It was to do with the ballerina that Evie had mentioned before. Their dance teacher had, to Samara's absolute fury, passed on Evie's concern that she might have an eating disorder. Instead of being flattered that Evie cared, the ballerina had decided that Evie Cheng was jealous because she was a fat, fucking bitch who thought she was better than everyone else. The friends who'd gone to Melbourne Central with Evie the day she saw the homeless man sculpted a version where she'd given them all sour looks when they ignored him, which was totally their right to do, and then ditched a bottle of Mount Franklin at the one girl who dared to say so. Classmates from maths with the prac teacher sniped about how snotty Evie was over some harmless jokes. Powered by the frisson of choosing a joint target, the other dancers theorised that Evie was in love with the maths teacher, wanted to fuck the homeless man. Was a lesbian obsessed with the too-thin dancer, envious of the smoothness of her chest under a leotard as Evie struggled to contain the udders that flopped from her own. It was why she'd bailed out and gone to hip-hop, they concluded. No one would be able to see her ugly body under a tracksuit. By the end of their conclave, the embarrassment and self-consciousness had evolved into an easier feeling: hatred. *Fuck Evie Cheng,* they thought. *She thinks she's better than us.*

'Jealous little shits,' Julia seethed. Samara nodded forcefully. 'She *is* better than them.'

They paused at the café for takeaway coffees. While their order was put through, Samara went on. 'The way they're exerting control is typical girl shit. Not outright bullying or anything the teachers could see. Like the other day at lunchtime, one told Evie she has fat legs. And the other girls all kind of nodded, as if this was true and an acceptable thing to say to another person.'

Evie in the schoolyard, standing up from a circle of girls and asking if anyone wanted something from the canteen. A kind offer, but not a suck-up one; something she would've done even without the coldness in the ranks. Her pleated skirt rising as she stands, and the bitchy ballerina letting her eyes bug as she announces, 'Wow, your thighs are kind of huge.' Evie freezing just long enough for every other set of eyes to snap around. 'Kind of like a slab of pork,' one comments. Another adds, 'The other white meat.'

'Jesus Christ,' Julia groaned.

'We had a big chat last week,' Samara said, taking the drinks from the barista. Outside, Julia untied Biscuit's leash and they set off back to Don's. 'She's going to change friendship groups. Obviously, she's upset. She liked those girls, until they turned nasty. She asked me if she did anything wrong.' Samara's voice stiffened, her eyes bright with withheld tears. 'I wanted to call up every single one of their mothers, but Evie wouldn't let me. Then we decided to visit you.' She tried to smile. 'So she could be with women she can trust.'

Soon they turned onto Don's street. 'I'd like to tear those girls limb from limb,' Julia said.

Samara looked thoughtful. 'I'd like to shave their heads.'

'I'd like to shred their trendy clothes and make them wear Laura Ashley dresses and Birkenstocks.'

'Birkenstocks are cool now,' Samara said regretfully. 'Make them wear Crocs.'

Their chuckles died away as they approached the house. The front door hung open and a dented white ute was parked in the driveway. The dog began to pull with agitation.

'Dad,' Julia said.

'Evie.'

Julia unclipped the lead and Biscuit bolted into the house, barking.

– TWENTY-THREE –

Inside, the tableau was much as they'd left it: Don in one armchair, Evie in the other. In front of them stood a man wearing heavy jeans and a pullover, bald-headed and red-cheeked. Instead of racing to Don, the dog threw himself at the stranger, back legs kicking wildly. It took a moment for Julia to realise Biscuit wasn't attacking. He was jumping for joy.

'Bix!' the stranger cried. His voice was as raw as his cheeks. He dropped to a knee so the dog could lick his face, sniff his ears. 'Bixie, mate, I've missed you!'

'Hello,' Julia called from the entryway. The two men looked around, and Evie got up and went to her mother. 'I'm Julia,' she continued, entering the lounge. 'Don's daughter.'

The stranger tilted his head away from the dog's flapping tongue and said, 'Hi.' He didn't offer his name.

'She's walked him every day since she got here,' Don said. At the sound of his voice Biscuit went to nuzzle the old hand hanging loose from the armrest. Don scratched his snout. 'He's in good nick.'

'I can tell.' The man pushed on his cocked thigh, heaving himself upright with a groan. 'Thanks a lot, mate. I really appreciate it.' He nodded to Julia. 'Thank you.'

Biscuit returned to the stranger. As he passed, Julia brushed her fingers along the soft fur of his back. 'What's going on?'

Her father shifted in the chair. 'Get Biscuit's things, would you please. The blanket and bowl. His tennis balls.'

'I'll do it,' Evie called. She tugged Samara down the hallway with her.

'I'll grab that,' the stranger told Julia, phlegm rolling in his throat. Julia followed his gaze to the leash hanging slack in her hand. 'He might be a bit confused on the way out to the car.'

She handed it over and Biscuit whined with anxious excitement as the man snapped it to his collar. Julia tried to make eye contact with her father, but failed.

'Was he a good boy?' the stranger asked, filling the silence. Don coughed.

'He knows a lot of tricks,' Julia said.

The man grinned, his cheeks glowing. 'Picked those up in a flash. He's a very intelligent dog. Reckon there might be some collie in him.'

Samara and Evie came back, the dog's blanket slung over Evie's arm and tennis balls in both her hands. Samara gave the empty food and water bowls to Julia, her eyebrows raised. Julia had no answers for her.

'Terrific,' the man said, taking the blanket from Evie. The

movement released the concentrated scent of dog, sharp and sour but comforting. 'Thanks. Thanks so much.'

Evie dropped the tennis balls in the bowls, then stepped back beside her mother.

'I mean it, mate,' the man said to Don. 'I really appreciate it. You don't know how much.'

'It's no trouble.' Don's voice had taken on the man's low rumble. 'You'd have done the same.'

'I'm feeling good about this, you know. I'm feeling confident.' The man winked at Julia and she stiffened, though it wasn't lascivious; just merry. 'I've slayed my demons now, I'm sure of it.'

'I believe in you,' Don murmured.

'Right-oh, Bixie,' the man said, shaking the lead so it swayed gently against the dog's flank. 'Time to say your goodbyes.'

Understanding the command, Biscuit went to Samara and then Evie, accepting their quick pats, before trotting back to Don. He pressed his chest to his thighs in order to accept the solemn, nuzzling canine kisses, and when Biscuit turned and pushed his muzzle into Julia's leg, she noticed moisture on her father's cheeks. Unable to scratch him with her hands full, she dropped down and put her forehead against a velvet ear. 'Bye-bye, Biscuit. Good boy.'

'Do you mind carrying those for us?' the visitor asked when she stood back up.

Julia followed him out to the ute, where he unlocked the driver's door and held it open. Biscuit jumped straight in and walked across the bench seat. Once the dog was sitting on the passenger side, the man went around to the tray of the ute and dropped the blanket in. He returned to Julia, taking the food bowls from her.

'Thanks,' he said again. The balls circled the curved edge of each dish; his hands were trembling. 'Your father is an absolute saint.'

She'd never heard anyone refer to Don that way. Not even Goldie.

'Ninety-two.' He shook his head. 'How'd he hurt the wrist? He wouldn't say.'

'He fell. It's just a sprain.'

'Poor beggar.'

'We didn't leave Biscuit alone at all,' she told him. On the other side of the windscreen, the dog seemed to grin at her. 'We made sure he was with people. Other than being in hospital, he was with my father all the time.'

Nodding firmly, the man balanced one bowl on top of the other, so his right hand was free to shake hers. Despite the tremor, his grip was strong and warm. 'You look after Don,' he said. 'He's a good bloke.'

Julia kept her eyes on Biscuit as the man got into the car, started the engine, and pulled out of the driveway. She wanted the dog to turn and look at her through the rear mirror as they sped away, but his gaze remained on the road ahead.

'Shut that door,' Don called as she went back into the house. She did so, then stepped into the front room. Samara and Evie were gone, and Julia saw how much her stepdaughter had managed to get done: the stack of items that once crowded Goldie's chair had been reduced to a neat boxful.

Don seized the remote control and the television burst to life, the volume cranked so high the midday movie actors were screaming.

'So that was Biscuit's owner?' Julia called over the din, knowing as the words left her mouth how silly the question was. 'Did you know he'd be coming back?'

Her father's shoulders fluttered in a not-quite-shrug. 'Not today.'

'But someday?'

'I knew he'd come for Biscuit when he was ready.'

'I thought you had the dog permanently.' Julia didn't want to yell at her father, but it was unavoidable. 'I thought the owners had to give him up.'

Don shook his head. 'Not permanently.'

'Where's he been, then?' She had the urge to stamp her foot. 'Why'd he need to leave his dog with you?

'It's a private situation,' Don snapped. 'You don't know him.'

'Exactly!' Julia pulled the remote control out of his hand and held her finger on the volume button until the level was halved. 'How do *you* know him?'

'It doesn't matter.'

'He called you a saint.'

Don frowned. 'When?'

'Just now. Outside.'

'Oh, well.' She handed the remote back and he fiddled with it. 'People get very emotional about their pets. They treat them like children, don't they.'

'So he's definitely nice to Biscuit?' Julia asked. Emotion crowded her throat; she felt like she could break down and bawl.

Don seemed to notice. He reached out and patted her arm. 'He loves that dog. You don't have to worry about that.'

Though time and again she'd thought the opposite, Julia said now, 'He was treated well here.'

'It was always going to be temporary.'

'You could have told me,' she muttered.

'It wasn't your business,' Don said. They gazed at one another, the house already emptier without the slurping snores of the dog. 'I knew the plan.'

Julia took a deep breath and released it shakily.

'Good timing, anyway,' Don said, eyes sliding to the screen. 'You can go back to looking for a home for me now.'

Her tears dried away. 'Really?'

'I told you I couldn't move while the dog was here,' he said. 'Now he's gone, we can get this show on the road.'

The three women moved like parts of the same machine. Each had her expertise: Julia understood the house and its quirks, could track down where items were likely to hide; Samara performed the grunt work, moving and cleaning more in an hour than Julia had in a day; and Evie stayed with Don, asking careful questions about the objects brought for his assessment. Whenever there was a moment of downtime, Samara was on her laptop, researching options for Don's next step and making a point-by-point list for Julia to follow after she and Evie went back to Melbourne.

On their last night, Julia took her stepdaughter to pick up dinner. Evie had her phone in her lap and kept glancing down and sucking her cheeks.

'Thanks so much for coming,' Julia told her while they were stopped at a red light. Rain had started that afternoon, and while it wasn't heavy, the car's wipers only had one, panicked setting. The whole vehicle ticked along like a metronome. 'You have no idea how much it cheered me up.'

Evie slid the phone under her thigh. 'It cheered me up, too.'

'It hasn't been much of a holiday for you.' The light changed and Julia took off carefully, wheels squeaking on the damp bitumen. 'Helping to box up Grandpa Don's things.'

'I didn't expect to go out and party.'

'That's good.'

Evie was quiet for a minute, sitting upright to look out at the darkening evening. The soft, steady rain made Julia feel calm, but she didn't know what it did for her stepdaughter.

'How's hip-hop?' she asked, trying to find her way into Evie's distress.

'Mum told you about those girls.'

The restaurant they'd ordered from was up ahead, and Julia concentrated on manoeuvring down the tight driveway before responding. 'She's worried about you.'

'I know.'

She parked. 'Are they being awful?'

'It's not that bad.'

'Evie—'

'I'm not in denial. I know they're trying to get to me.

It's lame, I'm annoyed, but I'm not crying my eyes out or something.'

Julia peered at her, trying to assess her face under the streetlight. 'Really?'

'Really,' Evie said. With a hard *click,* she threw off her seatbelt. 'Can we go in? I'm starving.'

They'd all been hungry when Julia put the order through, and when they got inside, the waitress handed over two full bags of containers and condiments. Evie licked her lips as Julia passed her credit card over the reader. 'I want to eat it all in the car.'

'We need to keep it clean, Eves,' Julia said. They had to hurry through the carpark, ducking from the fresh rain. 'It's going to be sold soon,' she added when they were back in the Commodore, its windows fogging immediately with the warmth of the food. 'If anyone in the world would want to buy it.'

Evie gave a mock pout and put the bags on the floor between her feet. 'Fine. But you'd better run all the red lights.'

They were halfway home, driving in patient silence, when Evie tapped decisively on the console between their seats. 'Mum saw I was sad, so I told her it was those ballet girls.' Julia glanced across, but traffic was banking up and she needed to keep an eye on it. 'Except it wasn't really that.'

The river setting, the shimmering silhouette of the older man. When Julia was awake, she could never summon his face – not that it would've told her anything – but the pressing humidity returned, the hum of insects, the stench. It was the river she'd walked along with Biscuit and Samara, but at the same time it wasn't. It was more vivid in her dreams than it was in waking life. 'What was it, then?' she asked.

Evie dug a fingernail into the old leather. 'It's kind of personal.'

The car in front stopped, and Julia braked hard, pushing them both against their belts. 'Sorry,' she wheezed. 'You okay?'

Evie rubbed her breastbone but said yes. A few tubs of food had fallen over in the bag and she bent to stack them up again. When the brake lights ahead disappeared, Julia rolled the Commodore cautiously forward.

'Nothing's too personal,' she said. 'Nothing's too private. Your dad and I – and your mum – you know that all we ever want is –'

'It's not personal about me,' Evie said. 'It's personal about you. You and Dad.'

'Me and –?'

Evie took a ragged breath. 'Are you going to split up?'

'Sweetheart.' She waited until they were safely stopped at another light before leaning over and pulling Evie into a side-hug. 'I'm sorry you've been stressed about that.'

'Because it's okay,' Evie said. She was crying but talking reasonably, as controlled as a confused fourteen-year-old could be, and Julia again wondered what magic mixture had made Evie this way. If it was just Rowan and Samara, their genes combining to create something that would never be seen again, or if Julia might be able to replicate the magic in another child of Rowan's. 'You don't have to stay with him,' Evie was saying. 'You don't need to worry about me. But not knowing ...' She wiped the back of her hand across her face.

The light turned green. In a couple of minutes, they'd arrive at Don's. Julia reached into the backseat for tissues and passed them to Evie. 'We didn't mean to upset you.'

'No, I know.' Evie dabbed at her leaking nose. 'I didn't want to add to everything by being crazy about it. I know that if you made a decision, you'd tell me.' They came to the top of Don's street. 'But I'm pissed at Dad. It's the second great wife he's messed things up with.'

'He didn't mess things up with your mother. It was a mutual decision.'

Evie's eyebrows narrowed. 'But he is messing things up with you.'

They pulled into the driveway.

'What did your father tell you?' Julia asked, setting the handbrake.

'Not much.'

The two of them got out of the car. The rain had mostly stopped, and the air had a freshly laundered feeling to it. Julia breathed it down to the bottom of her lungs, and Evie followed suit, though her nose was in the takeaway bag. She'd be all right, Julia knew. Whatever happened, Evie would be all right.

As they walked up to the house, Julia said, 'This is going to sound dumb, but when you said you were upset about something private, I thought it was something to do with a boy.'

She said *boy* and not *man*, she didn't mention dreaming about them. From what Evie had said in the car and Samara during their walk, Julia was almost positive her dreams had been what Evie called them a couple of weeks ago: the mind digesting, producing shit. Still, she needed to be sure.

The sensor light tripped, and Evie stepped aside so Julia could unlock the door. 'A boy?'

'Like bad news.' Julia knew she'd read the subtext. 'When I was your age, there was a flasher in the neighbourhood.'

'I told you how to deal with that, Jules,' Evie said as the key caught the lock. 'Scream your lungs out. Tell everyone. Don't let them get away with their bullshit.'

– TWENTY-FOUR –

'We need to talk,' Julia had finally told Rowan, two months after her conversation with Bethany.

She'd timed it with excruciating care. It was a Sunday of a non-Evie weekend, a warm, bright morning. Rowan made them breakfast and they wedged themselves onto the balcony. They had time and coffee. It was almost Lunar New Year, a time for renewal.

Cutting into his poached egg, Rowan made a comedic face. 'That's an ominous thing to hear.'

They'd been together for ten years without any problems. Neither liked conflict; they actively avoided fighting. Sometimes, often, that meant not speaking. Not in a cold way, but lukewarmly. Days without speech could feel effortless, but they could also make a person want to tear every hair out of their head.

'I'm wondering,' Julia began, carefully spearing a cooked mushroom, 'if you want to tell me about your friend Zoe.'

The guilt in his eyes was all she needed: he'd known it wasn't completely innocent.

Rowan didn't ask how she'd found out or what she knew. Actually, though his phone sat idle in the office for hours at a time, she'd never tried to find the texts. They'd either be exactly what she expected, or not what she expected. Or they would have been deleted. Any of these outcomes felt terrible to her.

'I'm sorry,' he said, pausing with cutlery in each hand to look her in the eye. After a beat, he went back to his food. Was that it? He continued, 'I know it was inappropriate. I don't talk to her anymore.'

'She had quite a crush on you.'

His cheeks pinkened. 'Yeah,' he told the remains of his egg.

'Would you like to tell me about that?'

Julia wondered where this therapist's voice and demeanour had come from. She'd certainly never had any kind of counselling herself.

'It was flattering.' His voice was quiet. 'I liked the attention. It was dumb, but that's all it was.'

'It's still bad,' she said. 'It still hurts.'

But as she said this, she'd felt an absence of pain; she felt hollowed out. She imagined the morning breeze passing right through her.

'Jules.' He dropped his fork and grabbed her hand. The table swayed. 'That wasn't my intention at all.'

'Because you weren't thinking about me.'

To be fair to Rowan, he gave this statement a few moments of consideration before responding, 'No, I wasn't.'

It gave her the courage to add, 'We don't think about each other enough. I don't flirt with other men,' she said, 'but that doesn't mean ...' Sighing, she shook off his hand. 'I don't know.'

Rowan was silent, and when she looked up, she saw his fear. 'What are you getting at?'

A small flicker of anger. All right, she was being obtuse, but what was the point of never communicating if it didn't mean they already understood one another down to the bone? 'We don't talk about the baby,' she began. 'About a baby. Are we still trying?'

'Jules,' he said, flabbergasted. 'Of course.'

'It's been years.'

'I've told you we can go to a specialist. See what's going on. You shrug it off. I thought we were leaving it up to whatever happens, happens.'

She pushed her plate away, disappointed even in that moment at the waste of good food. How could he not realise that if they went to a doctor, all they could possibly get was bad news? That with every passing month, even while the stress and frustration and grief of the situation grew, there was the comfort of what a miracle it would be if it worked *this time*? The absence of a baby was bitter, but how sweet if you could one day say, 'After three years.' 'After four years.' 'After five years, we'd basically given up ...'

But that was also bullshit. Julia would never tell anyone what it had taken. Her need for privacy overrode any desire to feel special, always. 'Is it worth it?'

'It's probably not worth your mental health, if we just keep—'

She shook her head. 'Not that.'

Maybe their unspoken connection was still there, because the colour disappeared from Rowan's face. 'Is our *marriage* worth it?' he asked, incredulous.

They'd both jumped as Julia's phone rattled against the table. Lifting it, she saw her brother's name on the screen. Paul never rang on a Sunday.

She answered with her hand shaking. 'Hey. Now's not the best time.'

Her brother spoke over her. 'I'm in Perth.' He sounded breathless, in the middle of many tasks. 'I just got to Dad's. What the fuck.'

'Paul?' She sat forward. 'What's wrong?'

His voice was hoarse. 'He's in a bad way. What the *fuck*!'

It was the first week of February.

Ten days later, when Evie returned to her mother's, Rowan took down the blow-up mattress and went to sleep in her room.

A few days after Evie and Samara returned to Melbourne, Julia drove back to the hospital. For the first time since she'd arrived, she was starting to feel on top of things. Order could be seen in the house, and her father had gone with her to tour one facility and was booked to view two more. There was a real estate agent coming to value the property. Impressed by the progress, Paul had agreed to fly over and help with the final move, whenever that turned out to be. The three of them would do it, the remnants of a family.

Julia arrived at the food hall first and chose a table set snugly against a pillar, out of sight of other diners. Patients and their visitors wandered along the path just outside the window, most of them slowly, their sicknesses marked by flapping gowns and drooping shoulders. A handful of staff stood metres from the smoke-free awning with their cigarettes, staring into the car park. A couple passed, both staring so avidly down at their tiny baby they almost bumped into a lamppost. Julia picked up a menu.

'Jules!' Kimmie's strong fingers squeezed her arm. 'Have you been waiting long?'

'A couple of minutes.'

Kimmie slid into the opposite chair and beamed. 'It's good to see you.'

Her lunchbreak was forty-five minutes, so they needed to be snappy. They both ordered and Kimmie got down to business. 'I have to say, I was very concerned when I heard you were spending time with Davina.'

'I wouldn't say I've been…' Julia stopped. Spending time with Davina was exactly what she'd been doing. 'She instigated it,' she said, aware of how peevish that sounded.

But the objection seemed to satisfy Kimmie. 'I know she can be persistent. I myself have had to actively avoid her at times.'

'Really?' Julia felt jealous. 'Because of how she was when we were kids?'

A voice called out Kimmie's order number and she stood awkwardly, knocking chairs as she went to collect it. Just as she returned with her vegetable soup, it was Julia's turn.

'I don't blame her, you know,' Kimmie said when they were both sitting down again. 'She was only a kid. I just find the whole situation very toxic, especially this preoccupation she seems to have about getting us both onside.'

'Probably she feels guilty.'

'It's misplaced.' Kimmie stirred her soup so the croutons dipped below the surface. 'Nothing that happened was her fault, of course. But she's the adult now, and her behaviour *is* her responsibility.'

'Did you know she's got two kids?' Julia asked.

Kimmie nodded. 'There you go.'

'I don't think she has custody of them. They're never there. Not that it means anything,' Julia continued, seeing the curious look on Kimmie's face. 'But she wasn't honest about it. Just kept saying they were out.' She shrugged. 'I guess it was technically true.'

'I'm sure she has ongoing issues, with parents like hers.'

Julia summoned an image of Pamela Weir, tall and glamorous, and Alec Weir, square and shy. 'I know they were kind of slack,' she said. 'Do you remember how the girls would call their dad stupid for asking weird questions? And Pamela just ignored it.'

Ignored it, or didn't see it? Julia had always wondered. At the dinner table, Pamela's eyes would be fixed on the window, one finger pressed into her thumb as if willing a cigarette to appear. Goldie never fell into those kinds of reveries, even for a second. She was alert for any slight against her husband, any inkling he might require her attention or support. 'Julia. Paul,' she'd say, if one of them even came close to the boundaries of Don's ego. A cold stone dropped into still water: 'Enough.'

An enormous bouquet for Goldie's funeral. What had

happened to their mothers' friendship? Davina never said.

There was no humour on Kimmie's face. Without her smile she looked like a completely different person, one who'd rip you to pieces if she had to. 'Do you not know what happened with Alec Weir?'

'What?' Julia's mind leapt on the most rational thing. 'Did one of the girls do something to him? Did Pamela?'

Kimmie's laugh was toneless. 'Did one of *them* do something to *him?* Did your parents not say anything to you?'

Julia's stomach roiled. 'About what?'

Kimmie's head and shoulders twitched. 'I can't believe—'

'What is it?'

'I don't know if I should be the one to tell you.'

'Tell me *what*?'

'He watched children,' Kimmie said. To give herself something to do she poked her soup, but like Julia, she was no longer eating. 'He looked at them when they were nude. I believe that's as far as it went,' she added. 'But it's abuse, plain and simple.'

Julia couldn't speak.

'I'm sorry I had to tell you here.'

'Davina knows?'

'She had to change schools,' Kimmie said. 'She must know something happened. Besides, she's so desperate to be friends with both of us. I guess she feels like she'd repair something by doing that.'

Mr Weir stumbling on their game of Light as a Feather, looking dazed. Mr Weir wanting everyone in their bathers, in the pool. Mr Weir and his need to crack open heads and hearts and get to the soft, dark stuff within. Stuff that preteen girls didn't understand, or if they did, would never in a million years tell their fathers.

'Did he look at us?' she whispered.

'They found out because of your brother. That's all I know.'

Baby Paul. Julia's to protect.

'But it was girls he was interested in,' Kimmie continued, glancing at the food hall clock. There were only a few minutes left. 'Four daughters meant access to a lot of friends.'

Baby Julia, then. Don's to protect.

Once, Julia went to the toilet at the Weirs' and came out to find Davina had gone off somewhere. She wasn't in her bedroom or the living room, and her older sisters were out and would murder anyone who went into their room without permission. Checking outside, Julia happened upon a dark pink figure doing laps in the pool. She didn't think it was Davina, but waited for the swimmer to pause. It was Mr Weir. Julia hadn't even known he was home. Seeing her, he smiled. 'Swim? You can have a hot shower after.'

The ripples created by Mr Weir's slow freestyle slowed and settled. Julia gripped the pool fence with both hands, feeling its warmth. 'I'm looking for Davina.'

Mr Weir ran his palms over the water's glassy surface. Julia shivered, knowing that sensation: sucking and smooth at the same time. 'She's a wayward one, that daughter of mine.'

Julia shifted her weight. The pool looked silky and fresh. Birds chirped.

Mr Weir stared at her for a moment, then his mouth opened slowly. Julia felt a whooshing in her stomach, but all he said was, 'There she is.'

Slow to cotton on, Julia was startled by Davina's thumping hand on her shoulder.

'What are you doing, ya dope?' her friend said.

'I was looking for you.'

'*I* was looking for *you*,' Davina argued, which hadn't made sense. She pulled Julia until her hands detached from the fence, and for a second the cool air on her palms had felt like the brush of still water. Like pressing against a window in order to look in. Julia turned from the pool and followed Davina inside.

Julia rang Paul as soon as she stepped out of the hospital, but his voicemail picked up. She ended the call and put in his number again and again. Finally, on the fifth attempt, he answered. 'What is it? Is it Dad?'

'He's fine,' she said quickly. 'Do you remember Alec Weir?'

'What?'

'Alec Weir. The family had four girls, Mum used to be friends with the mother.'

'I guess so. Why?'

She summarised what Kimmie Wessels had said, ending with her vague statement: *They found out because of your brother.*

She asked him what this meant.

'Jesus Christ, Jules. I was six years old.'

So, he did remember something. If he knew how old he'd been.

Paul let out an angry breath. 'I think it was when we stayed there the week Mum was sick. You remember how they had the bathroom with the two doors, one of them went out to the hallway and the other to the parents' bedroom?'

Julia remembered, faintly.

'The door to the bedroom would open, every night when I took a shower. I'd put the towel around me and go to close it, but the next time I looked it was cracked open again.'

A slippery clasp, Julia suggested. The house wasn't in the best condition, and six people used that bathroom regularly. The older girls slammed things and tried to lock each other out.

'That's what I thought, but one time I went to close it and Mr Weir was standing there.'

Hot, sickening fizzing at the base of Julia's stomach. She swallowed hard and looked out at the car park. 'What happened?'

'He said hi, sorry, it was an accident. He didn't realise I was there and wanted to use the toilet.'

'Well, maybe—'

'The shower was running, Jules. He knew I was in there.'

'Was he ...' she began. 'Do you think ...'

'Then he said, *Has your sister had her shower yet?*'

Speechless. A falling sensation, like leaping from the top of a staircase with your hands trapped.

'I told Dad about it. You remember, he came and got us

early. He said the Weirs' toilet was broken and it was better for us to stay home with him.'

Remember: The only time her father ever took off work, just to be there when they came home from school.

Remember: Asking if she could go and play at Davina's and being told no, she'd been staying there enough, give them space. But Davina wasn't allowed to come to Julia's house, either.

Remember: At the end of term the Weir girls left the school.

Remember: Goldie home from the hospital, unable to stop crying, gathering the children to her sides like life preservers.

An older sister and younger brother are staying with family friends while their mother is in hospital. Their father, working normal hours, wants to spend every evening by his wife's bedside. There are grandparents, but the other family lives close by, walks to the same school in the morning. It's a good idea all around.

What a favour to bestow, offering to cook and clean and care for two more kids, when you already have four, and quite a small house.

The father keeps in touch with his children by phone, calling from the hospital each night before dinner. The phone is passed: husband to wife, sister to brother. A few days into the arrangement, the father asks his son if he's having fun. He's paying attention, but not great attention. He doesn't expect an important answer. His son is six.

'The bathroom door's broken,' the son complains.

'Is it?' The father is stroking his wife's arm while she dozes. 'That's no good.'

'It keeps opening when I'm in the shower.'

The father thinks about steam letting the latch slide open. He's been to the house where the children are staying, had a piss in the cramped, ice-white bathroom. 'Put something in front of it, mate.'

'Last time Mr Weir tried to come in because he needed a wee.'

'Oops,' the father jokes. This is the last thing he will say that isn't serious.

Where are the other parents during this conversation? Where is the sister? There's a lot of commotion in the smaller house all the time. Four daughters, fighting, hugging, screaming. A mother who sits out on the back patio alone.

The boy says the man asked about his sister. How does he say this in a way that gets his father's attention? How does the father respond without frightening his son? What does he tell his ill wife?

The next day he's there to pick them up from school. The daughter comes out with her best friend, one of the girls whose house they've been staying at, but the father looks only at his children.

'Sorry, kids. Sleepover's over.' He takes their arms firmly. 'You're coming back with me.'

− TWENTY-FIVE −

Davina seemed unsurprised to find Julia at the door again. Though it was early afternoon, she was dressed for evening: skin-tight dark jeans, a low-cut top, fringed booties. Her dark hair was curled and sprayed into place, but she hadn't put on makeup yet, leaving her features flat and indistinct. 'Now isn't the best time,' she warned. 'I'm about to head out.'

'It won't take long,' Julia said, moving towards her with enough certainty that Davina stepped aside. In the kitchen, Julia sat on a stool with her handbag on the bench in front of her as if waiting for service at a bar. 'Where are the kids?'

Davina took the position of bartender, stretching her arms into an upside-down V, both palms on the counter between them. 'With their father. The usual.'

'Right.' Julia rolled her shoulders. Something in the room smelled bad, food on the turn. 'I just wanted to let you know, I'm going back to Melbourne soon. Things with Dad are almost sorted.'

Davina raised her eyebrows. 'Already? Wow.'

'And I wanted to thank you very much for your offer, but—'

Before the sentence was finished Davina went to the sink and poured an open bottle of whisky into an unwashed glass. She didn't offer any to Julia. 'I thought you wanted kids,' Davina said, keeping her back turned.

That stung, the way it was intended. 'I do,' Julia murmured.

Davina picked up her glass and held it to the light. 'Maybe not, if you aren't willing to take extraordinary measures.'

'I know you want to help,' Julia said slowly, lifting her chin. 'But I don't think you really understand the situation. How emotional it is. How complicated.' She paused. 'Actually, it's kind of bizarre that you want to be so involved, when we barely know each other anymore.'

Davina turned around. 'Some might say my offer is selfless.'

True. How could volunteering your body and time and emotions so that another person could have the thing they wanted most be considered anything else? And yet with Davina, it was only selfishness. Julia couldn't explain it, but it was. She rubbed a finger against the laminate, looking for patterns in the faux-marble stippling. 'You told me once that you knew someone who died because they fell from the top of a staircase with their hands in their pockets.'

Davina frowned and drained her whisky.

'Your dad told me,' Julia continued, forcing her voice to stay light, 'that if you don't put enough chlorine in a pool, it can grow a bug that goes up your nose and eats your brain.'

Twisting at the waist, Davina dropped the glass back in the sink. 'It's an amoeba, and it's true.'

'And the other story was true?'

'My mum saw someone,' she began, then backtracked, rolling her eyes. 'My mum *heard* about someone. It was at a hotel ball.'

'All right,' Julia said. 'No harm, no foul. I never smashed my head at the bottom of a staircase or got a brain-eating amoeba.' She crossed her arms and bowed her head. 'I caught up with Kimmie Wessels the other day.'

'Who?'

'Come on,' Julia said gently. 'You know.'

The wet sound of Davina swallowing burrowed into her ears. 'What did she have to say for herself?'

'She told me about your dad,' Julia said. 'What happened when we were kids.' Looking up, she took in Davina's twisted expression, the rage she was struggling to hold at bay. 'Do you know what I'm talking about?' she prodded.

'Bullshit.' Davina's voice was strong, steady, penetrating. 'Some fucking shit from when we were kids, is it? Maybe you should get the fuck over it.'

'We don't blame you,' Julia said. 'Actually, I think I understand you better now.'

'He didn't do anything.'

'Maybe not anything physical. But it's still wrong.'

'Are you fucking serious?' Davina asked. Only now was her voice becoming frayed, leaning towards a shriek, and droplets of sweat formed a chain along her hairline. 'Don't tell me now that you think it was wrong, when you kept winding him up.'

Julia gaped. 'I was *twelve*. I was having a *shower*.'

'Not *then*,' Davina snapped. 'Later.'

'What do you mean, later?'

'Oh, right, so you remember what my father supposedly did, but not how you made the most of it.' She stared with fury until it was clear Julia wasn't going to respond, then slapped her hand against the laminate. 'Having secret meetings with him, does that ring a fucking bell? Luring him out to see you over and over, just to get him in trouble?'

Chilled, Julia held the edge of the bench. 'What?'

'Sending your fucking *father* after him? Oh, poor old man Don, right? He's a fucking *thug*.' Davina's eyes shone with tears. Her throat pumped to keep them from spilling over. 'We should've had him up for assault.'

Julia is back at the river. It's twenty years ago. The sun goes behind a cloud and the face in front of her is revealed: Alec Weir. *Hey, don't we know each other?*

'Why did you want to be friends with me, then?' Julia asked. 'Why did you come up to me at the shops? Why not just ignore me?'

'I thought you might have changed.'

Julia couldn't suppress an incredulous laugh.

A clicking came from Davina's throat. When she spoke again it was slower, thinner, as if the engine of her rage was shutting down. 'You're such a bitch. Just get the fuck out.'

It's a year ten health class, not a whole-of-school assembly, though it does take place in the big hall with no air-conditioning, the girls' backpacks lining the walls. Last week, after the flashing incident, a Phys Ed teacher took them through self-defence techniques: what to do if someone grabs you from behind; what to do if someone runs at you; what to do if someone opens their coat and exposes their genitals. The answer each time was to scream as loudly as possible, then go to the police. The teachers seem to think this will come naturally, work instantly. There's no suggestion that shame and fear might make them freeze.

This time there's a talk about grooming. The danger of the people you know, not just strangers in the bushes. The importance of listening to your instincts. An adult male has no business being friends with a female child.

A ripple of defiance through the group. They don't consider themselves children.

One girl thinks of a man she knows, who's met her a few times on the river path. The focus of the lecture is on touching and compliments. There's nothing wrong with talking.

She's sure that, really and truly, they *are* just friends. The exception that proves the rule.

The teacher urges them, ignoring their titters, to be alert. Who's around? What are they saying and doing? She acknowledges that yes, as fourteen-year-olds, they're not little kids. But that doesn't mean there isn't a risk, either from strangers or people they know.

Afterwards, the girl is unsettled. She keeps running through the criteria in her head and deciding her friendship meets none of them. She isn't made uncomfortable. He doesn't ask her for anything. She hasn't been told or warned or threatened to keep it secret. That's a choice she's made for herself.

They've organised to meet that afternoon, as a matter of

fact. It's still humid as she collects her bike and rides in the direction of the river. At the highest point there's a tiny kiosk and an old swing set, with a track between them leading down to the river walk. Today she coasts to the start of the slope and brakes hard, feeling tired just looking down the incline. Easy enough to get to the bottom, but later she'll have to ride back up. Instead, she sits on a bench overlooking the water and fights the weight in her eyelids.

After a few minutes the man appears on the dirt path below. Her friend. She waves to get his attention, then gestures: *Come up here.* He has a hand in front of his face to block the sun. He shakes his head and points in front of him, lips curling into a smile. A cute little stand-off. She tilts her head playfully and crosses her arms.

Slowly, his smile drops away. He jams his thumb towards the ground forcefully. Mouths the words: *Come. Down. Here.*

Despite the heat, she feels a chill. She shakes her head lightly.

His eyes and mouth widen with shock. In one quick movement he's walking again, and within seconds he's around a bend, out of sight.

The girl is disappointed. She wanted to win, but not like that.

Her thoughts are derailed by someone calling her name. She looks over her shoulder. It's her mother, coming out of the kiosk. 'What are you doing?' she asks. The girl can see how hard she's forcing her expression to be neutral. 'Are you waiting for someone?'

'No.' Not a lie, now that he's gone.

'Let's go home,' her mother says.

The girl nods and collects her bike, and the two of them walk back to their house. They don't talk about it, now or ever.

She goes one more time to see the man, but he storms past her like they're enemies. His face is a clenched fist.

Julia came in breathless with anger, legs trembling like they wanted to kick. 'Dad?' she called, stumbling down into the sunken lounge. 'Dad?'

Don was fully reclined, injured wrist in his lap and his mouth hanging open. His rasping snores were like the ripping of Velcro. In front of him the TV played, the volume turned to low.

She took in his long thin limbs, the softness of his face. A fucking thug, Davina had called him. Don was far from that now, but Julia knew he hadn't been one twenty years ago either. Whatever he'd done, he was only protecting her.

Julia tried to shrug off the shame of her little sojourns, the warm, secret feeling she'd had when Alec Weir stood in front of her, shaded by trees, hidden from the world. All the time she'd been worried about Evie, what she was doing and who she was meeting, she never considered blaming her stepdaughter if the dreams turned out to be true. Now that she knew where they'd come from, she shouldn't blame herself, either. No matter what Davina said, it was Alec Weir who was at fault. Even if nothing had happened, he should have known better. He must have been aware of how it looked. The power that he had.

If she'd known her parents had cut the Weirs out of their lives and why, then surely she would have found Alec gross instead of alluring. Still, even though her teenage self was blameless, she must have sensed that something about the situation wasn't right. That was why she hadn't told anyone, and why, after it ended, she'd pushed it so far to the back of her memory that it could only come out in her dreams.

She fell onto the couch and tipped her head over the armrest. The ceiling in the front part of the house was cathedral-style, with dark wooden beams and a dirty drum light. The afternoon sun illuminated the dust motes, drifting back and forth as if on waves. Parts of the Lambetts, suspended in time.

Closing her eyes, Julia dozed along with her father. She didn't dream of Alec Weir, the way she had all the other times she'd seen Davina. Instead, Julia floated, a microscopic skin cell viewing the house from above.

Don woke before she did. 'Julia,' he called. 'How long have you been there?'

She dragged herself up on her elbows and looked at the clock, but didn't know when she'd got home. Outside, the sun had almost set.

'Did you have a nice time with Kimmie?'

Julia yawned and swung her legs around. 'Yes.'

'What did you two talk about?'

'Old times,' she said. 'Schooldays.'

Grunting, Don fumbled with the lever on the chair until it sat upright. He pressed the soles of his feet to the floor and glanced around the room. Aside from the television, the hutch was empty, wiped down with wood cleaner in preparation for the move. A box sat in Goldie's chair with its lid taped down tight. On it, Evie had written *Photographs and other mementoes.*

'It's a big house,' Don said, as if he'd only just realised.

'Yes, it is.'

'Too big for one person.'

Julia nodded. 'Good for a family, though.'

His gaze dropped to the floor. It was probably just shading in the carpet, but you could almost believe there was an outline of Biscuit. 'How do you think he's going?' he asked Julia.

'I think it's been a joyous reunion.'

'That's probably right.'

Don reached for his stick, wedging the end of it into the space below Goldie's chair so he could push himself up with his left hand. Julia watched, careful to let him do it for himself but eagle-eyed for another fall. Soon enough he was steady on his feet.

'How about dinner, then, love? I'm famished.'

– TWENTY-SIX –

Don's unit had a private courtyard accessed off the lounge room. They'd decorated the space with ferns and hanging baskets, and the garden's border was marked with the potted plants and gnomes that had survived the previous backyard's long drought. A three-piece wrought-iron outdoor setting, which Goldie had bought because it reminded her of the Parisian balconies she'd never seen in person, fit neatly on the sliver of deck. It had cleaned up well when Julia aimed a hose at it, murdering the redback families who'd lived in its crevices for generations. The little patch was cosy and manageable.

'Sit down,' Don insisted, touching Julia's shoulder as if to demonstrate how. 'I'll just get us a little nibble.'

He returned from the kitchenette with a serving tray – also purchased by her mother, evoking English tea parties this time – and put it down. A plate of Arrowroot biscuits, arranged in a fan, and two cups of water. 'My humble abode,' he said, taking the other seat.

The hanging baskets swayed in the breeze. 'It's very nice.'

Simultaneously, they reached for the plate, taking a biscuit each.

'The last pickup is scheduled for tomorrow.' Julia wiped crumbs from her mouth. The childhood taste of Arrowroots, a special treat in their family. Grown-up biscuits, dunked in tea. Try to catch the waterlogged chunks before they shed into the mug. 'There was a post online from a social worker with a client in emergency housing. She was thrilled with the stuff when she came and saw it. Said it's in amazing nick for its age.'

The social worker had offered to take everything left in the house: the guest bed and Paul's old bunks, the dining table and chairs, the TV and couch from the back room, the fridge and washing machine that were much bigger than Don needed. She'd spoken in broad terms about her client, a single mother fleeing domestic violence, and Julia had looked around at her childhood home and felt a flush of gratitude. Leaving, the social worker hugged Julia tightly and said it was a wonderful thing she was doing.

'My father's doing it, really,' Julia explained. 'They're his things.'

'Tell him for me, then,' the woman had said. 'Tell him I said he's a saint.'

Julia didn't use those words with Don. 'I think it's great,' she said now. 'Being able to pass things on to someone who needs them. Does it give you a good feeling?'

Don's back straightened with sudden alarm. 'Not the hutch, though.'

'The hutch is here, Dad.' It fit between the bedroom and bathroom doors as if it had been made for the space, or the space for it.

'And my chair?' he asked, still tense.

'Your chair's inside,' she said. 'You kept all the important things. You remember.'

'Oh, right.'

He'd been doing this lately, forgetting and fretting. At the intake appointment, Julia had pulled the facility's GP aside and given her the rundown. She was relieved when the doctor explained that Don would be seen regularly, whether he liked it or not. She had the blood results from the hospital and a comforting smile. 'We'll look after your dad. I promise.'

As Julia finished her biscuit, she thought of the days ahead. Tomorrow, once the social work organisation took the furniture, she'd do a final deep clean, then leave the keys with the agent. From there she'd check into the airport hotel, and the morning after would be on a plane back to Melbourne. It was only a week since she'd seen Rowan, who flew in along with Paul to help Don move, but she missed him badly. This time they were talking every day.

She swallowed water to clear crumbs from her mouth. 'So, what are the plans down at the social hall? Anything interesting coming up?'

The hall was a building at the centre of the complex that put on meals and entertainment for residents. During their tour, Julia had been amazed at the options: chess, board games, billiards, table tennis. An adjoining building housed a lap pool and a few exercise machines.

'We used to have air hockey,' the guide told Don, grinning, 'but there were a couple of broken knuckles.'

Don had waved his cane cheerily. 'Pity. I'd've had a great weapon if a fight broke out.'

'There's a poetry thing, and a card tournament,' Don said now. 'Roast lamb. A choir.'

'Sounds fun.'

'I'll eat the lamb. Maybe play cards. The rest of it …' He screwed up his face, then relaxed. 'Martin's bringing Biscuit round on the weekend.'

'That's fantastic.'

Don bit into an Arrowroot, then immediately spoke, spraying crumbs. 'Thank you for your assistance in this matter,' he said.

For a moment Julia didn't know what he was referring to. 'Helping you move?'

'Getting my rear in gear, so to speak.'

'That's okay, Dad,' she said. 'You're welcome.'

'I couldn't have had your mother with me in a place like this,' he observed. 'It's too old-farty.'

'I don't know. She'd like the choir.'

Don shuddered. 'Yes.'

They chewed and sipped. There was the faintest rumble of traffic from the arterial road beyond.

'Whatever happened with that friend of yours?' he asked after a while.

'Who, Kimmie?'

He shook his head. 'The Weir girl.'

Julia tried not to show her discomfort. 'We hung out a few times. We don't really have anything in common.' She swallowed some water, then added, 'She's pretty secretive.'

'That doesn't surprise me.'

Julia chose her words carefully. When he was there, she and Paul had talked about whether to bring the issue of the Weirs up with Don, but decided against it. He was too old, too much time had passed. And besides, what more was there to say? 'I think there's been a lot of pain in her life.'

'Well, of course. Her family was poisonous.' He seemed to take for granted that Julia knew what he meant. 'Like a well. She drank that water every day. What else was going to happen?'

'She thinks they didn't do anything wrong.'

'Self-protection. Bordering on delusion.' He snorted. 'Just like her mother. That Pamela knew what was happening. And if she didn't know, she was dumb as a rock.'

Julia tried to keep still, so as not to block the flood of information pouring forth. 'Oh?'

'Your mother couldn't be friends with her after that, knowing what she'd overlooked. Knowing that she'd decided to stay with him. Even when she screamed bloody murder about it, your mother didn't give in.'

Julia sucked in air. Surely Goldie would have cowered as Pamela, a giantess in comparison, berated her for ending their friendship. Julia wanted to leap between the two women, raise her own voice into the cold, nasty face of Pamela Weir.

'I never liked that woman,' Don went on. 'I found her

disingenuous. Of course, I had more experience with people than your mother did. She always gave the benefit of the doubt.'

'Mum never told me. I really thought they were still good friends.' Julia shook her head. 'I didn't even question why Pamela stopped coming around, why I never answered one of her phone calls.'

'Your mother would never lie.'

'I know.'

'Telling you would have been cruel. We said, oh, the toilet broke, you're coming back home. The two of you seemed happy with that.' Don snapped a biscuit in half, but didn't eat it. 'I suppose deep down you didn't want to be there, though you didn't say anything to us. You didn't ask to go over again. Didn't seem fussed when the girls left the school.'

'Did you go to the police?'

'We discussed it.' He rubbed the broken ends of Arrowroot together and a shower of crumbs landed on the deck. Ants flocked. 'But there wasn't any evidence, and we didn't want the two of you to be questioned.' To her surprise, he asked, 'What would you have done, if it were Evie?'

'Probably the same,' she admitted.

'Well, there you go.'

'Davina said you confronted Alec. Physically.'

Don frowned, puzzled.

'A few years later,' Julia said, trying to avoid the specifics.

'Oh,' Don said. 'Well, I gave him a talking to. I made my thoughts known.'

'She called you a thug.'

He blushed. 'There may have been some argy-bargy.'

'Dad!' she cried, delighted.

'Being a father was my most important job. That and being a husband. I took it very seriously.' He regarded the smoothed-down ends of biscuit. 'I advised Mr Weir to do the same.'

She reached over to rest her hand on his arm. 'You're a good man, Dad.'

'Thank you,' he said, watching the ants.

When it was time to go, Don walked her inside. His new lounge area was a little crowded, with the two recliners and the hutch and the roll-top desk, but it felt safer and tidier than the old house. Her father moved smoothly, unobstructed by forty years of junk. He stopped by the door and leaned on his cane.

'Travel safely,' he said. 'Give my love to Rowan and Samara and Evie.'

'I will.'

Julia steadied herself. There was a final question she and Paul hadn't been able to figure out the answer to. 'Can I ask you something? You don't have to tell me.' His expression was patient, neutral. 'Why was Mum in the hospital that time?'

'Oh, Julia.' His voice sagged with sadness. 'I thought you knew. She'd lost a baby.'

She sucked air through her teeth. 'A baby?'

'A pregnancy. Late.' Don's eyes shone; he seemed to be looking right into the past. 'We wanted scores more kids, of course. But after that we decided to stop.'

She embraced him gently, aware of his fragility. 'I love you, Dad.'

He touched his chin to her shoulder and breathed out. After a moment, she let go. 'I'll come back and see you soon.'

'Oh, yes,' he said. 'Unless I'm dead.'

She smiled, her heart blooming. 'I'll come back when you're dead as well.'

'Right,' he said, unbothered. He opened the door. 'Well, that's fine. You're always welcome.'

Waiting in the Arrivals hall at Tullamarine, Evie holds a piece of A4 paper with Julia's name in bubble letters. When Julia steps off the escalator, her stepdaughter grabs her and the two sway in place, humming with contentment. Julia feels as if she is truly home.

She releases Evie and turns to Rowan. When he came to Perth, things between them had felt easier, but not yet resolved. Now she presses her nose to the underside of his chin and breathes in deeply, comfort flooding through her. Rowan's hands tighten around her back. They don't need to speak.

The traffic is stop-start all the way to South Yarra, but Julia doesn't mind. She reclines her seat and listens to Evie's chatter from the back, her updates on school and friends and hobbies, pleased that she seems largely unaffected by the ballet dancers' bitchiness. They're still scowling at her in the corridors, she reports, but who cares? Evie has the hip-hop crowd now.

'Friends don't bring you down,' she tells Julia. 'They should always lift you up.' She clucks her tongue. 'You'd think a bunch of ballerinas could see that.'

'I'm very proud of you, you know,' Julia says.

'Okay,' Evie shrugs. 'Thanks.'

Rowan reaches to squeeze Julia's hand.

They need to have a conversation, but they're both prepared to wait. After a few days, Evie goes back to Samara's and the two of them are alone. Julia has been thinking how their space is only marginally bigger than her father's new unit. His deck is larger than their balcony. The time is coming, she feels, to follow Don's move, but in reverse. They need somewhere bigger, somewhere to make their memories.

She's told Rowan the bare bones of what happened, both when she was a child and the more recent events with Davina. She chose to tell him in the dark of their bedroom, her body curled into his and their whispers disappearing into the sheets, the way he once shared the story of Evie's birth. He held her and told her he was sorry she'd gone through that, and she said it was okay, she was okay.

'I'm just worried about Evie,' she said. 'About what can happen. I've never felt like she was in so much danger before, even when she was little. There are threats everywhere.'

'I know,' he said. 'It's terrifying.'

On their first Sunday morning they go for a walk in the Botanic Gardens. Melbourne is getting cold, heat evaporating from the earth into the ice-blue sky, so they wear jackets and get takeaway coffee.

Rowan starts. 'How's it feel to be back?'

'Good,' she says. 'Even better once I got my desk back how I like it.'

'Sruthi did a pretty good job, though.'

'I know.' Julia sips her coffee. 'I wonder if we should offer her the position full-time.'

He takes the suggestion in stride. 'What would you want to do instead?'

'I don't know. Maybe legal secretary stuff again. Maybe retrain.' Their feet move in unison along the path. 'I do see the clinic as our business, together. But I don't think that necessarily means we both have to work there.'

'That's true.'

When Julia returned to the office, Bethany hugged her warmly and asked about Don. Julia appreciated it, but her focus kept snagging on the neat bump beneath Bethany's shirt. She knows it's ridiculous to think she can avoid every pregnant person in the world, but it is possible not to watch Bethany getting bigger and bigger if she doesn't want to.

'I think we should move, as well,' Rowan says.

'Move out of the flat?' she checks. 'Or move the clinic?'

'Move houses. Move *to* a house. Not a big one,' he says, 'but somewhere not as crammed in.'

'With a backyard.'

'It'll probably just be a courtyard, with our budget,' Rowan says wryly. 'But yes.'

'I want to grow veggies.' Everything she's been planning for the past few days comes out, fully formed. 'I want a shed and space for bikes. I want Evie to have a big room to herself, and for there to be a spare room to use as an office. Three bedrooms at least.'

'For an office,' Rowan repeats. He doesn't look at her, and

she doesn't look at him. 'Not for anything else.'

'Maybe a guestroom. Yoga studio.' Julia knows she's being flippant. In reality, it's been on her mind for a while, the question coming to the forefront when for the past five years she's more or less successfully crammed it to the back: what is she willing to do, how far is she willing to go, to have a child of her own? Davina's accusation that Julia mustn't really want a baby was designed to be cruel, but it's made her think. How have she and Rowan been able to live in this limbo for so long without pushing things either forward or backward? What has allowed them to come to the threshold of one of the most important decisions a couple can face and not cross? Don's expression when he revealed the final lost pregnancy was still grey and harrowed, a quarter of a century later. The last few years have frustrated Julia, they've angered her, saddened her, made her prickle with envy at women like Bethany, but they haven't yet haunted her, and that makes her grateful.

And she has Evie. Rowan and Samara have shared their own child's life with her, and that's a gift Julia isn't willing to risk.

She up-ends her paper cup and drains the contents. A brown trail tracks down her chin and she wipes it away. 'Or, you know. If something were to happen, we could use it for that.'

'For a nursery.'

'If we ever end up needing one.'

He takes her hand and holds it still against the momentum of their strolling bodies. 'So, we keep doing what we've been doing.'

'I don't want to rule anything out.' Her voice is soft, but she knows he hears her. 'But I think the last few years mean that maybe, probably, it isn't going to happen.'

She waits to be devastated by this admission. Instead, it's like sitting in front of a pile of dirt and thinking of, believing in, a tiny emerald speck of growth.

'I've said we can get some stuff checked out.' Rowan squeezes their palms together. 'Just to see what's going on.'

'I don't want it to take over our lives,' she says. 'That's happened enough already.'

After a moment, he nods. 'And I guess that if we don't know for sure, it'll always feel like there could be a chance.'

Emotion clogs Julia's throat: Rowan does understand her. 'But I also want to feel like I'm doing something with my life. Not putting everything on hold for a *what if.*' She adds, 'Not putting my life on hold, full stop.'

'Getting things moving.' He grins. 'Working that muscle.'

'Exactly.'

Their hands drift apart, but naturally. They're on the final stretch now, heading for the footpath that leads them home.

'Anything else you'd like?' Rowan asks. 'While we're changing everything up?'

'Yes,' Julia says. 'Let's get Evie a dog.'

Acknowledgements

This novel was written and developed on Whadjuk Noongar Boodjar. I offer my respect to the traditional custodians of the land and to their Elders, past, present and emerging.

In bringing this book to publication, I've been immensely fortunate to have some of the strongest and most consistent advocates behind me. My most sincere and heartfelt thanks go to Fremantle Press and the Fogarty Foundation for awarding my unpublished manuscript the 2021 Fogarty Literary Award. The recognition and opportunity this award offers are second to none, and I am so appreciative of Annie and Caitlyn Fogarty and their team for their ongoing support of young West Australians. Their partnership with Fremantle Press is an inspired one, and I am in awe of the passion Jane, Georgia, Cate, Rachel, Claire and all the other fantastic staff have for writing and publishing in WA.

My editor, Georgia Richter, was an amazing teammate in developing this manuscript from the slightly wonkier original version. My thanks go to her, and to Rachel Hanson, for giving me great direction and for being so thoughtful, enthusiastic and easy to work with during what might otherwise have been an anxiety-inducing process.

Thank you to Dr Matt Hanson and Michelle Fyfe for sharing your professional knowledge with me, and for the vital work you do.

I've had the opportunity to learn from some amazing writing teachers over the years. Thank you so much to Brenda Walker for being the most incredible mentor, and for insights and reassurance from Van Ikin, Dennis Haskell, Deborah Robertson, Simone Lazaroo, and others at the University of Western Australia and Murdoch University. Thanks also to my high-school English teacher, Mr Stevenson, for your quiet confidence.

I am so grateful for the inspiration and camaraderie I get from relationships with other writers: Laurie Steed, Mel Hall, Nathan Hobby, David Allan-Petale, Shannon Meyerkort, Sue Braghieri, Brett Jenkins, Gina Perry, Marlish Glorie, Sanna Peden, Wayne Marshall, Delys Bird, Rashida Murphy, Daniel Juckes, Vivienne Glance and many others I have worked with. Our conversations are always terrific. I've also benefited from relationships with organisations and programs like the Peter Cowan Writers Centre, Writing WA, Centre for Stories, Fremantle Arts Centre, the Subcommittee, Words&Thoughts, the Loop, and Scottish Universities' International Summer School. Thank you to all my Home School Writing Group students for the fun, frivolity and thought-provoking workshops, especially my novel writing diehards Chenin, Kai and Riley.

I'm extremely lucky to have a very supportive family and friends. My parents, Peter and Lesley, encouraged my writing endeavours from the very start, as did my grandparents, Eve, Val and Bob, and my extended family, especially the equally artistic Epstein/Garlands. My in-laws, the Gays and Pfeiffers, are always keen beans – thanks for the interstate cheers. My brothers Chris, Tim and Drew taught me to fear an under-chlorinated pool and amoebic meningitis, so thank you for that, and for *The Simpsons* quotes and books snatched off your shelves. My childhood friends Laura, Mhairi and Brie have grown into wonderful, strong women – Kimmies, all of them. Unlike Julia, I have a wide net of trusted adult friends to fall back on as well: Maria, Kendall, Rhiarne, Shannon, Maryce, Kim, Neri, Ruth, Annie, Catie, Sandra, Angela and others. Jamie, you are my LOML.

If I've forgotten anyone, the mistake is mine. If you think you've helped me somewhere along the way, you're right. Thank you.

Finally, and most importantly, thank you to Andrew, who works so hard and gives me the time and space to be a writer. You're the best.